National Library of Australia Cataloguing-in-Publication
entry

        Creator: Amphlett, Rachel, author.
        Title: Scared to death / Rachel Amphlett.
        ISBN: 9780994433763 (paperback)
        Series: Amphlett, Rachel. Detective Kay Hunter
        ; 1.
        Subjects: Serial murderers--Fiction.
         Detective and mystery stories.
        ISBN: 978-0-9944337-6-3)

Scared to Death

Rachel Amphlett

Chapter 1

Yvonne Richards grasped the notepaper in her hands, the page creased within her grip. The writing had been scrawled in haste, slipping over the faint blue lines that intersected the sheet.

'Tony? *Hurry.*'

'I'm going as fast as I can,' he said, through gritted teeth.

The retort brought tears to her eyes as he cleared his throat.

'What's the name of the street again?'

She lifted her thumb off the paper, noticing the warmth from her skin had blurred the ink, and squinted at the handwriting.

'Innovation Way.'

She lifted the notepaper from where her hand had been resting on her leg, and peered at it once more. Tony's writing was appalling at the best of times, but now she struggled to read it. The writing had deteriorated because his hands had been shaking so much when he'd heard the caller's voice.

'East or West?'

'West.'

He turned too early, the car hitting a dead end within a few yards.

He hit the brakes, both of them straining against the seatbelts across their chests.

'No, no. The next one!'

'You said it was this one.'

'No – I said West. Innovation Way *West*.'

He swore under his breath, slammed the car into reverse, and swung it onto the main thoroughfare before turning at the next junction.

'I'm sorry.'

'No, it's okay. It's okay. I'm sorry.'

She let her hand drop to her lap, clutching the page for fear she would lose it before they could reach their destination, and stifled a sob.

A hand reached out for hers, and she wound her fingers around his, seeking strength.

She found none.

His hands were as clammy as hers, and he was still shaking.

'Both hands on the wheel, Tony,' she murmured, and squeezed his fingers.

She swallowed as her eyes swept across his tanned skin.

Even his hair had lightened in the glare of the Italian sun. Her own hair was frizzy from the humidity, her skin pale by comparison, and she'd envied him that healthy glow as they stepped off the plane three days ago.

Before they'd reached the house.

Before the phone call.

His hand retreated, and the car accelerated towards a mini-roundabout set into the road.

Yvonne tore her eyes away from the address written on the paper, and stared out the passenger window.

The industrial estate had never fully recovered from the recession, with only a few small businesses eking out a living on the outer fringes of the area. The glass and concrete superstructures of the bigger enterprises that had lined the inner sanctum of the centre of the estate lay dormant, while empty windows stared accusingly at the quiet roads that encircled them, and faded letting agency signs flapped forlornly against mesh fencing.

The ornamental landscaping that had been so carefully tended now resembled a hodgepodge of ill-placed tropical plants fighting off common weeds determined to reclaim their territory.

Yvonne shivered, and tore her eyes away, then cried out and wrapped her hand around the armrest.

Tony corrected the wheel as the rear tyre clipped a kerbstone before they exited the roundabout, then exhaled.

She relaxed her grip, and retrieved the notepaper from the foot well, smoothing it over her knee.

'Sorry.'

'It's okay.'

3

He'd never been a great driver, and Yvonne realised he'd probably never driven as fast as this in his entire life. Certainly not in the nearly twenty years they'd been together.

Melanie had already informed them she was taking over the organisation of the anniversary party.

'It'll be great,' she'd said.

Yvonne blinked, and wiped a tear away.

'It'll be okay.'

She didn't reply, and instead focused on the road in front of them.

'What number?'

'Thirty-five.'

'Are you sure?'

'It could be thirty-six.'

Tony swore under his breath.

'It's thirty-five. I'm sure.'

The car slowed to a crawl, and she peered through the window.

'I can't see any numbers.'

'Keep looking.'

Yvonne shaded her eyes from the sunlight cresting the buildings, and strained to find a clue to their whereabouts.

Here and there, kids had taken to the walls of the industrial spaces with spray cans, familiar graffiti tags dotted across doorways and signs that warned of CCTV cameras and security guards with dogs, which hadn't been seen on the estate for over two years.

'Fifteen,' Tony called out.

She spun around to face him, but he was peering through his window as he kept the car at a steady pace, his knuckles white as he grasped the steering wheel.

As the derelict buildings passed by, her mouth ran dry while she tried to push away thoughts of Melanie held captive within the confines of one of them.

She'd only been wearing a thin vest top and jeans when Yvonne had last seen her five days ago.

Five days.

The phone had rung late last Friday night, four hours after they'd returned from the airport. Tony had been sitting on one of the barstools at the kitchen worktop, an open bottle of wine next to him, a glass of red between his fingers while he'd flicked through the free newspaper. She'd dropped her bag on the surface, and accepted the second glass he'd held out to her.

'Where's Mel?'

'Not home yet.'

Yvonne had checked her watch. 'She'd better hurry up, or she'll get no dinner.'

Tony had grunted non-committedly, and topped up his own wine. 'Probably hanging out with that Thomas girl.'

'I wish she wouldn't.'

'Yeah, but you tell her that, and she'll do it anyway.'

Then the phone had interrupted them, and their lives had changed forever.

Now, Yvonne leaned forward in her seat, resting her hand on the dashboard as the car eased past the next padlocked fence. 'That's it. That's the one.'

Tony swerved the car over to the kerbside and cut the engine.

She heard his breathing, heavy on his lips, and wondered if she sounded the same to him. She couldn't tell – her heartbeat was hammering so hard, the sound of her blood roared in her ears.

He reached for the door handle.

'Wait.' She grabbed his arm. 'What if he's still here?'

Tony glanced over his shoulder. 'We just dropped a bag with twenty thousand pounds in it two miles away,' he snapped. 'Do you really think he's going to hang around here to thank us?'

Yvonne pursed her lips, and shook her head.

'Right, then.'

He shrugged her hand away, and she watched as he rocked his head from side to side, as if psyching himself up, before he placed his hand against the car door and pushed it open.

She launched herself out of the car after him.

When they approached the fence, Tony grasped the chain that looped through the wire openings.

It fell easily through his fingers.

'It's unlocked,' said Yvonne.

'He said it would be.'

She could hear it then, the fear crawling through his voice, replacing the brisk no-nonsense tone he'd tried to maintain since they'd left the house.

'Did he say where—'

'Yes. Follow me.'

Instinctively, she reached out for his hand, and he took hers between his fingers, gave it a squeeze, and then set off towards the side of the building.

She knew now how scared he really was. She couldn't recall the last time they'd held hands. Lately all they'd done was bicker and snipe at each other over the smallest inconsequential things.

Melanie had always been a daddy's girl, and Yvonne fought down the surge of jealousy that threatened.

She just wanted her back.

Now.

The building's windows mirrored their reflection as they passed. A dark-coloured privacy sheen had been applied, preventing her seeing into the rooms beyond. She craned her neck, taking in the three-storey concrete monolith. Any corporate signage had been stripped away when the tenants had vacated the premises, and walls that had been stained an off-white tone when first built now resembled something closer to off-grey. Dirt and grime fought an equal battle with graffiti, and faded signs depicting evacuation zones and fire exits hung to the surface in places, the doors boarded up and unwelcoming.

'How are we going to get in?'

'He said one of these would be open.'

Sure enough, towards the rear of the building, they discovered a solid steel door. Although it was closed, a discarded padlock lay on the pockmarked asphalt of the perimeter.

Tony reached out for the handle.

'Wait.'

He frowned. 'What?'

She swallowed. 'Shouldn't you cover your hand? In case the police want to check it for fingerprints?'

'I want my daughter back,' he said, and twisted the handle.

She paused while he stepped over the threshold, then took a deep breath and followed him. She shared Melanie's fear of enclosed spaces, and bile rose in her throat as she imagined the terror her daughter would feel at being held here.

She squinted as Tony pulled a torch from his pocket and switched it on, the beam blinding her before he lowered it, the light falling on discarded office furniture. She turned away, and blinked as she tried to adjust her eyes to the gloom beyond the torch beam once more. The pungent smell of rat droppings and damp from a leaking roof filled her senses, and she choked back the urge to vomit.

Tony had already begun to hurry towards the inner door, and she followed him through the derelict office into a narrow corridor that ran lengthways through the building.

Tony turned left, shining the torch ahead.

At the end of the corridor, a set of double doors blocked their path.

She leaned against them, and pushed.

They opened smoothly, and she breathed a sigh of relief before goose bumps prickled her skin as the door hissed shut behind them. She turned, touched the handle and pushed again, terrified that they wouldn't be able to get out.

It swung open with ease.

'It's on an automatic closer,' said Tony, and pointed to the upper framework. 'Come on. Hurry.'

Yvonne bit her lower lip, but followed, her arms hugging her chest. 'What *was* this place?'

'A biosciences company was here. Remember the protestors always used to gather at the town hall?'

Confusion filled her, then dread. 'The animal testing place?'

He didn't reply, but simply nodded and shone the torch around the walls.

The European-headquartered animal testing company had moved in over a decade ago, despite a several-thousand-signature petition being delivered to the local council within weeks of the original planning application.

Aluminium sinks were bolted to one wall, white tiles grimy through neglect above each. Shelving units dotted another wall, the splintered remains of glass crunching under their feet as they progressed through the room.

Their footsteps echoed; the tiled floor at an angle that Yvonne found difficult to keep her balance in her heels.

'What's wrong with the floor?' Her voice wavered.

'It's a soak away,' said Tony, pointing at the large grille in the middle of the room. 'All the water will wash towards that.'

He began to pace the room, his hands running over the tiles.

'Where is she, Tony?'

Yvonne cringed as her voice bounced off the tiles, before the fear wrapped itself around her insides and squeezed.

'He said she'd be here,' he said. He continued to run his hands over the tiles. 'Maybe there's a hidden door?'

Yvonne sucked in a breath. 'Did you hear that?'

'What?' He spun to face her. 'What?'

'Shhh,' she urged, and held up a finger.

Melanie wasn't a big girl; in fact, she was skinny for her age, with slender shoulders and hips. Yvonne had always marvelled that her daughter had never broken a bone – she looked so fragile, as if the slightest touch would shatter her.

'Tony?' She pointed at the grille in the tiled floor.

His skin paled as he followed her gaze, before he dropped to his knees, his fingers pushing through the grille. 'I can't see anything.'

Yvonne crouched, threaded her fingers around the grille, and met his gaze. 'On three.'

The steelwork groaned under their touch, and then lifted a little, its right-hand edge tantalisingly higher than the left.

Tony worked his fingers closer, and tightened his grip. 'Now.'

The grille slid away, exposing the dark opening.

'There's a ladder,' said Yvonne, and leaned closer.

When he shone the torch down the gaping maw of the hole, she frowned, unable to comprehend what she was seeing.

Then Tony began to scream, his terror echoing off the walls of the laboratory.

Chapter 2

Detective Sergeant Kay Hunter's hand shot out and gripped the handle set into the side of the car's door as Detective Constable Ian Barnes accelerated around a sharp left-hand curve.

'Uniform reported it twenty minutes ago,' he said, as he straightened the vehicle and eased his foot off the pedal. 'We're the nearest detectives, so guess what?'

'What?'

'Our day just turned to shit.'

Kay acknowledged the statement with a snort.

She was grateful though. Detective Inspector Devon Sharp could have insisted on running the scene as Senior Investigating Officer, but had instead phoned her with the assignment.

'You'll be my deputy SIO,' he'd said, before ending their brief phone call. 'You need this.'

She exhaled. She'd owe him after this one, that was for sure.

Up ahead, a silver saloon car and two patrol cars came into view, one with the emergency lights still flashing, the passenger door open.

'Pathologist is already here,' she said, and silently thanked the first-on-scene police officers for being so organised.

'Must have been a quiet day for him,' said Barnes.

As he slowed to approach the parked cars, he ran through the known facts.

'The father made the call. The woman from dispatch reported he was near hysterical by the time she spoke to him. Apparently, he and the wife discovered their seventeen-year-old daughter, Melanie, down a drain in one of the buildings here. Strangled.'

'How did she get here?'

'She was kidnapped – five days ago.'

Kay sighed. 'Dammit, I wish they'd told us.'

Barnes grunted a reply.

Despite the threats a kidnapper could make, common police practice meant many kidnappings in the UK were brought to a successful closure, simply because the police worked diligently behind the scenes, and with a total media blackout.

Kay loosened her grip on the door as her colleague swung the car to a stop behind one of the patrol vehicles.

She climbed from the car, and introduced herself to the two uniformed officers who were standing next to a couple in their late forties, a look of horror on their faces.

The elder of the two uniformed officers stepped forward. 'I'm Sergeant Davis. We were first responders.'

She introduced herself, and then led the way across the concrete apron of the building until they were away from the couple before she spoke.

'I understand they've found their daughter here, and that she's been strangled?'

He nodded. 'Seems she was kidnapped while they were on holiday,' he said. 'They paid the ransom money about an hour ago, and were told to come here to get their daughter. They found her body in the old testing laboratory, down a drain. It looks as if she's been strangled.'

Kay's eyes fell to the silver car. 'Pathologist here?'

'Yes. He was on his way from another call. Arrived ten minutes before you.' He jerked his thumb over his shoulder. 'He's in there now.'

'Nothing you could do to save her?'

His eyes clouded, and he shook his head. 'It's pretty bad. Girl's hanging down the drain by her neck.' He frowned. 'It's hard to ascertain from the parents what they might have touched. They definitely removed the drain cover to try to reach the girl. We haven't touched anything in there, and the scene's been preserved. We got fingerprints off the parents to eliminate those for forensics.'

'Good work, thank you.' She turned to the other detective who had wandered over. 'Right, Ian,' she said, 'you speak to the husband, I'll have a word with the wife.'

'Okay.' Barnes nodded, and made his way over to the couple.

Kay waited a moment, and then joined him, making a beeline for the woman. 'Yvonne Richards?'

The woman nodded.

'I'm Detective Sergeant Kay Hunter. I'm very sorry to hear about your daughter, but I need to ask you some questions.'

The woman looked to her husband, who was already conversing with Barnes. He glanced up, nodded, and turned back to the other detective.

A tear rolled down her cheek, yet she seemed oblivious, and it was all Kay could do not to wipe it away.

Instead, she turned the page of her notebook and pressed on, keeping her voice calm.

'Yvonne, when Tony made the triple nine call, he said Melanie had been taken five days ago. Why didn't you call the police then?'

The woman choked back a sob, and clasped her hands together.

'We didn't know she was gone. We've been in Europe. We – we only got back two days ago, and that's when he phoned. He said he'd kill her if we called the police. He said he'd rape her first, and make us listen.' She broke off,

15

and her hands fluttered to her mouth. 'He said he thought we didn't believe him, and then he made her scream.'

Kay glanced across to where Barnes was talking to Tony Richards. She frowned, and saw that DC Barnes had his hand on Tony's arm, and seemed to be steadying him.

'I'm sorry,' said Kay, directing her gaze back to Yvonne. 'I have to ask these questions.'

The woman flapped a hand. 'I know. I know. Oh, god—'

She sniffed loudly, took the paper tissue Kay handed to her, and blew her nose.

Kay took a moment, and then continued.

'Have you any idea why Melanie was taken?'

Yvonne shook her head. 'We're not rich,' she managed, 'despite what it might look like to some. Tony doesn't work – my business is doing well, so he stays home.' She gulped. 'It's nice for Mel to have someone there when she gets home from school in the afternoons.'

'What did the kidnapper say he wanted?'

'Twenty thousand pounds.'

Kay kept her face passive, and wrote the figure in her notebook, placing a question mark next to it.

'What timeframe did he give you?'

'Today.' Yvonne frowned. 'He was very precise – we had to drop it off between six-thirty and seven o'clock this morning.'

'How did you give him the money?'

'We had to put it in a padded envelope,' said Yvonne. 'He told us to put it in the post box on Channing Lane – the road that runs behind the industrial park.'

'In the post box?'

'Only enough so the end still poked out.' Yvonne shivered. 'Tony had to do it. My hands were shaking so much, I thought I'd let it go, and then what would we have done?'

Kay turned to the uniformed officer closest to her.

'Take your car. Preserve the scene. You know what to do. Go.'

The man didn't hesitate. He called out to his colleague and they ran towards their car, the lights flaring a second before the siren began to wail, and they tore from the kerb.

Kay watched them leave, and then turned back to Yvonne. 'What happened next?'

'We drove away, like he told us. We had to park in the car park next to the library in Allington. He called us, said he had the money, and gave the address of where we could find Mel. He told us to hurry, because time was running out.'

The roar of an engine interrupted them, and Kay turned to see a dark panel van braking next to the unmarked police car before its driver threw it into reverse and drew to a halt next to the open gates of the biosciences building.

The driver climbed out of the vehicle and made her way over to the side of the building.

A man in overalls emerged from the facility and joined her before they began to converse in hushed tones.

'Who's that?'

Yvonne's voice held a tremor.

'The head of the crime scene investigation team,' said Kay. She guided Yvonne away from the building, and turned so the woman's back was to the two figures.

Before long, the side of the van slid open, and the team began to assemble, their actions swift and well-rehearsed.

Kay's head snapped round at a yell from Barnes.

'Call an ambulance!'

Her eyes opened wide as she saw Tony Richards sink to the ground, before Barnes grabbed his arm to break his fall and helped the man to sit.

Kay didn't hesitate. She hit triple nine on her mobile phone and rattled off the details to the control room as she ran towards the stricken man, Yvonne's footsteps close behind.

They reached Tony at the same time.

'What happened?'

Barnes crouched next to the man, pulled his wrist towards him, and held his index finger against the thin skin. 'Chest pains.'

'Oh, god – Tony.'

Yvonne Richards sank to the ground next to her husband, whose face had whitened, and grabbed his other hand.

A croak emitted from his lips, and his eyes closed a moment before he slumped sideways.

Kay reached out and ripped open the man's shirt, buttons scattering over the ground, before she balled her hand into a fist and beat the man's chest once, hard.

Barnes leaned over, gently straightened the man's head, steadied it between his hands, and nodded to Kay.

She started the compressions, one hand placed over the other across Tony's ribs.

Sweat broke out between her shoulder blades, but the man remained unresponsive after several minutes.

'Sarge? You want me to take over?'

'I'm fine,' she said.

She swore inwardly.

Tony Richards didn't look an unhealthy man, but there was no telling what shock could do to a person.

Right now, she had to remain calm. She couldn't let the man's wife see her panic, not with what she was already going through.

'Boss, I'll take over.'

Barnes nudged her out of the way, and she rocked back on her heels, grateful for the respite.

Tony emitted a gasp, and his eyes fluttered open.

'Tony!'

Yvonne Richards shoved Barnes aside, and wrapped her arms around her husband's chest.

'Mrs Richards, please,' said Barnes. He gently pulled her away. 'Let him get some air.'

The sound of approaching sirens carried on the wind, and Kay straightened as the ambulance rounded the corner.

She hurried to meet it; pointing out the access route they should take to reach their patient, and waited while they hurriedly pulled overalls, gloves, and plastic booties over their uniforms to avoid contaminating the scene.

She followed the path they took with the stretcher, the rattle and clang of wheels across the cracked concrete surface setting her teeth on edge.

She stood close as they assessed Tony's vital signs, their voices calm as they worked. The elder of the two stood and gestured to her to step to one side with him, out of earshot of Yvonne.

'We're going to have to take him,' he said. 'You've done well, but we need to get him to hospital now. It's too risky to wait.'

'You were told on the way over what's happened here?' Kay raised an eyebrow.

The paramedic nodded. 'We'll let the hospital know when we get there, and request they keep you informed.'

Kay handed him one of her business cards. 'Thank you. Go.'

He nodded, and within minutes they had loaded Tony onto the stretcher and wheeled him towards the back of the ambulance.

Kay hurried over to Yvonne Richards, who was being comforted by one of the police officers, her hand over her mouth and her eyes wide as she watched her husband be stretchered away.

The woman looked over her shoulder towards the industrial building where the body of her daughter had been found, then back to the ambulance.

Kay stepped forward, and put her hand on the woman's arm.

'Go with your husband. I'll stay with your daughter.'

The woman's eyes met hers, confusion crossing her face, and Kay saw then that it was the right decision. The woman needed to get to hospital anyway, before shock set in and she too suffered any kind of medical condition.

'Go with this man,' she reiterated. 'He'll take you to the hospital with your husband.'

One of the paramedics nodded, and began to steer the woman towards the waiting ambulance, its blue lights blinking across the wall of the biosciences facility.

Yvonne squeezed Kay's fingers before she was out of reach.

'Thank you,' she whispered, and then hurried through the back doors of the ambulance to be with her husband.

Kay flipped her notebook shut and tucked it into her handbag, then rolled an elastic band off her wrist and tied back her shoulder-length blonde hair.

'Right, you bastard,' she muttered. 'Let's see what you did to her.'

Chapter 3

Kay left her bag on the floor next to the uniformed police officer who guarded the door, and signed the attendance sheet he handed to her on a brightly coloured clipboard.

She'd returned to her car, broke open the seal on fresh plastic booties and overalls she'd retrieved from the back of the vehicle, and pushed a tendril of hair out of the way before she pulled the hood over her head.

'Left down the corridor,' the police officer said. He pointed. 'Through the door at the end.'

'Thank you.'

She tugged on gloves, and then stepped onto the plastic sheeting that covered the tiled floor. Her footsteps rustled on the temporary walkway that had been set out to preserve the scene, and echoed with a dull thud off the walls of the corridor.

Despite the murmur of voices that emanated through the open double doors at the end of the passageway, an involuntary shiver crossed her shoulders.

Outside, the building had resembled many of the other abandoned glass-and-concrete structures on the tired industrial estate. Once the pinnacle of modern-looking business complexes, the scuffed and worn outer shell now appeared dated and forlorn.

Inside, the history of the business clung to the walls.

Kay averted her gaze from the various ageing safety notices, and tried not to think about the experiments that might have been carried out within the walls.

She reached the double doors at the end of the passageway, both of which had now been wedged open to allow better access for the crime scene investigation team.

She paused at the threshold, her eyes roaming the scene before her.

Pale-coloured tiles laced with dirt lined the walls from floor to ceiling, the overall effect one of confinement. No other doors led from the room. There was one way in, and one way out.

Pipework had been removed from the space above the sinks lining the wall, taped-over joints protruding from recesses.

A coppery scent wafted on the air, along with the unmistakable stench of urine and faeces, and she wrinkled her nose at the smell.

Two floodlights had been set up on tripods, the feet on more plastic sheeting.

Lucas Anderson, the forensic pathologist, was crouched next to a large open drain in the middle of the room with two of his colleagues, pointing out different details and providing instructions to them. A Crime Scene

Investigator circled the room, the flash from her camera further illuminating the space with bursts of light.

She moved, stood to one side of the drain, away from the light that provided Lucas and his team with a clear view of their working area, her gloved hands cradling the camera. She glanced up at Kay's arrival and beckoned to her.

'Come on in,' she said.

Lucas turned. 'Morning, DS Hunter.'

'Hello, Lucas.' She nodded to the CSI. 'Thanks, Harriet.'

Kay kept a wide berth as she walked around the perimeter of the room to join Lucas. Only once she was standing next to him did she peer down the hole.

She knew better than to ask questions at this point. Lucas and Harriet would tell her what they knew, when they knew, and they would never hazard a guess.

The rungs of a ladder were the first thing she noticed, then on the fourth rung she saw a rope knotted around the length of it, the end taut, disappearing into the darkness.

Severed ends of a thinner rope were entangled around either side of the upper rung, a splash of blood covering one of them.

The pathologist finished talking with his two assistants and straightened. 'We're going to be here for some time,' he said. 'She's been strangled using the noose tied to the ladder. At some point, her hands were tied above her head to the sides of the third rung of the ladder. She was able to place her feet on the rungs below until recently.'

Kay frowned. 'Until recently?'

The pathologist nodded, and pointed at the items arranged next to the hole. 'It appears that whoever did this to her made a conscious effort to enhance her terror,' he said, his grey eyes fierce. 'That bottle of motor oil is connected to the plastic tube, which has then been fed down the hole so that it drips onto the ladder rungs.'

'She lost her footing?' Kay stepped forward.

'Eventually,' said Harriet. 'He tied the noose around her neck, secured her hands to her chest, and let the oil do the rest.'

Kay leaned closer. 'Is that – is that a *camera* down there?'

'Yes.' Harriet crouched and gestured to her to join her. 'It's one of those small models mountain bikers and the like use. Lightweight.'

'So he was filming her?'

Harriet nodded. 'The record light isn't on, so it's probably operated remotely. I'll get the tech team onto it as soon as possible.'

'How would he view it – computer? He obviously wasn't planning on coming back here to collect it.'

'Or via a mobile phone app, yes.'

Kay exhaled, and stood with her hands behind her back as she peered down the hole, keeping her weight on her back foot.

The girl's pale neck hung at an impossible angle, her face hidden by a tangle of auburn-coloured hair.

Kay swallowed, and resisted the urge to run a gloved finger around her collar. 'How long did it take?'

'We'll let you know, but perhaps ask the parents what time they were given the location, and how long it took them to get here – that will help.'

'Will do.'

They turned at the sound of running feet, and Lucas's brow creased.

'Whoever that is better be staying on that bloody path,' he said.

Barnes appeared at the doorway, his overalls twisted where he'd dressed hurriedly. He held up his mobile phone in his gloved hand.

'Just had a call from the hospital, Sarge. Tony Richards didn't make it. Died on arrival.'

Chapter 4

Kay strode across the car park towards the back door into the police station.

Barnes swiped his security card against a panel fixed to the wall, then held the door ajar for her before leading the way through the building and up a short flight of stairs along a carpet-tiled corridor to an open plan office.

Already, a sense of urgency had gripped the area nearest her desk where the rest of the team were organising themselves, the atmosphere tense.

She saw DI Devon Sharp walking towards her.

Older than her by five years, he was ex-military, and walked with the upright posture of a man trained on a parade ground.

He'd brought with him a solid no-nonsense approach to his work that Kay had immediately acknowledged upon joining the ranks of the town police station.

'Which room are we in?'

'Invicta,' he said, 'but before we start, a word in my office, if you don't mind.'

Kay gestured to Barnes to proceed without her, and then followed Sharp to a small box-like office set against the far wall of the main room.

As she passed the groups of desks that comprised the detectives' space, her eyes ran over the stacks of paperwork that lay across the surfaces, all live cases in the process of being worked through and solved. Near Sharp's office, two older DCs bickered over a recent football score, their voices growing louder as the good-natured arguing progressed.

She shut the door behind her as she entered the office, cutting off the voices mid-commentary, and took the seat opposite Sharp's desk.

He waited until she'd settled, and then leaned forward, his hands clasped.

'Good work at the scene. I presume Lucas and Harriet are still there?'

She nodded. 'And they'll be there for a while yet.' She went on to explain what had happened, and how she had handed over the scene to the crime scene investigator when she'd turned up.

Sharp grunted. 'Harriet's a good CSI,' he agreed. 'What happened with the father – Tony?'

'He collapsed during questioning. We performed CPR at the scene, and he responded to that, then the ambulance arrived. Yvonne, his wife, went with him. We were where Melanie's body was found, with Lucas and Harriet, when

DC Barnes received a call from the uniforms who accompanied Yvonne saying that Tony died on arrival.'

'Christ, what a mess.' Sharp ran a hand over his close-cropped, brown hair. 'What about Yvonne Richards?'

'We've heard nothing from the hospital yet. Again, uniform reported that the doctors insisted on keeping her in for observation. The Family Liaison Officer arrived there half an hour ago. Barnes gave his details as first point of contact for any news.'

'Okay. Keep me posted if you hear anything. Obviously, we need to interview the mother again as soon as possible, but we'll play that by ear.'

'Who's on the team?'

Sharp leaned back in his chair. 'Yourself, Barnes, and Carys Miles – she's not worked a case like this before, but she's a hard worker, and I think she'll be an asset.'

'Agreed.'

'We'll also get a couple of uniforms to act as exhibits officer and provide general administration assistance.'

'Good.'

Two uniforms processing the administrative side of the investigation would free up the detectives to pursue more pressing tasks.

'There is one more thing,' said Sharp, his eyes wary.

She peered through her fringe at him. 'Boss?'

'Detective Chief Inspector Angus Larch is going to be following this one closely. Orders from the top. Sorry.' He gestured to the paperwork covering his desk. 'They're anticipating how the media are going to react when they find out about this one, so they want it monitored from the start.'

She swore under her breath, and he raised his eyebrow. 'Is that going to be a problem, Hunter?'

'No, sir. Not for me.'

His mouth twitched. 'Come on, then.'

Chapter 5

Kay returned to her desk, grabbed her notebook, water bottle and a spare pen, and made her way out of the room, along the corridor, and into the meeting space that had now been designated as a critical incident room. The IT experts had overhauled the meeting rooms a few years ago, ensuring that at any time there were enough phone sockets, internet connections and power boards to support a major investigation.

Already, Ian Barnes and Carys Miles had taken up station at two desks they'd pushed together, while a young police constable, Gavin Piper, bent over a table, plugging in computers that would soon link the team to the Home Office Large Major Enquiry System database.

Carys had joined the team six months ago, relocating from the Thames Valley force, and appeared to be settling in well. In her late twenties, her dark brown hair framed a heart-shaped face with green eyes that could bore into the most hardened of suspects, and Kay felt the woman had a promising career ahead of her.

She hadn't worked with Piper before, but Barnes had, and she knew the young constable was keen to pass his exams and become a detective. The blond streaks through his light-brown hair hinted at an outdoorsy-type, and Kay reckoned he'd be a safe pair of hands if she needed someone to depend upon. The broad-shouldered police officer had already turned heads among the younger members of the admin team since joining the busy town station, but he kept his personal life private and seemed oblivious to the attention.

Kay waited a moment at the door, the excitement of a new investigation tempered with the thought that she owed it to Melanie's mother to find out who had been responsible for her death, and that of Tony Richards.

The next few hours would be critical, and she knew DCI Larch would push the team to deliver a result – and fast.

She turned her head at the sound of footsteps behind her, and then stood to one side to let Sharp pass.

'How are we doing?'

'We're ready.'

She dumped her water bottle, notebook, and pen on a desk near the door, and walked over to the whiteboard the other PC, Debbie West, had pulled away from the wall.

'Morning, Sarge,' she said, as Kay approached.

'Morning. Please, call me Kay. Have you got everything we need?'

'Yes. Admin brought a stack of stationery up here half an hour ago,' said Debbie, and pushed her hair out of her eyes. 'I've chased IT to see if we can get an extra printer though.'

'Good work.'

Coloured marker pens sat on the shelf under the board, together with an eraser.

Kay chucked the eraser onto a worktop that ran the length of the meeting room. Nothing would be rubbed out, not until the case was closed.

It was just one of the rules she lived by, instilled in her by Sharp.

Kay kept what she hoped was a neutral expression on her face as DCI Larch entered the room.

It was the first time she'd been in close proximity to him since the Professional Standards committee had ruled out any action against her, and she wasn't sure how he was going to behave.

His eyes flickered over her, and his jaw tightened before he turned away and surveyed the rest of the team gathered around the whiteboard. He moved over to a desk near the door, pushed some paperwork to one side, and perched there, his ankles crossed and his arms folded casually across his chest.

Kay exhaled, then blinked and unclenched her fists.

Although the matter had been drawn to a close nearly four weeks ago, the distrust he'd held for her still stung. As did the effect of the rumours that had swirled around the station during that time. Of course, there were those who saw her predicament as an excuse to get the knives out. She'd certainly found out who she could trust, and who would stand by her assertions of innocence after the whole debacle.

'Focus,' she muttered to herself.

***

'Before he collapsed, Tony Richards stated that the kidnapper had warned them not to go to the police, otherwise he'd hurt Melanie,' said Barnes. 'During the second phone call they received after Melanie was taken, she screamed – Tony said it wasn't a scream of someone who was scared. She was hurt.'

'Lucas reported that the little finger on her right hand had been severed,' said Kay. 'It appears that the suspect used a knife, but it wasn't a clean job. He'll have more detail after the post mortem.'

The room fell silent for a moment.

'Bastard,' murmured one of the uniformed officers.

'Indeed,' said Sharp. 'Right. Immediate thoughts?'

'There are no reports of anything like this happening locally before,' said Carys. 'We're waiting to hear back about national cases.'

'Perhaps a gang new to the area?' suggested Barnes. 'Trying to make an impact?'

Sharp turned to the whiteboard, and spoke over his shoulder as he wrote. 'Whoever it is will be panicking. A kidnapping gone wrong like this is unusual. Especially with the father dying as well.'

'Twenty thousand pounds isn't a lot of money though, boss,' said Kay.

A few heads swivelled to look at her, but she kept her eyes on the whiteboard.

'Go on,' said Sharp.

'Well, initial enquiries indicate Yvonne Richards' business is doing well. They live in a nice house – and they were able to get the money together relatively quickly without alerting anyone. Surely, if the kidnapper was watching them for a while to work out a routine, he or she would have latched onto the fact they were well off, and would've asked for more?'

'Keep going.' Sharp said.

'I can't help thinking this wasn't simply a kidnapping. Maybe Melanie's death was deliberate.'

'Murder, rather than a kidnapping gone wrong, you mean.'

'Yeah.' She shrugged. 'I keep wondering if there's more to this than what we're seeing at the moment.'

Sharp nodded, and wrote her suggestion on the whiteboard before drawing a question mark next to it. 'Fair point. Anyone else?'

The room fell silent.

'All right,' he continued. 'It's early days. There's going to be a lot of information coming in. Based on what we have, I want two separate lines of enquiry until one gets ruled out. DS Hunter, I want you leading the angle of non-monetary gain – find out if it's personal, rather than opportunistic. Any bad debts, threats to the family, grudges against them with regard to the business. Carys, you'll lead the monetary angle, and keep Kay up to date with anything you find. I want everyone back here at six o'clock daily for a full update, and we'll reconvene at eight o'clock every morning. Any questions?'

The room remained silent.

Sharp checked his watch, and then turned to DCI Larch. 'Anything you'd like to add?'

'Thanks, Sharp,' said Larch, and stepped forward. 'A murder of any kind is a tragedy,' he said, his voice even. 'However, when it involves a young girl, and the effect of that murder results in her father dying…' He met each of the officers' gazes in turn, 'I can't think of anything more horrific.' He turned his attention to Sharp. 'I'll make some phone calls; see what I can do to get you more resources.'

'Thank you.' Sharp tossed the whiteboard pen onto a desk next to where he stood. 'Right, everyone. Go make the necessary phone calls to your families, let them know they're not going to be seeing very much of you for a while. We're going to be in for some long hours.'

Chapter 6

'What have you found out about the building Melanie's body was found in?'

Kay sipped her coffee, and stared at the aerial map pinned to the wall with the industrial estate at its centre, then turned and faced the team.

'Until two years ago, there was a biosciences company based there.' Carys leafed through some pages on her desk. 'Although they had a licence to conduct animal testing for the purposes of evaluating the toxicity of a new drug, they also had dealings with the cosmetic industry – high-end make-up products, shampoos – things like that.'

'Has it been abandoned since they left?'

The detective nodded, and held up a page. 'They closed up shop twelve months before their German head office put out a press release saying they were entering into voluntary administration. From the records online, it looks like the cosmetics end of their business was propping up the biosciences half. After the global financial crisis, they never really recovered – people stopped buying high-end goods, discovered good cheap alternatives, and never went back.' She tossed the page aside. 'The building never got re-leased.'

'What about security patrols?'

'I spoke to the agency that lets the buildings on the estate – apparently, after the last tenant vacated, the landlord decided to cancel the patrols. Too expensive, given he couldn't pass on a portion of the costs to a new tenant.'

'Did they give you a list of key holders to the property?'

'Working through it now.'

Kay turned to the young PC. 'Gavin. How are you progressing with getting hold of the CCTV footage?'

'It's patchy, Sarge. A lot of the cameras have been vandalised over the years, and I guess because there are no tenants in the buildings, the cameras haven't been replaced.'

'Noted. Do what you can to chase it up. And we're going to be working together for a while, so why don't you call me Kay while we're here? We'll leave the formalities outside this room.'

He nodded in response.

'What was the outcome of the search of the money drop?' Her eyes swept the room, then fell on Barnes as he raised his hand.

'Ian?'

'Forensics took what fingerprints they could from the post box. They said the surface near the posting slot was sprayed with bleach though.'

'Damn.' She sighed. 'Let me know if they come up with anything we can use. The sooner we can confirm forensics for both crime scenes, even if it's fragmented information until they have the whole picture, I want to know.'

'Sarge.'

'Right. Kidnapping timeline.' She turned back to the whiteboard, and picked up one of the pens. She drew a line across the top, and marked off five sections. 'Melanie was taken on Tuesday,' she said, writing in the first box on the left. 'Her parents didn't arrive back from holiday until three days later.' She marked an 'x' in the middle box. 'They received a call that night from the kidnapper, giving them their instructions.' She scribbled in the last box, and recapped the pen before facing her team once more. 'Thirty-six hours later, Melanie was dead.'

She was met with silence as all eyes fell to the right-hand side of the whiteboard. She flipped open her notebook, and skimmed through the brief interview she'd had with Yvonne at the crime scene.

'What time on Friday night did Tony Richards say they received the first call, Ian?'

Barnes cleared his throat. 'Seven o'clock. Their taxi dropped them off at home that afternoon, and they were about to start cooking dinner. Tony said they fully expected Melanie to turn up any minute – she knew they'd be home from holiday, and they'd arranged to have a family meal together at eight o'clock.'

'So Melanie told her kidnapper the routine?' said Gavin.

'Or he was watching the house,' said Kay. She gestured to Barnes. 'Go on.'

'Tony's mobile rang, he answered it, and the kidnapper asked if he and Yvonne were alone in the house.'

Kay frowned. 'Either he didn't have eyes on the house then – or he was testing them.'

'Tony confirmed they were alone, and then he was told to put the phone on speaker so Yvonne could hear.'

'Yvonne said he waited until Tony switched to speakerphone before stating he had Melanie,' said Kay. 'According to her, he said "I have your daughter. If you want to see her alive again, follow these instructions". He then went on to tell them to have twenty thousand pounds in used ten- and twenty-pound notes available within thirty-six hours.'

'It's strange he gave them so long to get the money together,' said Gavin, scratching his chin.

'Most banks won't let you withdraw more than a few thousand at a time,' said Kay.

'Or he wasn't ready,' said Carys.

'Could be, though the way he had everything set up at the site, he looked pretty organised to me,' said Kay. She checked her watch. 'I'm going to head over to the hospital after this. See if the doctors will let me talk to Yvonne. At least that way, we might have more to work with when we reconvene here in the morning.'

'What if he was working with someone else?' said Barnes. 'What if he had to liaise with them to arrange the collection of the money?'

Kay wagged her finger at him. 'Good point.' She turned and scribbled on the whiteboard. 'Yvonne said the next call came the next day. They'd been instructed to leave the house only to go to the bank, and not to phone the police, or anyone else for help if they wanted to see Melanie again. The kidnapper phoned at exactly the same time as before, to ask if they had the money. Then he said he'd phone the next day with further instructions.'

'At which point, Tony said Yvonne grabbed the phone from him, and screamed at the kidnapper. Said she told him to let Melanie go,' said Barnes. He flicked his notebook shut. 'That's when Tony says the kidnapper made Melanie scream.'

'The drop off,' said Kay. 'This morning. What went wrong?' she mused.

'Nothing,' said Barnes. 'Tony said they got a phone call at five forty-five this morning. They followed the kidnapper's instructions. Put the twenty thousand pounds in a padded envelope, and placed it in the opening of the post box on Channing Lane before driving away. They were told to wait in a library car park about a twenty-minute drive from the drop-off point for another call.'

'Yvonne Richards stated that they received a message from the kidnapper on Tony's mobile phone that told them where to find Melanie.'

'How far away were they?' said Carys.

'The other side of Maidstone.' Kay chewed her lip. 'They were never going to make it. Not from there.'

Chapter 7

Kay swung the battered pool vehicle into the last remaining
space of the hospital car park, and tried not to look at the
driver of the BMW who glared at her through his
windscreen before powering away.

She locked the door, hurried over to the ticket machine,
and jammed the last of her loose change into the slot before
ripping the paper ticket from its housing.

After she'd thrown it onto the dashboard, she weaved
between five rows of parked cars, and ran through the
afternoon's events in her mind once more.

The main building of the hospital loomed above her.
Built in the early 1980s, the structure had been modernised
and expanded over time, with specialist units for oncology
and physiotherapy now housed in their own low-lying
buildings to either side of the original footprint.

A breeze lifted the collar of her blouse as she
approached the entrance to the building, sending a chill
down her spine as she recalled the teenage girl.

She clenched her fist tighter around her bag, and
shoved the door open with her free hand.

After speaking with a woman on reception, she made her way over to the lifts.

All around her, the scent of disinfectant and worry permeated her senses. Muted voices tumbled from partly closed doors, and somewhere further along the ground floor, a child cried.

She bit her lip, forced herself forward, and kept her eyes downcast.

She knew it was unlikely any of the staff would recognise her; they saw so many patients every day, and she hadn't told them her occupation, only that her husband was a vet. They had quietly congratulated him; his quick thinking in getting her to hospital when he did, meant they could operate before her life was endangered further.

Their baby girl hadn't survived.

She clenched her fist, and forced herself to concentrate. She'd found out she was pregnant only a few weeks before the miscarriage. Accidental, the pregnancy had caused shock, which gradually turned to excitement as she'd begun to make plans for the future.

All of that had been snatched away.

Only a few weeks in the womb, their baby didn't stand a chance. The consultant who met with them afterwards had explained in guarded tones that the miscarriage had probably been brought on by stress.

Neither she nor Adam had mentioned the Professional Standards investigation that had begun the previous week.

Nor had they mentioned that her whole career lay in the balance, and that criminal charges were threatened against her.

Instead, they'd thanked him, and returned to their home, then battened down and awaited the results of the investigation while Kay recuperated and tried not to think of the children she'd never be able to have.

The lift doors opened, and Kay stepped back to let a porter pass, his face animated as he chatted with the old man he pushed in a wheelchair. She met his eye, managed a smile, and then pressed the button for the second floor.

The machinery groaned in protest before the lift began to rise through the building. Kay reached into her bag for her notebook and pen, her eyes skimming the facts she'd jotted down from the short briefing while she formulated her questioning in her mind.

She snapped the notebook shut as the lift juddered to a halt and the doors opened.

PC Hazel Aldridge, the Family Liaison Officer, had arrived at the hospital forty minutes after the ambulance, and now sat in a plastic chair in the corridor. She stood as Kay approached.

'Detective.'

She inclined her head towards the closed door. 'What's the latest?'

'The doctor's with her now,' said Hazel. 'They've given her a mild sedative, but she's demanding to go home.' She shrugged. 'There's a relative on the way – her sister.'

Kay exhaled, and wondered how strong a sedative had been administered by the doctor.

The longer she had to wait to question Yvonne, the more she worried that events of the past three days would be blurred by grief. She knew some might think of her as heartless, but her priority was to catch a killer.

'How long has he been in there?'

'About ten minutes.'

At that moment, the door opened, and a tall, broad-shouldered man in a shirt and tie appeared. He took one look at Kay, stepped out into the corridor, and pulled the door shut behind him.

'Detective…?'

'Detective Sergeant Kay Hunter,' she said, and extended her hand.

His grip was surprisingly gentle, and Kay relaxed hers to suit.

'How is she holding up?'

His lips pursed, and then he ran a hand over his closely-shaven head. 'You can imagine. I've given her a sedative to keep her heart rate settled. She's a little drowsy now. Hopefully she'll sleep for a few hours.'

'How long do you plan to keep her in?'

'Just for tonight.'

'I need her to answer some preliminary questions.'

'I thought you might.' He checked over his shoulder towards the closed door, then glanced at his watch and turned to Hazel. 'What time did her sister expect to be here?'

'She left Dover an hour ago. Given the rush-hour traffic, I expect she'll be here within the next twenty minutes or so.'

The doctor sighed. 'No more than five minutes, all right?'

'Right,' said Kay. 'I realise you're busy, but could you sit in on this with me, just in case we need you?'

He nodded. 'I would've insisted anyway.'

'I know.' She gestured towards the door. 'Lead the way.'

Chapter 8

The doctor pushed open the door to Yvonne's room, and stood to one side to let Kay pass.

The walls seemed to encroach upon the figure swathed amongst blankets in the bed, but as the door clicked shut, Kay was grateful the woman had been allowed some privacy instead of being placed on one of the main wards.

A lamp affixed to the wall pushed its dull light across the bed and cast a yellowish glow over the pillow, yet couldn't reach the corners of the room where shadows crept across the tiled floor. A heart monitor pulsed a steady *beep*, the machine on the far side of the bed blinking red and green lights as it recorded Yvonne's vital signs.

'How is she, health-wise?' said Kay.

'Fit and healthy. I understand from her notes that she was a regular at her local gym.'

Kay picked up the unspoken words. It appeared that Tony Richards could have done with his wife's healthy discipline.

She grazed her arm against the doctor's as she turned, and lowered her voice. 'What about her husband?'

'We've been in touch with the pathologist from the scene. He'll take care of things from here.'

'Thanks.'

Kay moved closer to the bed, and held her breath as Yvonne's eyes eased open, then widened.

A gasp escaped the woman's lips, before a tear rolled down her cheek.

'Hello, Mrs Richards,' said Kay.

The woman coughed, and then tried to raise her head.

The doctor moved across the room, and moved the pillows to support her. 'Take it easy, Yvonne. It's okay to sleep.'

'I'm sorry for your loss today,' said Kay. She pulled the lone chair from under the curtained window closer to the bed and sat.

'I won't keep you long,' she said, and kept her voice low. 'I understand your sister is on her way, and that you need to rest.'

Yvonne nodded, and then sniffed. 'And you have a job to do,' she said.

'I do, that's right.'

'You can call me Yvonne.'

'Thank you.'

'What do you want to know?'

'Did Melanie have a boyfriend?'

Yvonne shook her head. 'No. Well – not that I knew about.' A sad smile crossed her features. 'Seemed more interested in whatever band was hitting the charts each week than anyone around her.'

She ran her tongue over her lips.

Kay reached out for a jug of water and a glass next to the bed. Filling it, she crouched next to the bed, and helped Yvonne take a sip before returning the glass to the small table beside her.

'Thank you.'

Kay retrieved her notebook. 'Did she belong to any sports clubs or anything like that? Places she'd go after school?'

'No,' said Yvonne. Her voice wavered. 'A bit like her dad in that respect. Liked watching television and playing computer games. Didn't really like the outdoors much.'

'Did she have a job?'

'She used to come to my office after school and help out some afternoons. Thought it'd give her some good experience.'

Kay leaned back. 'When was she seventeen?'

'End of last month,' said Yvonne. She balled up her fist, and rubbed at her eyes. 'I can't believe she's gone,' she whispered. 'I can't believe they're both gone.'

The heart rate monitor skipped a beat, and then increased.

'Detective Hunter?' The doctor moved from his position in the shadows. 'I'd like my patient to get some rest now, please.'

Kay caught his eye. There would be no compromise. 'Okay.'

She lowered her gaze to Yvonne. 'Thank you, Yvonne. I'll be in touch once you get home.'

The woman nodded, but Kay couldn't be sure she'd heard her words. Tears streamed down her face now, and her breath escaped in biting sobs.

Pushing her way out into the bright corridor, Kay pulled the door shut behind her, closed her eyes, and took a deep breath.

'Everything okay?'

She opened her eyes to find Hazel staring at her, concern in her eyes.

'Yes, thanks.' She gave herself a mental shake. 'All right. I'm going to head off. Could you let me know once the sister arrives, in case we need to speak to her?'

'Will do.'

Kay made her way back through the hospital. As she pushed open the double doors that led out to the car park, she inhaled the fresh air, trying to rid her senses of the cloying smell of disinfectant.

She pulled her mobile phone from her bag, saw that no messages or missed calls had been logged while she'd been talking with Yvonne Richards, and reached for her car keys.

Aiming the fob at the vehicle as she drew closer, she tossed her bag onto the passenger seat, and sat for a moment, recalling their conversation.

'I'll find you, you bastard,' she murmured, and started the engine.

Chapter 9

Eli Matthews threw the battered canvas sports bag over the wooden fence, the soft crunch of it hitting the gravel next to the dilapidated garden shed reaching his ears.

He checked the keys to his moped were tucked safely into his pocket, and then looked both ways in the alley.

Satisfied that he hadn't been seen, he hitched himself up onto the palings, and peered through the gloom to the back door of the terraced house.

No lights shone through the windows, and once satisfied he wouldn't be seen, he hoisted himself over, landing next to the bag.

He crouched for a moment, waiting, his eyes picking out the debris that littered the lawn, the stone path overgrown with weeds and cracked from age and neglect.

Finally, he stood, grabbed the bag, and hurried to the back door. He extracted a key from his jeans pocket, thankful that he'd thought to oil the lock several days ago, and stepped over the threshold into a small kitchen.

He closed the door, careful not to let the panes of glass rattle in the kitchen window next to it, then removed his boots.

He was tired now, as all the adrenalin of the past week dissipated and sapped his energy. He fought to keep his wits about him. He had to reach his room without stumbling into her. Especially now.

He shouldered the canvas bag, clutched his boots in his other hand, and padded across the linoleum floor towards the hallway. An open door to his right led to the living room, which he avoided at all costs. That was her domain, and it wasn't safe.

He took a deep breath, and began to climb the stairs. Although carpeted, the fourth and seventh treads housed a formidable squeak. He took long strides over these, and reached the top landing without a noise.

There, he paused, his ears straining for any sound from the main bedroom at the front of the house.

He'd considered whether to enter the house by way of the bedroom window at the rear of the property, but discarded the idea almost immediately. He couldn't risk the neighbours saying something to her, or one of them seeing him in the act. It would raise too many questions he wasn't prepared to answer.

He held his breath.

A faint snore emanated from behind the closed door, and his shoulders relaxed. It would be several hours before she woke now, and with any luck, he'd be gone for the day.

He'd made the mistake a week ago of walking through the back door, his mind elsewhere, before he realised she was still in the living room.

She'd launched herself at him, a well-aimed fist catching him on the back of his arm before he'd managed to slam his bedroom door shut.

He rubbed his hand over the fading bruise, and instead focused on the memories of the past few days.

He stifled a yawn.

All in all, it had been a productive week off work. Everything had gone as planned. Better, in fact.

Much better.

He reached the door to the back bedroom and pushed it open, slid the brass bolt across the back of it, and dropped the canvas bag onto the threadbare carpet. The room stank; a mustiness that was beginning to permeate his clothing the longer he stayed there, but it would have to do.

For now.

There was nowhere else he could go.

He put his boots next to the door, then wandered over to the window, and opened the smaller of the two panes before he twitched the curtains closed.

He peeled off his socks, threw them onto a pile of dirty laundry in the corner, and lowered himself to the bed. A smile began to form on his lips, and he closed his eyes before lying back and resting his head on the pillow.

As sleep began to claim him, his right hand travelled down his chest and stomach to his waistband, then continued under it.

Yes, it had been a good week off.

Perhaps he should take a holiday more often.

Chapter 10

Kay stood back as a figure appeared through the frosted glass a moment before the front door to her house was yanked open.

'Hey, blue eyes.'

She smiled, and dropped her keys back into her bag.

Adam wore one of his old sweaters pulled low over jeans that had seen better days, and clutched a pair of wellington boots in his hand. His hair was wet, the smell of shower gel wafting over the threshold. 'I didn't think I'd see you before I left.'

His tone wasn't accusatory; it was simply the truth. He was one of two local vets who specialised in livestock and racehorses in the area, and so he often spent his evenings attending various emergencies at nearby farms and villages at short notice. With both of them working long days, it sometimes felt to Kay that they spent most of their time chatting on the doorstep – or in the hallway.

'What is it this time?' She kissed his cheek, and then pushed the door closed behind her. She shrugged off her jacket, and hung it on the newel post.

'Stables over at Tonbridge. A mare has been having difficulties for the past three months of her pregnancy. She took a turn for the worse tonight.'

She could hear the weariness in his voice as he crouched and checked through the bag on the floor, making sure he had everything he needed.

'How bad?'

He shrugged, and scratched the stubble on his chin. 'Not sure. The owners have a tendency to panic, but we'll see.'

She met his eyes, and he bit his lip.

Only a few weeks ago, they would have made light about the neurotic owners.

Only a few weeks ago, things had been normal.

Adam cleared his throat, and then straightened. 'What about you?'

'We've got a nasty one. Kidnapping gone wrong.'

He closed the gap between them, and tilted her chin up to his. 'Well, they've got the best detective on the case by the sounds of it,' he said, and kissed her.

He knew she could never talk about a case, not while it was still open. He also knew how badly the Professional Standards investigation had hit her confidence, especially as it had ended her chances of promotion to detective inspector so brutally.

And their chances of a family of their own.

The key piece of evidence that would have put away one of Kent's most unsavoury characters for life had gone missing a few days before his trial, reducing the case against him to shreds. According to the records, Kay had been the last one to access the locked safe where the small pistol had been kept, and despite her assertions she hadn't removed it, Angus Larch had thrown every disciplinary action he could at her, culminating in the Professional Standards investigation.

Kay knew she'd have done the same if faced with the same situation. It didn't make it any easier to deal with the aftermath, though.

She bit her lip.

Adam glanced at his watch, and sighed. 'We're like passing ships at the moment, aren't we?'

Her mouth quirked. 'Well, tell all those bloody racehorses to stop shagging, then.'

He chuckled. 'I'll bear that in mind.'

She smiled, and left him to sit on the stairs and pull on his boots. She slipped off her shoes, picked up her briefcase, and padded along the hallway to the kitchen, then flipped on the light switch as she walked through the door.

She yelped, and her briefcase hit the tiles with a clatter. 'What is it?'

Adam's footsteps pounded along the hall carpet before his head popped round the corner of the door.

Kay pointed at the glass case on the worktop, its contents writhing.

'There's a bloody snake in the kitchen.'

Adam chuckled. 'Meet Sid,' he said.

'Sid?'

Kay looked back at the glass case, and took a step away. She was used to Adam bringing a sick animal home occasionally, but last time it had been a cat expecting a litter they had ended up delivering at two in the morning. Something fluffy. Something *normal*. 'How long is he here for?'

'Just a few days. He was taken ill as his owner was leaving for a holiday in Budapest.'

He cleared the gap between them, and pulled her into a hug. 'He won't hurt you. He's perfectly safe in there.'

'Hmm.'

'I have to go.'

He kissed her hair, then spun on his heel and rushed from the room.

Kay heard the front door close, and the house fell silent.

She rubbed at her right eye. It always itched when she was tired, and the investigation was only in its early stages. She knew part of the problem was seeing DCI Larch again, even though it was only a matter of time before they had to work together again.

She sighed, pushed the thought from her mind, and turned her attention to food.

She and Adam had got into the habit of cooking meals in large batches so they always had something healthy in the freezer to warm up, and now she pulled out a bag of bolognese, careful to avoid eyeing the contents of the bottom drawer where the snake's frozen mice had been stashed.

While she waited for the microwave to work its magic, she flipped through the pages of her notebook, refreshing her knowledge of the facts so far.

The landline began to ring, closely followed by the cheery ping of the microwave.

Kay checked her watch and groaned. There could be only one person who would phone at this time of day.

'Hello, Mum.'

'Have you only just got home?'

Here we go, thought Kay. 'About half an hour ago.' She crossed her fingers. 'Just about to sit down to eat.'

'I think it's disgusting the hours they make you work, on top of how they've been treating you. You should find something else to do. At least that way, you'll be home for Adam more often.'

Kay felt sure the grinding of her teeth would be heard down the phone. 'Mum, I'm tired. I'm not having this conversation now.'

'Look at your sister,' her mum continued. 'Nice nine-to-five job, earns twice as much as you, and two kids.'

'Mum—'

'She does what she wants at weekends, has lots of hobbies in the evenings – a life.'

Kay turned her head, and eyed the cooling bolognese in the microwave. Then her gaze fell to the half-full bottle of pinot noir on the worktop next to it.

'Mum, I've got to go. There's an emergency. Talk soon.'

'Oh, well, that's just typical isn't it? They call you. Why don't they call someone else?'

'Bye, Mum.'

Kay hung up the phone, and placed it gently into the cradle, despite wanting to throw it across the room. She took a deep breath.

Her mother knew how to rattle her. Had done for years, with constant comparisons to her older sister, her dislike of her job – she'd only recently stopped berating her for living with Adam without being married, and that was after several years of telling her he wasn't good enough for her.

Before that, growing up, it was about the way she dressed, who her friends were, how her exam results hadn't turned out to match her mother's expectations.

Kay had been quite pleased with her exam results. It meant she could take an offer from a university several counties away from her mother, for a start.

And her degree had led to her joining Kent Police within months of graduating. It was either that, or return to her hometown.

The thought made her shiver.

It also irked her that, so many years later, her mother could still get under her skin so easily.

She took a deep breath. She hadn't told her mother about the miscarriage. If she was honest, she didn't know how to start the conversation. If she was really honest, she was also slightly relieved that she hadn't.

It would simply have encouraged her to become even more overbearing.

She pressed the microwave button to give her food a quick blast, pulled a wine glass from the cupboard above it, and poured a small measure of the pinot.

'Cheers anyway, Mum,' she said, toasted the silent telephone, and took a sip.

63

Chapter 11

Eli Matthews climbed off the moped and stowed his helmet in the box on the back.

He cricked his neck, then ran a hand through his straw-coloured hair and ambled towards the wide open doors of the depot, his lanky frame casting a long shadow over the asphalt.

The early morning air washed over him, a freshness that tugged at his hair and filled his nostrils, despite the urban sprawl of car dealerships, industrial units, and interlaced roads that surrounded the building.

No doubt, by the time he was halfway through his shift today, the humidity levels would have gone through the roof once more, and the air conditioning in the van would fail.

The grating squeal of the wire mesh security gate rolling back into place across the entrance to the car park filled his ears as he sniffed the air a final time, a feeling of expectation seizing him.

After a week off work, he was almost looking forward to returning. If it hadn't been for the little side project he'd concocted for his absence from the bedlam of the depot, he would've gone out of his mind being in the same house for a whole seven days trying to avoid his mother.

Her sniping remarks echoed in his mind even now, and he gritted his teeth, forcing the memories away.

He needed to concentrate today.

Especially today.

Act normal.

Except it was going to be hard, because everything was so different now.

He'd done it. Finally done it.

A small smile tugged at the corner of his mouth.

'Blimey, Eli. You should piss off on holiday more often. Never seen you looking so cheerful.'

Eli scowled.

Bob Rogers, one of the depot managers, leaned against one of the steel doors, and took a long drag on a half-consumed cigarette.

'It's because I wasn't here,' said Eli, as he walked past.

Rogers chuckled. 'Good to see you, too.'

Eli entered the depot, before he turned left through a wide entryway. He swiped his security card at a turnstile, and then walked along a passageway to the locker room.

He held his breath as he opened the door, then exhaled with relief when he saw the space was empty.

He hated having to make small talk; didn't see the point of it, and didn't want the others to spoil his good mood. Rogers had already tried that, and it had nearly worked.

The air in the locker room was musty, a tangible fug of sweat and damp clothes seeping into the whitewashed brick walls.

He pulled a small key from his pocket, opened his locker, and stuffed his leather jacket inside. He kept a fresh set of work clothes in the locker at all times, as well as spare pairs of socks and a towel. A storm was predicted for later in the week, and he wanted at least one set of dry clothing.

As he went to shut the door, an envelope on the top shelf caught his eye, and he reached in, pulling it towards him. His good mood returned; he'd forgotten about the pay rise they'd been awarded two weeks ago – his mind had been on other things.

He shoved the envelope back in place, and closed the door. He wouldn't take it home – his mother would find it, and then the arguing would start when she wanted to know why he wouldn't give her more money.

He'd given up months ago explaining to her that he wasn't responsible for her smoking and drinking habits. She received enough on benefits, as it was.

No, he'd keep the news to himself, tuck it away out of sight when he had the chance.

He had a special place for secrets like that.

A place his mother knew nothing about and never would.

He dropped the key into his pocket as the door to the locker room swung open.

'Hey, the straggler returns.'

Eli turned, and nodded. 'Steve.'

A second man followed in the first's wake. 'Good week off?'

'Yes, thanks.'

'What you get up to?'

'Nothing much.'

He forced a small smile, then brushed past the second man, and hurried from the room, making a point of checking his watch.

His shift started in five minutes.

***

Eli released the handbrake, and the van rolled out of its space and towards the security gates.

He tapped his fingers on the steering wheel while he waited for a space big enough to get the van through, and then turned right and pressed the accelerator.

For the rest of the morning, he drove out of the town, through the outlying villages of Leeds and Chart Sutton, looping through farmland and criss-crossing the A20 then north over the high-speed train line. All the time, he hummed under his breath, content to make his deliveries and enjoy the relative solitude.

At five to eleven, he pulled the van over, outside a village convenience store, the bright signage of a national chain hanging above the low doorframe.

He nodded at the cashier, pulled an energy drink from the refrigerator at the back of the shop, took a plastic-wrapped, thick sausage roll from the display in the chiller cabinet, and made his way to the cash register. A stack of local papers had been placed on the floor near his feet.

His brow creased as his eyes scanned the headlines.

'Anything else?'

He glanced up, then crouched and picked up one of the papers. 'I'll take this, too.'

The cashier's eyes fell to the bruises on Eli's forearm as he took his money, before he blinked and looked away, added up his purchases, and handed him his change. 'Have a nice day,' he muttered.

Eli snatched the change away, and spun on his heel.

Returning to the van, he cracked open the can of soft drink, and took a swig before placing it in the cup holder between the front seats. He put the sausage roll on the dashboard, then flicked open the paper, turning page after page.

Nothing.

He frowned.

Maybe it was too early. Maybe they missed the print run?

He threw the paper onto the passenger seat, unwrapped the sausage roll, and pressed the power button for the radio.

He hated commercial radio, but he needed to know. Needed to hear.

The digital clock set into the dashboard counted down the seconds to the hourly news, and he increased the volume.

The news announcer began on time, right after the last commercial had aired, and the last notes of the station's jingle faded, but started with a story about something the prime minister was doing in London.

Eli munched in silence.

The next story came and went; a thirty second spiel about the drink driving campaign that Kent police had rolled out across the county, and then a third story. Followed by the sports headlines, and finally the weather.

Eli stared at the radio, swallowed the last mouthful of sausage roll, and then blinked.

Nothing was being reported.

Fuming, he scrunched up the empty wrapper, shoved it into the pocket in the side of the driver's door, and reached for the energy drink. He took a long swallow, slammed the can back into the cup holder, and gunned the engine.

'Patience,' he reminded himself. 'Be patient. Give them time.'

Chapter 12

Carys swung the car into the small business park, and Kay ran over her tactics in her mind while noting the sign at the entrance to the area that touted it as the region's newest innovation centre.

There seemed to be renewed effort to pull down the derelict buildings around the town, and replace them with housing and business parks as soon as possible. She couldn't help but wonder what history might be lost along the way, especially as some of the developments seemed to be taking months to complete, despite the haste with which the old landmarks were demolished.

She roused herself from her thoughts as the vehicle eased to a standstill outside a business unit, one of four in a row that backed onto the main road. Each building comprised a large roller door that stretched from the ground to the roof eaves, a single glass door next to it, and two windows above the entrance door.

Kay unclipped her seatbelt, climbed out, and stretched her back while she waited for Carys to lock the car, then made her way to the reception door.

It was locked, and there was no answer when she pressed the intercom.

'Tradesman's entrance it is, then,' she said to Carys, and led the way to the open roller door. 'I'll find out more about the business generally, and I'll leave you to speak with whoever's in charge of the accounts to see what you can turn up, sound good?'

'Works for me.'

Kay peered into the gloom.

'Hello?'

'Over here.'

Kay moved into the warehouse space, and registered movement towards the back as her eyes adjusted to the gloom.

She weaved between boxes and packing crates that lined an ill-formed aisle. Most were open; those that were sealed had been taped shut with generous layers of sticky tape.

'Can I help you?'

An older woman who looked to be in her early sixties approached, adjusting her hair that had been tied in a loose topknot, and was now trying to escape its bindings. Curled tendrils fell into the woman's eyes, and she brushed them aside as she squinted up at Kay.

'I'm DS Kay Hunter, this is DC Carys Miles. I wondered if I could speak with you and your colleagues about Melanie Richards?'

The woman bit her lip, her eyes watering.

'Of course,' she said. She held out her hand. 'I'm Sheila Milborough. I look after the warehousing and stock. Come on up to the office.'

She moved past the two detectives, reached out for a cord next to the warehouse entrance, and hit a button.

The door began to slide down from the ceiling, and Sheila checked its progress before she returned to them and beckoned them to follow her. 'This way.'

Kay inclined her head towards Carys, and she followed them both through the maze of boxes to an internal door that opened into a reception area.

Sheila checked the front door was locked, and then led them past an overstuffed sofa that faced a sparse reception desk, and up a flight of stairs.

Kay was surprised at the compact size of the office space. It was evident that the warehouse took up the majority of the building's footprint, leaving the staff with a cramped space they had somehow managed to squeeze four desks into. Three filing cabinets filled the space in front of the window, obliterating much of the natural light.

Sheila introduced Belinda and Annie, who she described as customer service officers, and looked at Kay expectantly.

'Is there anyone else?' said Kay, surprised.

'No, it's just us,' said Annie. She sniffed, and dabbed a paper tissue at her nose. 'Unless Melanie dropped by to help.'

Belinda snorted, and looked away.

Annie managed a small smile through her tears. 'It's why Yvonne's so successful. She runs a lean operation.'

Her colleagues nodded, and murmured in agreement.

Kay let her eyes roam the space.

A tiny meeting room had been partitioned off in the left-hand corner of the open-plan office at the rear of the room, and Sheila gestured towards it.

'Yvonne sometimes uses that as a private office when she needs to get away from the hustle and bustle. You can use it if you want.'

'That's fine. Thank you.'

'I'll put the kettle on, and we'll get started, shall we?' said Carys.

Again, there was a murmur of agreement, and Kay stood to one side as chairs were pushed back and mugs were collected, and Carys was shown where to find the small kitchenette set into the rear right-hand corner of the office space.

By the time mugs of tea and coffee were handed out, the three staff members had relaxed.

'Sheila, do you mind if I start with you?' said Kay. 'Carys can speak with Belinda and Annie, and then we'll let you get on.'

'Of course.'

Kay took her mug of tea, and led the way over to the meeting room. She left the door open after Sheila had joined her – at the moment, they were only there to conduct preliminary questions, and there was no need to make the staff nervous by splitting them up; it was just easier to focus on answers if there were fewer involved at any one time.

'Right,' said Kay. 'You mentioned that Melanie would drop by to help. How often did that happen?'

'Maybe once or twice a week. It depended on what she had planned after school.'

'What did she do while she was here?'

'Answer the phones. Help out with the filing. Sometimes, if we had a lot of orders to get out the door, she'd help me pack the boxes. I think she thought it was all a bit of a giggle, to be honest.'

'Did she get paid?'

Sheila shrugged. I don't know. Maybe.'

'It would show on the books, wouldn't it?'

'I suppose so. You'd have to ask Annie.'

Kay made a note for Carys to check.

A bell suddenly rang out in the office, and a frown creased Sheila's brow.

'Hang on.' The woman moved to the door. 'Belinda? Could you see who that is, please?'

She sat back down, and picked up her tea mug. 'Sorry. Probably just the courier.'

Kay waited until the woman had settled. 'What about Tony Richards?'

The woman's expression hardened, and she shuffled in her seat. 'I hate to speak ill of the dead.'

Kay leaned forward slightly. 'Anything you tell me won't be repeated to Yvonne, or the other staff,' she assured her.

Sheila sighed. 'It was awful,' she said, and jutted her chin towards the door. 'Yvonne gave him a job here after he was made redundant. Annie nearly quit, he was so rude to her. And he kept making mistakes, then blamed us.' She shook her head. 'Yvonne tried, she really did, but after he was rude to a client on the phone, she had to put her foot down.'

'How long did he work here?'

Sheila leaned back and blinked. 'Well, let's see. Maybe a few weeks? No longer than a month, I'd say.'

Her eyes moved to a spot behind Kay's shoulder.

She turned to see a man in a short-sleeved shirt and long shorts appear at the top of the stairs.

He held his hand up in their direction, then moved to a desk next to Carys, and picked up a large box, his voice carrying over to where she sat.

He made a comment that sent Belinda and Annie into giggles, and a smile crossed Carys's face, before he turned and made his way back down the stairs.

Kay turned back to Sheila. 'He seems friendly.'

'He'll be devastated when he finds out about Melanie. They always used to flirt when she helped out on reception.' She stopped and blew her nose.

'Excuse me,' said Kay.

She left the woman sipping her tea, and hurried out to the main office. Carys saw her approaching, and stood up.

'What's up?'

'Catch up with that courier. Get his details. Apparently he and Melanie used to flirt when she worked here.'

'Onto it.'

Kay nodded her thanks, then returned to Sheila who was watching her wide-eyed.

She smiled. 'Don't worry. We need to talk to everyone who knew Melanie, or saw her these past few weeks.'

The woman nodded. 'I know.' She sighed. 'I still can't believe she's gone.'

Kay gestured to the office. 'Will the three of you be okay while Yvonne's away?'

'Oh, yes. Belinda and Annie are more than capable of running the admin side of things, and I've got the warehouse under control,' said Sheila. 'Yvonne usually does the marketing side of things, and meets with new clients. There's nothing in the diary at the moment because she's only just got back from Milan. Oh dear.' She broke off as tears welled up once more.

Kay leaned forward, and patted the woman's hand. 'Thanks for talking with me, Sheila. We'll be on our way now.'

The woman nodded, and led Kay out of the meeting room.

Kay handed business cards to all three staff members, then followed Sheila down the stairs.

Carys was walking through the front door when they reached the reception area, but stopped short when she saw them.

Kay raised an eyebrow at Carys, but the woman gave an almost imperceptible shake of her head.

Nothing.

'Right, I think that's all for now,' Kay said. 'If anyone does recall something that you think might help us – anything at all – please get in touch.'

Kay pushed through the double doors, but she waited to speak until she and Carys had reached the car.

'What's the story with the courier?'

'His name's Neil Abrahams. Been a courier around here for about five years. He confirmed he used to have a bit of fun with Melanie when he came here. Seemed genuinely shocked about her death.'

'Alibi?'

'Says he was playing cricket with friends yesterday at the same time Yvonne and Tony said they received the kidnapper's phone call telling them where Melanie was. I've got the name of a friend who can corroborate that. Apparently he gave him a lift home.'

'Okay. Give him a call when we get back.' Kay opened the car door, and inclined her head at the warehouse door. 'What do you think?'

The young detective glanced back at the front windows to the unit. 'There are no large cash withdrawals from the business account. They're running a good profit, and appear to have been audited by the tax office last year with no issues.' She shrugged. 'Everything seems above board.'

Kay drummed her fingers on the steering wheel, then checked her watch before starting the engine and steering the car away from the industrial park. 'We've got a couple of hours until the next briefing. Let's make a start with Melanie's friends. Who's first on the list?'

Carys flicked through her notes. 'Emma Thomas. According to Belinda, Emma and Melanie used to hang out here after school sometimes, supposedly to help out.'

'Yeah, Sheila said Melanie used to come here. Didn't mention Emma though.'

'I'm not surprised – Belinda and Annie said she was a pain in the backside.'

'Interesting. What's the address?'

Carys read it out, and Kay nodded. 'I know it. Just the other side of the A20.'

She manoeuvred the car into a turning lane, and pressed the accelerator as soon as the opposite carriageway was clear.

'All right. Let's see what Emma Thomas has to say for herself.'

Chapter 13

'I always did like this area,' said Carys, as the car drew up to the kerb. 'Your place is near here, isn't it?'

Kay laughed. 'Yes, but the Maidstone end. This part is way out of my price range.'

She climbed from the car, and peered over the roof at the village green. The gastro pub on the corner of the encircling road was doing a brisk lunchtime trade, and she knew at the weekend a couple of local cricket teams, vying for space among those who preferred to kick a ball, would take up the grassy area.

They made their way towards a red brick house further up the lane from the pub. A tall privet hedge provided the home with privacy from the road, and as they approached, a curtain in the top left-hand window twitched.

'We've been spotted.'

Kay concentrated on keeping her eyes lowered. 'I expect they've been waiting for this call.'

She reached out, and rang the doorbell.

They didn't have to wait long. The sound of feet running down a flight of stairs reached them, and then the door was opened.

'Emma Thomas?'

'Yes?'

'Are your mum and dad in?'

A woman appeared at the daughter's side, wiping her hands on a towel. 'I'm Sarah Thomas, Emma's mum.'

Kay held up her warrant card. 'Good morning, Mrs Thomas. Detective Sergeant Kay Hunter. This is Detective Constable Carys Miles. I wondered if we could speak with Emma, please – about Melanie Richards?'

Sarah Thomas stroked her daughter's head. 'You okay to talk to them, sweetie?'

'Yes,' said the teenager. She sniffed. 'If there's anything I can do to help, I want to.'

Kay noted the girl's red-rimmed eyes. 'We could really use your help to find out more about what Melanie was like as a friend,' she said, gently.

'Come in,' said Sarah, and beckoned to them to follow her.

Kay let the mother and daughter lead the way through the house to a bright conservatory that had been added onto the back of the building, flooding the kitchen and dining area with light.

The surfaces of the worktops were spotless, save for an array of the latest cooking and coffee-making gadgetry that seemed to have been placed for aesthetic purposes, rather than for any practical use.

'Please, have a seat,' said Sarah, gesturing to a suite of armchairs in the conservatory. 'Would you like coffee?'

'No, that's fine,' said Kay. 'We won't take up too much of your time today.'

She gestured to the garden. 'You have a lovely home,' she said.

'Thank you,' said Sarah, and visibly preened. 'My husband's business does very well, and we're blessed to live in such a nice area.'

'So, Emma – can you tell me about Melanie? I understand you've been good friends over the past year or so?'

The teenager nodded, then reached forward and plucked a paper tissue from a box on the low table between the chairs. She blew her nose, then clutched the crunched-up tissue in the palm of her hand. 'We were in different classes at secondary school. So I didn't really get to know her until we started our A levels last year.'

'In September?'

'Yes.' Emma sighed, and then threw the tissue in a wastepaper basket next to her chair before taking another from the box. She held it between her fingers, and tore absently at the material. She frowned. 'I can't remember how we first got talking. I think I made a joke about something.'

'What happened then?'

A smile stole across Emma's face. 'There was a really loud laugh from the other side of the room, and I turned around to see who it was, and it was Melanie. We ended up hanging out at lunchtime, and found out we had loads in common.'

She sniffed again. 'I can't believe she's gone.' She dabbed at her eyes with the remnants of the tissue, and then dropped it into the wastepaper basket. 'What happened?' she said, raising her tear-streaked gaze to Kay.

'I'm sorry, Emma. I can't divulge any details of an active investigation.' She held up her hands. 'When I can tell you something, I will – does that sound fair enough?'

The teenager nodded.

'Right, so you latched onto one another when you started studying for your A levels. How much time did you spend together?'

'Oh, loads,' said Emma. 'She liked the same music as me, we went to the same hairdresser, we hung out at the same shops at the weekend.' She drifted off, her face wistful. 'We used to go up to London on the train some Saturdays. Camden Market, Covent Garden.'

'And they were always home before it got late,' interjected Sarah.

Kay smiled. 'Good,' she said. She turned her attention back to Emma. 'Did Melanie ever mention that she might be in danger?'

Emma shook her head. 'No. No – never.' Her bottom lip quivered once more.

'Okay,' said Kay. 'Where else did you go with Melanie?'

Emma thought for a moment. 'Oh – sometimes we used to go over to her mum's business after school. Her mum doesn't have that many staff, so we used to help out answering the phones or packing boxes in the warehouse.'

Sarah leaned forward. 'Yvonne and I felt that it would be good experience for the girls, so they'd have something on their CVs before leaving school.'

'It was fun,' said Emma. 'We'd do the post, and sit at reception and stuff. We used to get paid, too.'

'How much time did you spend on reception?' said Carys.

Emma's brow creased. 'Um, maybe a couple of afternoons a week? Yes, that's right – especially the last three months. It's been really busy,' she said, with authority.

Kay smiled. 'I understand you got on well with the courier.'

Emma's lip curled. 'That was Melanie. He never really took any notice of me. Thank goodness.'

Kay noted the edge of jealousy in the girl's voice, despite her words. Her mother seemed oblivious, and so she changed the subject.

'Mr Richards used to work there as well, didn't he?' said Kay.

Emma nodded, and looked down at her hands. 'Yes. He was fun.' She shook her head. 'I can't believe Tony's dead, too.'

'When was the last time you saw Melanie and Tony together?'

'The week before he and Yvonne went on holiday. Although, it was a business trip for Yvonne. Tony thought it was a holiday,' Emma added with a smile.

'And Melanie stayed behind?'

'Yes.' Emma's face fell. 'The last time I spoke to her, she was meant to be going with them. If she'd gone, she'd still be alive, wouldn't she?'

The girl burst into tears once more, and Sarah pulled her daughter into her embrace.

'Do you need anything else, Detective?' she said, peering over her daughter's head.

'No, thank you.' Kay leaned forward. 'And thank you, Emma. You've been really helpful.'

'Excuse me,' said Sarah. 'I'll take her up to her room, and then I'll see you out.'

She rose from the settee, and coaxed Emma out of the room, their muffled voices trailing through the kitchen and hallway in their wake.

Kay rose from her chair, and paced the conservatory.

'What do you think?' murmured Carys, gathering up her notebook and bag.

'I think she misses her best friend.'

Sarah returned after five minutes, and stood on the threshold between the kitchen and the outer room, hugging her arms across her chest.

'Thank you for letting us speak with Emma,' said Kay. She held out one of her business cards. 'We'll need to talk to her again at some point, but if she thinks of anything that might help us in the meantime, please call me.'

'We've kept her here ever since we heard about Melanie,' Sarah said. 'She'll go back to school next week, but we'll be setting some ground rules.' She visibly shuddered.

'What does Emma's father do?' asked Carys.

Sarah waved her hand dismissively. 'Oh, he's long gone. I remarried about three years ago. Vince is a superb father to Emma. Runs his own import and export business.' She gestured to the interior décor. 'Doing very well for himself.'

'Well, thank you for your time,' said Kay. 'We'll see ourselves out, if you like?'

Closing the front door behind them, she set a quick pace down the driveway and back to the car.

'What's the rush, boss?'

Kay tapped her watch. 'School finishes in half an hour. I want to speak to the headmaster. See what our girls were really like.'

Carys stopped next to the car while Kay unlocked it, and looked back at the house. 'Too good to be true, you think?'

'Definitely. Maybe Emma and Melanie were getting up to some things Sarah Thomas never knew about.'

Chapter 14

Kay's lips thinned. 'I never really liked school.'

'Why not?'

Kay shrugged. 'I liked learning. I didn't like the bullying that came with it. Couldn't wait to get out.' She glanced at her watch, then across to the woman behind the desk. 'The headmaster does realise this is urgent?'

'Of course,' the woman said, primly.

At that moment the door next to the desk opened, and a wiry-looking man poked his head out.

'Detective Sergeant Hunter? Would you like to come through?'

Kay stood, arched an eyebrow at Carys, then made her way across the reception office and through to the headmaster's room.

He held out his hand as he ushered them through. 'I'm Geoffrey Hatchard.'

As Kay entered, she was struck by how bare it was. Two chipped and dented grey filing cabinets stood propped against one wall, a pile of paperwork on top of each. A frosted glass window let light into the cramped space while allowing its occupant some privacy from the playground outside. The headmaster's desk was a cheap affair, and looked as if it had been built from a flat-pack kit in a hurry.

The headmaster himself seemed to have absorbed some of his environment's less flattering features.

He loosened his tie from his collar, and removed his threadbare jacket from his shoulders before placing it on the back of his chair and running his hand through thinning hair with an audible sigh.

Kay lowered herself into one of the visitors' chairs he indicated, and waited while he pushed some more paperwork to one side and leaned his forearms on the surface.

'I presume this is about Melanie Richards.'

'It is. Thanks for seeing us at short notice,' said Kay. 'I understand she was close friends with Emma Thomas. Can you tell us more about them?'

Hatchard exhaled, and leaned back. 'A lot of potential. But, unfortunately, a lot of hard work to try to get them to focus.'

'Care to elaborate?'

'We've had some – issues – this past year. Melanie's grades were fine at the end of the last school year, and then she and Emma Thomas were placed in the same class in September. I hate to say it, but Emma has been a bad influence on a few of the girls in the school. Tends to exert her authority.'

'You mean she's a bully?'

Hatchard spluttered. 'Well, I don't suppose it's bullying in the sense that no one is getting hit. They're just words.'

'What sort of words?'

The man sighed. 'Name calling, that sort of thing.' He shrugged. 'We had words with them both on several occasions – especially Melanie. It seemed such a shame that she was more interested in being part of Emma's clique than concentrating on her schoolwork. She really was an excellent pupil.'

'Do you think anyone she bullied would harm her?'

The man's face whitened. 'You can't mean—'

Kay remained silent, and let the man mull over her question.

He opened and closed his mouth a couple of times, and then shook his head. 'No. No, really I wouldn't.'

'We'll need a list of the children who've made complaints,' said Kay.

'I don't know if that's possible.'

'We'll seek permission from their parents to speak with them first.'

'No – that's not what I mean. You see, no one ever made a formal complaint.'

'What?'

The man lowered his eyes and blushed. 'I only found out about it because two of my staff reported incidents to me. None of the kids who were bullied have ever said anything.'

'Why ever not?'

He shrugged.

'Were Melanie and Emma intimidating them so much they were scared?'

'I don't know,' he murmured. 'I'm sorry,' he added, his eyes meeting hers. 'I have no idea.'

***

Kay finished her call to DC Barnes, and having received an update from the incident room, stuffed her phone into her bag.

Her eyes fell to the graffiti scrawled across the red brickwork of the bike shed next to the visitors' car parking bays. It appeared that, at some point, effort had been made to scrub the walls clean; in places, the untarnished surface stood out in stark contrast to the scribbled tags that surrounded it.

When she glanced up, Carys was staring over the car roof at the school's main building.

'What are you thinking?'

Carys shrugged. 'I was wondering how desperate a bullying victim would be to end the torment.'

'Yeah. Definitely something we're going to have to keep in mind,' said Kay. She exhaled. 'Okay, well Barnes says Gavin has managed to get hold of the CCTV footage from the industrial estate, so that's something I suppose.'

'Excuse me?'

She spun round.

A small, thin girl stood in the shadow of the bike sheds, hands clasped in front of her.

'Where did you come from, love?'

The girl pointed over her shoulder to a pathway that cut between the bike sheds and a tired-looking tennis court. 'I heard your voices,' she said.

'Everything okay?'

The girl peered back over her shoulder. 'I guess.'

Kay dumped her bag on the driver's seat, and nodded to Carys before turning back to the girl.

'Did you want to have a chat?'

The girl bit her lip.

'It's okay,' said Kay. 'You won't get into trouble.'

'Is Melanie Richards coming back?'

'Um, no. No, she isn't.'

'Good.'

The girl spun on her heel.

'Wait.'

The girl's eyes widened as she glanced back towards Kay, her whole stance signalling she was ready to flee.

Kay took a deep breath, then took a punt. 'How bad was the bullying?'

'Bad.'

'I got bullied at school, too.'

The girl didn't look convinced.

'I don't know if I'd have gone as far to kill someone who bullied me, though.'

'Me neither.' The girl seemed to relax. 'I don't think any of us would, to be honest. We just wanted to make sure the news was true. That she wasn't coming back.'

'What's your name?'

The girl took off, and Kay swore under her breath.

'What do you think, Sarge?'

They climbed into the car, and Kay started the engine.

'I'm wondering who else Melanie Richards bullied.'

Chapter 15

Kay steered the car between two red brick pillars, the wrought-iron gates to the Richards' driveway already open, and slowed as the wheels crunched over a newly laid, gravel driveway.

A plain pool car from the station had been parked nearest the closed garage doors, and she exhaled as she realised the FLO had transferred from the hospital with Yvonne Richards. A second vehicle, a mid-range silver SUV, stood sentinel on a paved area to the far side of the property.

'Have you ever worked on a kidnapping case before?' asked Carys. She shifted in the passenger seat, unclipped her seatbelt, and stared at the front door.

'Not like this,' said Kay. 'You?'

Carys shook her head.

'Right, I'll lead with the questions. You take notes. If you think I've overlooked something, or want something clarified, jump in. Okay?'

'Got it.'

Kay pulled the key from the ignition. 'Let's go, then.'

Their shoes crunched on the gravel as they made their way to the front door. Carys reached out and pressed the doorbell. From within the house, an electronic bell sounded. A few seconds passed, and then the family liaison officer from the hospital opened the door.

Kay's shoulders relaxed. Hazel had a formidable reputation as an FLO, and she was glad she'd been assigned to Yvonne Richards.

'Morning, Hazel.' She closed the door behind Carys, and immediately noticed the cloak of silence that enveloped what had once been a family home.

'Do you want to wait in the living room?' said Hazel. 'They're in the kitchen at the moment. I'll go and get them.'

Kay nodded, and went through the door to the right that the FLO indicated. She and Carys remained standing while they waited, and she cast her eyes over the expensive soft furnishings that had been carefully placed within the large room.

The space would have echoed with their footsteps except for the thick, plush carpet that covered the floor, and for a moment Kay felt the urge to check the soles of her shoes before discarding the thought. Hazel would have told them if Yvonne required them to remove their shoes at the door.

An enormous television took up a third of the space on the long wall that ran the length of the house, while the far wall had been replaced with concertina-style patio doors that overlooked a medium-sized landscaped garden. Several vases of flowers had been arranged around the room, a false sense of cheer in a house devastated by a double tragedy.

'Serious money, Sarge,' said Carys, eyeing up the sound system hardware that sat on a low unit under the television, then at the speakers set into the ceiling.

Kay acknowledged the remark with a nod, but said nothing. She'd learned before that appearances could be deceptive.

A strong tang of furniture polish clung to the air, and she noted with sadness that often, the only way people could cope with grief was to clean – as if they tried to retain order in a world that no longer made sense to them.

She turned as the door opened, and Hazel entered and stood to one side to let Yvonne pass. She was followed by an older version of herself, with dark-coloured hair tied back in a ponytail, and wearing jeans and a polo shirt.

'This is Dawn, Yvonne's sister,' said Hazel, and made the other introductions.

Kay waited until Yvonne had settled, and noted that Dawn took hold of her hand as soon as she'd sat down, giving it a squeeze.

Yvonne ignored her sister, weary eyes meeting Kay's.

'You're no closer to finding out who did this, are you?'

'It's very early in the investigation,' said Kay. 'Which is why I'm here.' She leaned forward. 'Yvonne, we'd like to make a statement to the media later today. To seek help from the public to find who did this.'

Yvonne dabbed at her eyes, then lifted her chin and stared at Kay. 'You do whatever you need to do to find the bastard. Do you need me to be there?'

Kay shook her head. 'Not at this time. It's likely it'll be just my boss, Detective Inspector Sharp – he's the Senior Investigating Officer assigned to this case. He'll work closely with our media advisors, and it'll be on the evening news. Hazel will be assigned to you while the investigation continues. Is that okay?'

'Thank you.' Yvonne glanced at Hazel. 'But you don't mind?'

'I don't mind at all,' said Hazel. 'I'll be around as long as you need me.'

Yvonne exhaled, and Kay noted the relief in her eyes. For a moment, she wondered what the relationship between her and her sister was like, then pressed on.

'Do you have a recent photograph of Melanie I could take with me, so we can show it to the media?'

'Of course. Hang on.'

Yvonne lifted herself out of the armchair, straightened her skirt, and hurried from the room.

Dawn leaned over to look through the door, and then turned to Kay.

'Do you really think you're going to catch him?'

Kay took a moment before she answered. 'At the present time, my focus is getting as much information as possible to my team. As soon as we have something to act on, we will.'

She glanced up as Yvonne returned and held out a photograph.

'I printed this one off just before we went away.'

'Thank you,' said Kay. She handled the picture with care, and looked at the smiling face of Melanie Richards. Her throat tightened, as it always did when she first saw a murder victim as a normal human being. She'd never baulked at the horrors her job entailed, but it was this, this human element that kicked her in the gut and kept her focused.

'I thought it'd probably be the last time I'd get a photo of her in her school uniform,' said Yvonne. 'The school is changing the rules for the sixth formers, so they can wear what they like.'

'How did she get on at school? Any problems?'

Yvonne shook her head. 'No – she's always had excellent school reports,' she said, and then her face fell.

'I'll look after this,' said Kay.

Yvonne sat next to her sister once more, and Kay tucked the photograph into her bag.

'Yvonne, I need to have a chat about what your routine was like before you went on holiday.'

'It wasn't really a holiday.'

'Oh?'

Yvonne sighed. 'I have a client in Milan who's been particularly difficult these past few weeks. In the end, I took the decision to fly out there and deal with him face to face. Tony came with me as we thought we'd tack on a couple of days at the end to have a break before coming home.'

She wiped her eyes, and Kay could see the guilt seeping into the woman's gaze.

She heard a faint *click* as Carys popped the spring of her pen, and glanced across to see the nib poised over her notebook, before turning her attention back to Yvonne.

'What day did you leave?'

'On Tuesday morning. I had to go to the office first thing for a video conference with the client before we got on the plane. Tony came with me – we got a taxi from the office to the airport.'

'I understand from Emma Thomas that Melanie was going to travel with you.'

Yvonne sighed. 'She was, but she and Tony had a row on Monday night, and she changed her mind at the last minute?'

'What did they argue about?'

'Silly stuff. Tony put his foot down about what Melanie could take to wear, and she didn't like it.'

'And you had no communication with Melanie after you left the house?'

'No. She'd always been very mature for her age, and it wasn't the first time she'd been left on her own for a few days.' Yvonne managed a weak smile. 'I think she liked it, being made responsible.' Her smile faded, and her voice shook. 'We agreed she'd only phone or text us if there was an emergency.'

'Can you take me through the events of that Tuesday? Say, from when you got up?'

Yvonne sniffed, and dabbed at her nose with a scrunched-up tissue she'd pulled from her cardigan sleeve.

'Tony was up first. He liked to have coffee before eating anything, and was always an early bird. As soon as I heard him get the newspaper from the letterbox, I got in the shower. By the time Melanie appeared in the kitchen, we'd had our breakfast.'

'Melanie didn't have breakfast with you?'

'Melanie didn't have breakfast full stop,' said Yvonne, and Kay noted the exasperation in her voice. 'Stopped about a year ago. Said she couldn't face eating first thing in the morning.'

Kay saw a frown crease the sister's brow, and made a note to talk with her in private.

'What time did you leave the house?'

'Just after seven thirty. Melanie wasn't ready, so she would've walked to the end of the road to catch the bus into town.' Her shoulders sagged. 'The video conference was due to start at eight. Otherwise…'

Kay nodded.

Otherwise, Melanie would have been chauffeured into town in the safety of the taxi with her parents.

Otherwise, perhaps Melanie's kidnapper wouldn't have been able to snatch her away.

'What time did Melanie plan to leave the house to catch the bus?'

Yvonne swallowed. 'About seven forty-five.' She gulped back a sob. 'Fifteen minutes. After all that, I could have waited. Bloody client cancelled the video conference anyway.'

Chapter 16

Hazel respectfully suggested a short break from the questioning, and Kay felt inclined to agree with her, so Dawn offered to make coffee, and everyone concurred.

Kay followed Dawn out of the living room and along the hallway to a kitchen that any estate agent would have called 'well-appointed'. Everything that could have been expected to have been there, was there. All in its place, functional, and gleaming.

And clean.

Very clean.

'Are you staying here?'

Dawn nodded, picked up the kettle, and held it under the tap. 'Yes. For a while. I've explained to work I can't leave her at the moment.'

'It's good of you to do that.'

Dawn shrugged and flipped the tap off, then plugged in the kettle. 'She'd have been no good on her own. I would have worried about her.' She grabbed a tea towel, and began to wipe up the mugs that had been tipped upside down on the draining board.

Kay wondered why she hadn't simply placed them in the top of the range dishwasher, but said nothing, and let her eyes wander around the room. 'They've done well for themselves.'

'*She's* done well for herself,' said Dawn. She tossed the tea towel onto the draining board, spun around, and pointed her finger at Kay.

'Tony was nothing until he met Yvonne,' she hissed. She dropped her hand, and leant back against the worktop, her chest heaving.

Kay gestured to the barstools tucked underneath the central kitchen worktop. 'Shall we?'

She waited until Dawn pushed away from the sink and pulled out one of the stools, an almost petulant expression crossing the older woman's face, before she joined her.

Dawn busied herself with retying her hair elastic, smoothed her fringe into place, and then sighed.

'I'm sorry. I know you're just doing your job.'

'It's okay,' said Kay. She pushed her bag out of the way, leaned an elbow on the worktop as she swivelled in her seat to face Dawn, and lowered her voice. 'So, what can you tell me about Tony?'

Dawn snorted. 'Tony? He landed on his feet the day he married my sister.'

Kay raised an eyebrow.

'Listen, he doted on Melanie, and I think he loved Yvonne too, but he was a difficult man to deal with sometimes.'

'In what way?'

'He lost his job two years ago, just as Yvonne's business was starting to take off. Yvonne had moved the business out of the house the year before – it had grown so fast, she had to get proper premises, or start losing contracts.'

Dawn reached out and traced her finger around a rogue coffee stain on the worktop. 'Our father died years ago, and when Mum went, we did okay for ourselves money-wise. Yvonne got a commercial mortgage with her half of the inheritance, and bought the freehold of the unit on Sparks Way.'

Kay pulled her notebook towards her, and wrote a reminder for herself.

Dawn watched, and stayed silent.

'So, what happened when Tony was made redundant?'

Dawn pulled a face. 'I said "redundant",' she agreed, 'although I suspect he pissed off so many people while he was there, they were probably desperate to get rid of him.'

'Did he have a temper on him?'

Dawn shrugged. 'He was more of a verbal bully. Rude to everyone. Always putting people down. Ridiculing them.' She glanced down at her nails.

'Did he do that to you, too?'

Dawn's head snapped up, her eyes glistening. 'Yes. And Yvonne.'

'Did he find more work?'

Dawn shook her head. 'Yvonne decided she'd employ him.'

Kay caught the mocking tone in the woman's voice. 'How long did that last for?'

'About three weeks. Tony began to bully the two other staff members Yvonne had taken on. They were too important to the business for Yvonne to lose them, so she had to let Tony go.'

'How did he take it?'

'Sulked like a five-year-old for a week. It's, *was*, his usual defence. It was never his fault, in his mind.' Dawn reached out for a roll of kitchen towel on an upright spindle in the middle of the worktop, ripped off a sheet, and rubbed at the coffee stain. 'Luckily, I guess, about that time Mel got into trouble at school, so it made sense for him to be around more for her at home.'

'What did she get into trouble for?'

Dawn's mouth twisted. 'Bullying. Like father, like daughter, right?'

Chapter 17

Kay dumped her bag on the hall carpet as she passed, and made her way upstairs.

She crossed the landing to the main bedroom, kicked off her shoes, and then unbuttoned her blouse, pulled off her trousers, and threw both garments into the laundry bin behind the door.

She tugged on her favourite jeans, the ones with holes in that Adam reckoned would fall apart before she agreed to throw them away, and slipped a long-sleeved T-shirt over her head as her stomach rumbled.

She tried to remember when she'd eaten that day, and then gave up.

The afternoon briefing had been delayed by DI Sharp's attendance at the media conference, and by the time he had arrived back at the incident room, it was already late.

The team pushed on regardless, reporting back their findings over the course of the day, with Sharp setting tasks for the morning before he dismissed them.

Kay paused at the top of the stairs, and her gaze shifted to the small room at the back of the three-bedroom semi-detached house.

She hugged her arms around her stomach, and moved closer.

The door had been left ajar; Adam had forgotten to close it in his haste to get to the clinic that morning, and as she peered through, it swung open on its hinges to reveal its contents.

A breath caught in her throat.

They hadn't started painting the room, but had put all the "office stuff", as Adam called it, into boxes, ready to be redistributed around the house once they'd got their heads around the fact that a baby was on the way.

The boxes had stayed packed these past few weeks, neither of them wanting to be the first to suggest that they give up the idea of a nursery and put the office back together.

A packet of two new paintbrushes lay unopened on an old sheet, discarded but not forgotten.

Ignored.

Kay bit her lip, reached out, and pulled the door closed.

She moved down the stairs, picked up her bag, and walked through to the kitchen.

Her eyes fell onto the worktop, and the reptile that lay curled up at the bottom of its temporary home.

'I know you're not feeling well, Sid,' she muttered, 'and don't take this the wrong way, but the sooner your owner's home, the better.'

It flicked its tongue out, and sat unmoving while she edged around the stools that were tucked under the bench.

She'd missed the six o'clock news, and with it the broadcast of the live media statement that Sharp and Larch had made to the press, simply because she'd had to ensure as deputy SIO that all the relevant paperwork had been updated before leaving the incident room for the night.

She'd caught a snippet of the statement on the radio during her drive home, but wanted to catch the late evening news to see what had been presented to the public.

Any investigation had to weigh up the pros and cons of getting the media involved and what to tell them, and it was often a careful balancing act. By finding out what had been publicly released, she could prepare herself for the phone calls they could expect to receive from the public the next day.

Her eyes fell onto a yellow sticky note stuck to the chopping board, Adam's familiar scrawl across it.

It's twins!

She smiled. He'd spent long hours up at the livery stable, and she shared his relief that in the end, everything had turned out okay for the mare and her foals. No doubt he'd remain at the stable until he was satisfied there would be no post-birth complications, and so her mind turned to dinner.

Her hand hovered over the door to the freezer, and then she snatched it away. She'd never get used to Sid's snacks being kept in there while he recuperated.

She opened the fridge door instead, threw together a salad in a bowl, making enough for two, and heaped a generous portion onto a plate while she waited for the microwave to heat up a jacket potato. She added a sticky note of her own next to Adam's.

Salad in fridge. Cans of tuna in cupboard – eat!

The microwave pinged, and she set down her plate on the kitchen worktop, and picked up a knife and fork.

Sid lifted his head and stared at her, his tongue flickering as he scented the air.

Kay glared at the snake, then picked up her plate and placed it on a tray.

'Can't eat sitting next to you, Sid.'

She grabbed a glass of wine, balanced it on her tray, and padded through to the living room.

Adam had left two of the large, floor-standing lamps on before he'd left, and a glow softened the edges of the room. His pride and joy, a large flat-screen television, hung over a low-slung cabinet that housed all the sound system equipment.

Bookshelves lined the long wall opposite the bay window that looked out onto the street, half of which were taken up by a DVD collection they'd amassed between them while Adam was still at university.

Kay put down her tray, and ran a finger along the spines of the films; most were thrillers, along with a rom-com or two they'd enjoyed together at the cinema several years ago, and a few foreign language titles mixed in between. She pushed an errant box back into line, made sure everything was still in alphabetical order, and smiled as she imagined Adam's response to her actions.

He'd always teased her about her need to file the films alphabetically – he'd managed to coerce her into leaving the books alone – but he'd understood once she'd explained to him that after some of the cases she dealt with on a daily basis, she needed something to give her a sense of order in her world.

Satisfied, she turned back to the sofa, and picked up the remote control for the television.

She balanced the tray on her lap as she flicked between channels, until she found the local broadcaster that would soon show the news on the hour.

She ploughed through the salad, and realised she hadn't eaten since breakfast. A smile crossed her lips as she thought of what Sharp would have to say about that – he was a stickler for making sure his team kept up their energy levels, and skipping meals was something he'd managed to drill out of her.

Until now.

She pushed the tray aside when she was done, and turned up the volume on the television as the news programme's familiar theme tune played out.

The kidnapping and death of Melanie Richards was the top story, and she settled back to watch.

Sharp had spent an hour with the media officer prior to going in front of the cameras. Every word of his statement had been analysed, tweaked, and rephrased until it contained enough information to engage the public without releasing valuable intelligence that only the killer would know. The decision had been taken early on in the meeting that the exact details of Melanie's death would not be mentioned.

The method used had been so elaborate, so calculated that any leads from the media appeal would be treated as a priority if a member of the public brought information to their attention that linked to those particular facts.

In addition, they needed the public to be vigilant, not scared.

The photograph Yvonne Richards had provided of her daughter now appeared on a one-page briefing sheet that would have been handed to each attendee at the press conference. It provided a precis of the facts known – at least, the ones they were releasing to the public at this time – as well as the names of the senior officers leading the enquiry, and the national Crimestoppers telephone number.

Finally, they had brainstormed and worked through the questions they anticipated from the press.

Sharp had been reticent upon his return to the briefing room, and Kay wondered if that was because the media conference had gone well, or otherwise.

She reached out for the remote control, and increased the volume as Sharp approached the podium.

He began by thanking the press for their attendance, and then read out the prepared speech.

'It is with great sadness that I also have to report that Tony Richards, Melanie's father, passed away this afternoon due to suspected heart failure,' he added at the end. 'The perpetrator of this terrible crime is now responsible for taking two innocent lives, and we will not rest until that person or persons is brought to justice.'

Kay listened intently while the gathered journalists fired questions at Sharp. The media officer and DCI Larch stood to one side, their faces grim.

There were no surprises; the journalists were respectfully well behaved, and the newscaster repeated the Crimestoppers number, the image of Melanie displayed in the background replacing the footage of the media conference.

Kay switched off the television, checked her watch, and decided to have an early night.

Tomorrow would be a busy day.

Chapter 18

The mobile phone on the sofa next to Eli began to ring.

He cursed under his breath. It was rare to get the house to himself, but his mother had disappeared – to the off licence or pub in all likelihood. She wouldn't return until she passed out, or was kicked out. Either way, he had a few precious hours to relax, and could watch the local news.

He silenced the television, picked up the phone, and checked the number. He'd been expecting the call for the past three hours. In fact, he was surprised it had taken the other man so long to get in touch.

The local six o'clock news had been an extended edition as the police had tried to elicit help from the general public in tracking down Melanie's kidnapper. The story had even made the national news, and had been repeated at nine o'clock on all channels.

He'd slid from the sofa to his knees when the detective revealed that the girl's father had perished, too.

A cry of ecstasy had escaped his lips as Melanie's photograph was displayed on the screen, and he recalled the terror in her eyes as she'd tried desperately to maintain her balance.

He wet his lips at the memory. He'd seen a recording of her demise the day before, watching again as she'd teetered on the brink of death, slipping from one foot to the other as the oil snaked down the rungs.

Somehow, though, it hadn't been as satisfying as watching it happen live.

It hadn't been as thrilling.

Eli had been surprised at the police's decision to appeal to the public so early on in the investigation, and then it hit him.

They didn't know who he was.

No motive.

No suspect.

Nothing.

He answered the phone after the fourth ring, silencing the factory-installed melody.

'What do you want?'

There was an intake of breath at the other end of the line, before a wavering voice replied. 'We need to talk.'

'You picked up the money?'

'You've seen the news?'

'Did you get the money?'

'The girl died, Eli.' The caller paused, and took another deep breath. 'She *died*.'

Eli changed the phone to his other ear, and muted the volume on the television. He checked the football score displayed in the top left hand corner of the screen. 'Did anyone see you taking the money?'

'No. The lane was deserted, like you said it would be.'

'Are you sure?'

'Well, I – I think so.'

A sly smile stole across Eli's face as an idea began to form. The sensation began between his ribs, slipped over his stomach and washed across his groin. 'Where's the money right now?'

'Here.'

'In your *flat*?'

'Yeah.'

'Jesus.' Eli stood, and injected a level of concern into his voice. It was easy. He'd heard other people do it, and had studied how to mimic their reactions. Eli could hear the other man pacing back and forth, back and forth.

'Yeah.'

'What if they went to the police?'

'What?'

'What if the girl's parents *did* go to the police, and we didn't know?' said Eli.

'What do you mean?'

'The police. If they got involved, that money could be marked with something. To make it traceable.'

'Oh, *Christ*.'

'You need to leave your flat. Right now. Keep your head down for a few days.' He almost laughed out loud, and instead expelled the air as a cough at the last minute.

'Where do I go?'

'I don't know. Better still, don't tell me. Then, if the police find me, I can't tell them where you are, right?'

'Shit, Eli. This is huge. This is really bad.'

'I know. We just have to wait until it's safe.'

'But when will I know it's safe?'

'I'll phone you. Don't call me, remember? Delete all your call logs. I'll do the same.'

'Okay.'

'And for fuck's sake, don't phone me again.'

'What do you mean?'

The panicked tone had increased; the pacing stopped.

'Eli – wait!'

Eli pulled the phone from his ear, and held his forearm over his mouth. Tears welled in his eyes as he relished the fear emanating from the other man's voice. He could hear him, shouting his name at the other end of the line. Eventually he answered.

'What?'

'What are we going to do?'

'I don't know. But I have to go.'

'Go where?'

'Best I don't tell you, just in case, yeah?'

A fractured silence filled the phone line.

'She was never meant to die, Eli.'

The man's voice wavered, and Eli smiled.

'I have to go,' he hissed. 'I think there's someone coming.'

He ended the call, ripped the battery and SIM card from the rear of the phone, and set the components on the scuffed coffee table.

He smiled, checked his watch, and then sank back onto the sofa, picked up his can of soft drink, and increased the volume on the television remote.

Fear could be a powerful motivator.

He'd give it an hour, and then follow the other man, to make sure.

Chapter 19

Guy Nelson peered out through the curtains of the double-glazed window at the front of the flat.

Two storeys up, he rented the building with three other tenants, a central hallway and landing bisecting the building that had once been a grand Victorian terrace. He kept to himself, paid the rent in cash on a weekly basis, and made sure to mind his own business.

The realisation that his meagre wages would mean he'd never escape the monotony of his day-to-day life had led to this.

An accomplice to murder, and in hiding from the police.

With twenty thousand pounds in tidy bundles of five hundred pounds poking out from a ripped-open padded envelope on the threadbare sofa behind him.

His hands trembled as he let the curtain fall back into place.

The street below was quiet and poorly lit. No lights shone from the houses across the street, and no sounds escaped from the other flats around him. His immediate neighbour across the landing had switched off his television an hour ago.

It was just him, and his thoughts.

He blinked away tears.

Eli had seemed genuine about ensuring no harm be done to the girl when he had first brought up the idea.

'It's an easy way to make some money,' he'd said.

Nelson had swallowed the last of his can of beer with effort, the warm liquid sticking in his throat. He'd wiped his mouth with his sleeve, and turned to see Eli staring at him, waiting.

'What?'

'I'm serious,' he'd said. 'Twenty thousand pounds. We'd have it within forty-eight hours.'

Nelson had glanced over his shoulder. The rest of the group had fanned out across the car park, and no one was within earshot of them.

'What about the police?'

'They never call the police.' Eli shrugged. 'Too scared. Too embarrassed it's happened to them.'

'But what if they do?'

'Then we walk away. Tell them where the kid is, and say nothing. No one would ever know it was us.'

Nelson's eyes had narrowed. 'Have you done this before?'

Eli had pursed his lips, his gaze moving away as his eyes scanned their work colleagues. 'Once.'

'What happened?'

A smile twitched at the side of the other man's mouth as his eyes met Nelson's. 'I made fifteen thousand pounds.'

Nelson stepped back. 'Really?'

Eli nodded.

'And you never got caught?'

'I'm here, aren't I?'

No more had been said that day. Eli's manager had wandered over, complaining that they should make more of an effort to socialise with the rest of the group, and the afternoon had progressed to evening, the staff members gradually becoming more and more drunk.

Except Eli, Nelson now recalled.

He'd smiled, made small conversation, but had seemed to flit around the edges of the crowd, watching, almost waiting for something.

Eli's shifts changed the following week, and it had been four days before Nelson cornered him.

'How easy would it be?'

'Very.'

Nelson had shoved his hands in his pockets. 'What do you need me to do?'

And Eli had told him.

Nelson had been relieved he wouldn't be involved in the actual kidnapping itself. All he had to do was carry out a reconnaissance of the parents' house, and the industrial building Eli had selected, and report back. Then pick up the money. Eli said he'd take care of the rest.

Now, he wiped angrily at the tears that blinded him.

It had all seemed so simple.

He'd spent the past four hours pacing the small flat. His hand hovered over his mobile phone, first to call Eli, then the police. Each time, he'd snatched his hand back, cursing Eli, cursing himself for being so stupid, so greedy.

Eventually, he slipped out onto the landing and down the stairs. He sat on the last stair tread and pulled on his shoes, lacing them tightly.

His stomach rumbled painfully. Between bouts of throwing up, his stomach had twisted and cramped so much since he'd seen the first news report he'd barely left the bathroom for an hour afterwards.

How could Eli sound so relaxed?

He leaned forward, and held his head in his hands.

If only he hadn't been desperate for the money. If only he'd stopped Eli before it got this far.

He hadn't seen the girl, hadn't been there when Eli had snatched her and taken her to the biosciences building. Eli had told him to stay away, to forget all about it, and simply ensure the money was collected.

And now she was dead.

Nelson stood on shaking legs, zipped up his jacket, and pushed his way out the front door, making sure it didn't slam shut behind him. He jogged down the path, checked the road left and right, and turned in the direction of the park.

He kept a brisk pace, determined to reach his destination before he changed his mind. His pockets empty of house keys and mobile phone, he felt strangely liberated now that his mind was made up.

The night air held a freshness to it, as if the silent town revelled in the lack of traffic and pedestrians.

Ahead, a ginger and white cat scurried across the pavement before diving into the sanctuary of a privet hedge that bordered one of the larger houses on the street.

At the end of the road, Nelson turned right, and then jogged across the pitted asphalt to an alleyway between a house and a block of garages.

He stopped, and checked over his shoulder.

No shadows moved amongst the triangles of light under the street lamps, and yet the tiny hairs at the back of his neck prickled.

He shivered, and then turned back to the dark maw of the alleyway.

The stink of dog shit filled his senses as he hurried along the narrow thoroughfare, the shadow of the house to his right looming over him, blocking out any natural light the waxing moon might have offered.

A fence ran the length of the property, while to his left the solid brickwork of the garages faced the alley. At the end of the fence line and brickwork, the alleyway ended, opening out into a small wooded area that bordered the local park.

He paused for a moment, hands in pockets, as his eyes adjusted to his surroundings and familiar forms began to take shape.

The wooden goalposts that had been rotten when he was a kid, kicking ball after ball into the net; the swing set from which his younger brother had tumbled after a dare too many, breaking his wrist in the process.

He blinked, and the goalposts and the swing set disappeared.

His familiarity with the local area had been what Eli had relied upon.

'Find the perfect place to hide her,' he'd said.

Nelson fought the retching sensation that clawed at his throat, and tried again not to think about how terrified the girl would have been.

He avoided the open expanse of the park in front of him, and instead turned left, keeping close to the brambled hedgerow that lined the perimeter.

He cursed under his breath as his foot slipped down the shallow entrance to a rabbit hole, and then choked back a snort at the thought of his plan being thwarted by a broken ankle.

No.

He would see this through. See this finished.

The scent of mulch and fertiliser drifted over the hedgerow from the vegetable allotments beyond, a heady aroma of rotting organic matter and whatever chemicals the gardeners had added to their prized crops.

Debris lay strewn across the hedgerow and into the path he walked; rubbish that the allotment owners had neglected to take home and dispose of properly, preferring instead to toss it out of the way, out of sight.

Nelson glanced down as his foot kicked something wooden, then bent down and picked up the small crate.

It would come in handy for what he had planned.

He stuffed his right hand back into his jacket pocket, his fingers touching the folded paper there.

He'd agonised over the words, wondering how to explain his remorse to his younger brother, and the mother and wife of the dead girl and husband.

His ballpoint pen had scoured scars into the wooden surface of the cheap coffee table, as time after time he'd torn the page from his notebook and started again. Before he'd left the flat, he'd placed the unwanted pages in the kitchen sink before setting them alight with a cheap cigarette lighter he kept for emergencies.

The stink had filled the small room, but he'd managed to prevent the smoke alarm going off and waking his neighbours by drenching the ashes as soon as they'd started to smoulder, before washing the remnants down the drain.

He picked up his pace.

The allotments ended with a cluster of sheds built with their wooden backs to the hedgerow, and Nelson became aware of the sound of running water.

A breeze tugged at his hair.

He wondered what Eli would do when he found out, a split second before he realised he didn't even know where the man lived. They had only spoken at work.

The thought made him stop in his tracks.

Had this been Eli's plan all along? To engineer the kidnapping so that if anything went wrong, Nelson would take the blame?

Were the police at his flat right now, hammering on the door to get entry? Wasn't that what they did? Raids in the early hours of the morning to catch their suspects unawares?

He checked over his shoulder again.

No one followed; the park remained silent except for the trees rustling in the light wind.

He squinted at the dials of his watch.

Half past four. It'd be sunrise soon.

His eyes found the post in the distance that marked the entrance to the park.

No one moved in the shadows.

He gritted his teeth, and marched on, determined.

He wouldn't go to prison. *Couldn't* go to prison.

Because that's what would happen. Even if he told them about Eli, he would still be charged as an accomplice.

Better to do it this way, and give Eli the chance to start his life over again and put this mistake behind him.

He had his elderly mother to care for, after all. That's why Eli said he needed the money.

She shouldn't have to suffer for her son's mistake.

He reached the lake at the far edge of the park, the water lapping at reeds on the shallow banks.

A memory resurfaced, of him and his younger brother using cheap fishing nets – bright coloured plastic nets on bamboo sticks – to catch water boatmen and small fish every summer, before returning the creatures to the water and watching them dart away.

The oak tree was still there, a majestic, towering canopy that dwarfed the nearby willows.

He paused, his neck craning, but he couldn't see the topmost branches from where he stood.

No matter. The branch he sought was still there, thick and gnarly with age.

Strong.

He removed his hands from his pockets, unzipped his jacket, and began to unwind the rope he'd coiled around his waist.

He hadn't wanted any of his neighbours to wonder where he was going in the middle of the night with a length of rope. He didn't know what he would say to them if asked. Simpler to tuck it away from sight, until it was needed.

It took three attempts to throw it high enough so it arced over the branch and fell to the other side, the end snaking down towards him as he clenched the other end. He flapped the rope in his hand until the higher end began to drop towards him, then looped the ends together, and tied a knot to form an efficient loop.

He left it lying on the ground while he fetched the wooden crate, positioned it under the branch, and then checked the knot once more.

The crate wobbled as he stepped onto it, his shaking legs almost giving way under the added momentum of trying to keep his balance.

He looped the noose over his head, and adjusted the length of rope.

He exhaled, and felt some of the tension from the past week leave his body, at the same time experiencing an urgent need to take a piss.

'Too late for that,' he murmured, and stepped off the wooden platform.

Chapter 20

Kay stamped her feet, and shoved her hands into her pockets in an attempt to seek some warmth from the thin jacket she'd thrown over her shoulders when heading out the front door of her house at six that morning.

Beyond where she stood, a fine mist lifted off the lake as the sun began to ease heat into the day, and the fresh breeze that had sent chills down her neck when she'd first arrived now started to drop. She took a deep breath of the fresh air, and tried to suppress a yawn.

Adam had arrived back late, nearly three o'clock, and despite his best efforts to sneak into bed without disturbing her, she'd turned and snuggled up against his back before drifting off to sleep.

Until her phone rang, and she'd stumbled out of bed, making her way to the park while it was still dark outside.

Now, she turned at the sound of Barnes's voice.

'There's a suicide note.'

He'd left the crime scene investigators to their work beyond the cordoned-off area below the tree, and was heading towards her, the hemlines of his suit trouser legs damp from the morning dew that clung to the long grass.

'A note?'

He held up his notebook. 'It says, "I'm sorry. I didn't mean for her to die".'

'Is that it?'

'Yup.' Barnes snapped his notebook shut, shoved it into his pocket, and turned to face the tree. 'Bastard.'

Kay said nothing. She knew what he meant. By killing himself, the man had escaped justice. She chewed her lip. 'Anything to suggest it wasn't suicide?'

'Sarge?'

'Well, it's a bit convenient, isn't it?'

He shrugged. 'Saves the taxpayers some money.' His head turned at movement to their right. 'Lurch is here.'

She glanced over her shoulder. 'There's a surprise,' she said, not rising to the humour in Barnes's nickname for the detective chief inspector.

'I'll go rustle up some hot drinks for us,' said Barnes. 'Good luck.'

'Thanks.'

Barnes nodded at DCI Larch as the two men passed, and Kay watched his retreating figure, wondering how much her team knew about the Professional Standards investigation, and which of them still held an allegiance to her. She sensed Barnes would be loyal, but she'd have to have a quiet word with him – by making his allegiances too public, he might be in danger of ruining his own career chances if Larch took umbrage to it.

She forced her thoughts back to the task at hand as Larch approached.

'You're rather reticent,' he said. 'Had coffee yet?'

She managed a small smile. 'I'm not that bad. And, no, I haven't.'

'So, what's on your mind?'

He led the way over to the cordon, and they watched as the forensic team worked.

One of the crime scene investigators had hold of the man's legs, and was steering the body into position onto a stretcher as the rope grew slack.

A ladder stood propped against the trunk where one of the investigators had clambered up to cut the rope from the branch, leaving the noose around the dead man's neck, ready for the post mortem examination that would take place.

'It's too simple,' she said. 'Too neat.'

'I wouldn't call that neat,' said Larch, inclining his head towards the body.

The blue-purple hue of the man's face did little to disguise the glass-eyed look of horror etched into his features. Lucas had already told her that the man hadn't tied the noose properly, so rather than a quick death caused by a broken neck, he'd have choked slowly, and would have been unable to lift his own weight to prevent it.

The hanged man's trousers stank of piss and shit, and Kay didn't envy the person who was assigned to clean him up prior to the post mortem.

Larch moved until he was standing next to her, their elbows almost touching as they took in the scene before them.

'Remorse, guilt – it's a strong motivation for suicide,' he said. 'The problem with you, Detective, is that you have a habit of jumping to the wrong conclusions.'

She swallowed, refusing to look at him.

She knew he'd try to bait her at some point, try to make it look as if she was incompetent, or unable to be trusted, but she'd be damned if she'd let him see how much it angered her. One of them had to remain professional, after all.

'Sir,' said Kay, 'with all due respect, that first scene at the biosciences building – that was *nasty*.' She shivered. 'Melanie was made to suffer. This—,' she flapped her hand towards the tree, 'I can't see someone with that much evil in them hanging themselves out of remorse.'

Larch frowned. 'There's nothing to suggest he was murdered. Driver's licence in his wallet. Suicide note in his pocket. No signs of foul play.'

Kay exhaled. 'I just think someone capable of doing what he did to Melanie wouldn't choose to end his life like this.'

Larch snorted, and began to walk away as Barnes approached. 'Well, you might just have to change your thinking on that one, DS Hunter,' he said, over his shoulder. 'I'll see you back at the station.'

'Sir.'

'What did he want?' said Barnes.

'To share his opinion about motive,' said Kay. She took the other coffee he held out to her. 'Cheers.'

Barnes sipped at his hot drink, and then used the takeout cup to point at the DCI's back as he stalked across the park towards the path that led to the road and his waiting car.

'What does he think?'

'Suicide.'

'Well, it is – isn't it?'

Kay sighed. 'Maybe. Looks that way.'

The coroner's vehicle started to bump its way across the grass away from the tree and past two uniformed officers, leaving the crime scene investigation team to glean what they could from the area before they too moved on.

'Come on,' said Kay. 'Let's get back to the station. There's nothing else left for us to do here.'

Chapter 21

Kay glanced up from her computer as Sharp walked through the door to the incident room.

She frowned at his wet hair, and then craned her neck to see out the window.

Dark clouds gathered on the horizon, but the promised storm hadn't reached them yet.

Sharp shrugged his jacket off, slung it over the corner of a chair, and noticed her staring at his wet hair.

'Shower – and a change of clothes,' he said. 'I had to, after the post mortem.'

She nodded her understanding. The stench of the pathologist's rooms clung to clothing – and a person's mouth and nostrils. A hot shower was often the only way to eradicate it.

'That was fast.'

'I know,' said Sharp. He shrugged. 'High profile case, though. It helps. Anything to report here?'

'You haven't missed anything.' Kay sighed, and pushed her chair back. 'We've been going through the call logs from Crimestoppers.'

'Anything of interest?'

'Not yet, but we've only just started.'

'Are you and DC Barnes still convinced there was an accomplice? Someone else involved?'

'Involved, or masterminding it? Yes.'

'Motive?'

'I don't know. I'm not sure. Yet.'

Sharp used his coffee cup to point at the photograph of Guy Nelson on the whiteboard. 'So, what happened there?'

Kay pursed her lips. 'Maybe Nelson found out that Melanie died, and he wasn't expecting that. What if he believed it was just meant to be a kidnapping, and once Yvonne and Tony dropped off the money, Melanie would be returned to them?'

'And his accomplice had other ideas, you mean? That Melanie was never going to leave that building alive?'

'Yes.'

Sharp scratched his chin, and then looked over his shoulder. 'Let's get everyone together. I'll give you all a debrief on the post mortem findings.'

He waited until Kay signalled to the rest of the team and they'd all pushed chairs closer to the whiteboard, and then turned to Barnes.

'Why don't you kick things off by giving us a run-down on the search at Nelson's flat?'

'Boss.' Barnes cleared his throat. 'Crime scene investigators were there for four hours in total. They report finding a mobile phone, some payslips – from a garage up near the Tonbridge Road – and a bag of cash.'

'The ransom?'

'Yeah. All twenty thousand pounds of it.' He jerked his chin at Kay. 'You're right. I saw them logging it for evidence. It doesn't look like much.'

'Maybe he only asked for that much because anything bigger wouldn't have fitted in the padded envelope to fit in the post box,' said Gavin.

'Maybe,' said Sharp. 'Go on. What about the phone?'

'Call logs were clean,' said Barnes. 'The only message found on there was the one Nelson set up for his voicemail greeting.'

'Plan, or pay-as-you-go?' asked Kay.

'Pay-as-you-go,' said Barnes. 'Found a receipt for the last top-up card he bought at the local supermarket three days ago. We've passed it onto the digital forensics team.'

'I'll go and speak to the owner of the garage in the morning,' said Kay. She checked her watch. 'There'll be no one there now.'

Sharp nodded. 'What about the camera in the drain?'

'I'm not sure about that,' said Barnes. 'He didn't have a computer at home, which is weird in this day and age, and CSI found no apps linking to that remote camera on his phone.'

'Did he live alone?'

'Yes. Only one set of clothing found – all his size. Not much food in the refrigerator. Looks as if he lived on microwave ready meals.'

'Okay, well if CSI report back with anything else, let me know,' said Sharp.

'There's one more thing, boss,' said Kay, and jerked her chin towards Barnes. 'Ian says they found no other documents at the flat that are written in capital letters. Guy Nelson used a loopy sort of handwriting.'

'Makes me wonder about the suicide note, that's all, guv,' said Barnes, and shrugged.

'It's a good point,' said Sharp. 'Okay, keep following that line of enquiry unless and until we can disregard it.'

He turned his attention to Carys. 'How did you get on interviewing the other residents?'

'There are two other tenants in the house,' she said. 'The ground floor flat has been empty for three months. The landlord says there's a new tenant moving in next week, but whether they will now, he doesn't know. Nelson's lease wasn't due for renewal until August, and the landlord said he'd had no problems with him in the two years he's lived there. Gets behind on paying the rent on time occasionally, but that's it.'

She checked her notes. 'The woman who lives on the top floor uses separate side access stairs to get to her flat, and rarely saw Nelson. Couldn't even give an accurate description of him, so I don't think we'll get much more from her. The man who has the flat opposite Nelson's on the middle floor works shifts – he'd just got in from work early this morning, he says about half past two, and was about to get his head down when he heard the door to Nelson's flat shut, and then footsteps on the stairs. He said he thought it was unusual, as he didn't usually hear him leave for work at that time. He didn't think anything of it until we knocked on his door.'

'All right. Good work,' said Sharp. He took a step back, and leaned against one of the desks, folding his arms across his chest. 'While you were working on those tasks, I went over to attend the post mortem of Melanie Richards.'

The room fell silent.

No one liked to be the one to have to attend a post mortem, let alone that of a teenage girl, and Kay was grateful Sharp had chosen that task for himself. It said a lot about the way he ran his investigations, often taking on the worst tasks for himself.

He reached across the desk he sat on and picked up the autopsy report, then took the reading glasses he kept in his shirt pocket, flicked them open, and began to read.

'First up, no signs of sexual intercourse, nor any traces of illegal drugs, although that comes with the caveat that if our suspect used a date-rape drug, it wouldn't show up in her system by now.'

He sighed, and flipped the page. 'Based on Lucas's findings though, I doubt very much Melanie was drugged to keep her quiet, especially given the location where she'd been kept. It would seem that our suspect was determined to ensure that Melanie remained conscious and fully aware how dire her situation was.'

The team remained silent, hanging onto his words.

Kay bit her bottom lip, aware she was holding her breath.

'Lucas says Melanie didn't die by strangulation,' said Sharp, and waited while the news sank in.

'Then, how—,' began Barnes.

'Heart attack.'

Kay frowned. 'Any medical history of a weak heart?'

'No,' said Sharp. 'But, what *is* interesting is the presence of a large amount of insulin in Melanie's body. The family GP has been contacted, and he confirms that Melanie wasn't a diabetic.'

'It would've raised her heart rate,' said Kay.

'Exactly,' said Sharp, and threw his copy of the report onto the desk. 'So, it is suggested that the terror from her predicament, and trying to keep her balance on that ladder knowing if she slipped she would hang – would have sent Melanie's heart rate through the roof. Aided most effectively by the insulin.'

'Jesus,' said Kay. 'He scared her to death.'

Chapter 22

The scent of oil, grease, and sweat hit Kay the moment she approached the large double doors of the garage.

A radio played in the background, the pounding beat of that summer's hit song belting out, only to be drowned out by the punch of an air line being used to rhythmically ratchet wheel nuts into place.

Three vehicles stood on hydraulic jacks, raised several feet above the ground while men worked underneath them.

Kay shaded her eyes and squinted through the gloom, and tried to figure out which one of them was the owner.

Each and every man was wearing blue overalls, smudges of oil and grease on their faces.

She wrinkled her nose. She glanced down, noticed a hubcap turned upside down, full of cigarette butts, and stepped away to fresher air.

A sign nailed to the wall demanded visitors wait before entering the space, warning of dangers and legal waivers should anyone dare to ignore it.

Kay read through the faded lettering twice before she heard footsteps approach.

'Can I help you?'

The man who spoke wiped his hands on a dirty rag, his face quizzical.

He loomed out of the shadows, and she had to raise her chin to look him in the eye.

'I hope so,' she said, and held up her warrant card. 'I'm looking for the owner of this place.'

He smiled. 'That would be me.' He held out his hand. 'I'm Darren Phillips.'

Her eyes must have shown her surprise, as his face turned rueful. 'Yeah, I know – everyone says it – I look too young to run this place.' He shrugged. 'It was my dad's business. Until he got dementia.'

'I see,' said Kay. 'Is there somewhere we can talk in private?'

'And away from this noise, you mean?' He grinned. 'Sure – come on through to the office.'

He led the way into the garage, and Kay followed him across a dusty and oil-stained concrete floor to a small room that had been created at the back of the space by placing partition boarding in a square and adding a door.

Phillips closed it, blocking out some of the noise, and gestured to a seat placed against the wall.

Kay resisted the urge to dust it off with her hand before sitting, and placed her bag on the floor before removing her notebook.

Phillips sank into a chair next to a small table that seemed to serve as a desk, picnic table, and all-round storage dump. 'What's this about?'

'Guy Nelson,' she said.

Phillips snorted. 'Haven't seen him in over a week.'

'When was the last time you did see him?'

'Friday before last. Pay day. He said he wanted a few days off, which I agreed to. He never came back.'

He shrugged. 'The business only employs casual labour,' he elaborated. 'It keeps the overheads down. Some people are more reliable than others.' He nodded towards the two men in the workshop. 'Those two have been with me for ages – worked for my dad before that. Guy Nelson was only here three months.'

'He was found hanging from a tree in Mote Park this morning.'

Phillips' jaw dropped open. 'That was him? I heard on the news a body was found.'

'We're in the middle of a murder investigation. We haven't released the full details to the press yet.' She held his gaze. 'And I'd appreciate it if this conversation remained confidential at the present time.'

'Of course, of course.' Phillips sat back in his chair, a stunned expression on his face. 'Well. I never took him for being the suicidal type.' He rubbed his chin. 'Jeez.'

Kay gestured to the vehicles outside the double doors. 'You have a lot of courier vans here.'

'Dad won the contract before he got too sick to work.'

Kay peered through the window between the office and the workshop, and then ran her eyes over the sports car that was being lowered to the floor on one of the hydraulic platforms.

'Some of the cars you get in here must be worth quite a bit. What do you do to ensure no one can get to them?'

Phillips pointed to a safe next to the office door. 'All the keys are in there, apart from the ones we're working on. At night, if we're halfway through a job, we'll lower the jacks, lock the vehicle, and put the keys in here until the next morning.'

'Who has access to the safe?'

'All of us. There's no cash in there,' he added. 'It's a deterrent in case we're broken into.' He pointed to a laptop on the desk. 'We've got cameras on the outside of the building, too. One over the front door, one over the fire exit at the back – that one also covers the window at the back of the shed.'

'Do you mind if I have a look at Nelson's personnel file?'

'I suppose it wouldn't be a problem.'

He heaved himself out of the chair with a grunt, and moved towards a two-drawer filing cabinet in the corner of the room, returning with a thin plastic folder.

'Thanks,' she said, and began to flick through it. Her fingers ran over the usual paperwork – copy payslips, tax forms, terms of employment. She paused at the page that listed Guy Nelson's contact details. 'No emergency contact provided?'

'No. Said both his parents had died. Has a sister in New Zealand, I think.'

Kay nodded, and made a mental note to find out what arrangements had been made by the pathologist for formal identification. Nothing had crossed her desk yet, so she wondered if the sister had been contacted already.

She closed the file, and handed it back. 'What was he like as an employee?'

Phillips shrugged. 'All right, I suppose. Turned up on time. Did the work. Left.'

She gestured to the two men in the workshop. 'Did you socialise much with him?'

'Not really. We go to the pub when we close up here on a Friday sometimes.' He frowned. 'Actually, yeah. Last time was about two months ago. Some of the blokes from the courier company organised a barbeque and cricket match. We all went to that.'

Kay jotted down the details. 'Whereabouts?'

'The main courier depot.'

'I know it. Do you have details of any friends of his?'

He shook his head, and tapped the personnel folder on his knee. 'He never mentioned anyone. I think he preferred to stay at home and play console games. Seems to be all he ever talked about during his breaks here.'

Kay snapped her notebook shut. 'Okay, I think that's all the questions I have for now,' she said, and handed over a business card. 'If you think of anything else though, feel free to contact me.'

'Will do.' He rose, and opened the door for her. 'I'll see you out.'

Kay watched where her feet fell as she walked across the workshop floor.

Piles of tyres were stacked against the front inside wall of the building, while boxes of parts and tools filled a steel shelving unit off to one side.

Phillips held up his hand and stopped as a whirring noise began. She paused next to him, and drummed her fingers on the strap of her bag as they waited while the nearest van was lowered to the concrete floor. The machinery stopped, and they carried on.

'Thanks again for your time,' she said, and shook Phillips' hand before returning to her car, her mind racing.

What sort of game enthusiast wouldn't have a console or computer at home?

Chapter 23

Kay put her mobile phone away as the front door opened, and nodded to Hazel as she stood to one side.

'How's things?' she murmured.

Hazel shrugged. 'A bit tense between her and her sister,' she said, in a low voice. 'I think she'd be happier if her sister went home, to be honest.'

Kay bit back a response. If her sister was anywhere near her house, she'd be packing up and moving to a hotel. Most likely one in a different country, too.

Instead, she rummaged in her bag and pulled out her notebook. 'Any new thoughts on the weeks leading up to the kidnapping?'

'No. She's angry, though. I think that's helping her through her grief. She's determined to find the bastard who did this.' Hazel checked over her shoulder to make sure the doors to the living room and kitchen were closed. 'She insisted on watching the press conference, even though it was incredibly upsetting for her. Now she wants to know when we're going to arrest someone.'

Kay nodded. Yvonne's reaction was natural, and very common among families of victims. 'Where is she?'

'Living room. I let her know you were on your way. She suggested to Dawn that she pick up some things from the supermarket about five minutes ago. Dawn wasn't happy about it, but she went.'

They shared a knowing smile, and then Kay followed Hazel along the hallway. She knocked on the door, and then led the way into the living room. 'Go on in,' she said. 'I'll get some tea.'

'Have you caught him?'

Yvonne rose from the settee, her eyes hopeful.

'Why don't you sit down,' said Kay, keeping her voice even, 'and I'll walk you through where we're up to?'

The other woman sank back into the plush upholstery, and sighed. 'You've got nothing,' she said. 'Have you?'

Kay didn't answer straight away. Instead, she placed her bag on the floor, shrugged off her jacket, laid it on the arm of the matching chair, and sat. She opened her notebook.

'When you received the phone calls from Melanie's kidnapper, Yvonne, did he ever indicate to you that he was working alone, or with others?'

'Why?'

'Please, answer the question.'

Yvonne frowned, and bit her lip. 'I can't remember. Tony was the one who spoke to him, you see.'

'Did Tony talk to the same person every time?'

'I think so, yes.'

'When you went to the place where Melanie was being held, did you see anyone else?'

Yvonne shook her head.

'Okay, going back to the phone calls you received, did you ever hear the caller's voice?'

'No.' Yvonne sat back, and held up her finger. 'Wait. Yes. Just that once. I snatched the phone away from Tony, and yelled at him.' She sniffed. 'And then he… he hurt Melanie,' she gulped. Her eyes found Kay's. 'What's this about?'

Hazel appeared at the door, a tray of steaming mugs in her hands, and made her way across the carpet towards them. 'Has there been a development?' She handed one of the mugs to Yvonne, pushed another to Kay, and sat down.

'This morning, at sunrise, a jogger found a man hanging from a tree in Mote Park, near one of the paths above the lake,' said Kay. 'A suicide note was found in his jacket pocket.'

Yvonne's hand flew to her mouth, and she set the tea mug down on the small table in front of them with a clatter.

'The note indicated that he was involved in Melanie's kidnapping,' said Kay.

'Oh, my god.' Yvonne stood on shaking legs, her face white.

'A sum of money was found at his house,' added Kay, 'in keeping with the amount you indicated had been paid to ensure Melanie's return.'

'The bastard,' said Yvonne, pacing the carpet. 'All I wanted was my daughter home safe. He took her, he took my husband, and now he's not even going to get justice for what he's done to me!'

'Yvonne, I need your help,' said Kay. She crossed the room to where Yvonne stood, placing her hand on the other woman's arm. 'The crime scene investigators found a mobile phone at the suspect's flat.' She took a deep breath. 'It has his personal voicemail message recording on it. I'd like you to listen to it. To confirm it is the man you heard on the phone.'

Yvonne's eyes opened wide. 'Why?'

'We want to be sure,' said Kay.

Chapter 24

Yvonne Richards had offered to attend the police station immediately, much to the obvious chagrin of her sister.

'You can't go!' she'd insisted. She'd spun round in the hallway to face Kay, a plastic supermarket shopping bag banging against her leg. 'Tell her – she's not well enough to go.'

'Don't be ridiculous,' Yvonne had said, as she wrapped a scarf around her neck and shrugged on a jacket. 'Stay here. I won't be long.'

With that, she'd led Kay out of the house and across the driveway to her waiting car.

As Yvonne had settled into the passenger seat and Kay pulled into the street, she'd emitted a sigh. 'Well, at least this gets me out of the house for a while.'

Kay had bitten her lip, and emitted a non-committal, 'Hmm.'

She'd been saved from having to respond further by the rush hour traffic, and had concentrated instead on getting Yvonne across the town to the station as quickly as possible.

Pulling up into the car park, she'd eased the saloon into a space near the emergency exit at the back of the station, and switched off the engine.

'There are a few reporters lurking around the front,' she'd said to Yvonne by way of explanation. 'I thought we'd use the back door instead.'

'Thank you,' Yvonne had murmured.

Now, they waited in an office off the incident room that Sharp had commandeered. Kay had phoned ahead to announce their arrival, and he'd rushed off to get a copy of the voicemail message.

They didn't have to wait long.

Kay had settled Yvonne into one of the soft chairs next to the desk when she heard footsteps approaching.

Sharp knocked twice, then entered, nodded to Kay, and introduced himself to Yvonne Richards.

'Mrs Richards, I'm so sorry for the loss you've had to bear this week. Thank you for coming over.'

Kay always admired the way Sharp's manner softened when he spoke to victims or their families.

He had a knack for putting them at ease, showing compassion and empathy, while at the same time ensuring he got the results he sought, without appearing too tough.

'That's okay,' said Yvonne. 'I want to help.' She glanced across at Kay. 'Kay said you had a voicemail recording of the man who was found dead this morning.'

'That's right.' Sharp pulled a USB stick from his trouser pocket, leaned over, and plugged it into the side of the laptop on the desk. He lowered his eyes to Yvonne. 'Are you okay if we listen to this now?'

Kay held her breath, and waited for Yvonne's response.

The woman's shoulders slumped as she studied her hands in her lap, and Kay heard her exhale, a shaking breath that seemed to wrack her body. Eventually, Yvonne raised her head. 'You can't do this without me, can you?'

'No,' he said. 'We can't.' He pulled out the chair next to Yvonne and sat down, leaning his elbows on his knees. His brown eyes bored into Yvonne's. 'We have to make absolutely sure we have the right man. I won't rest – nor will Kay, or the rest of my team – until we're one hundred percent certain.' He straightened. 'I'm sorry, Yvonne. I know this won't be easy, and I wish there was another way.'

The woman plucked at the hem of her cardigan, a loose thread growing in length as she worked. 'No, no,' she croaked. She cleared her throat. 'That's fine.'

'All right,' said Sharp. He rose, and leaned over the laptop once more. 'To clarify, this is a voicemail message found on the man's mobile phone. It's the sort of message you record when you want someone to leave a message for you when you can't take their call, okay?'

Yvonne nodded. 'Okay.'

'We'll play it once, all the way through, and then if you need to listen to it again, just say so.'

Kay stood behind Yvonne, her arms folded, doing everything in her power not to pace the room.

Sharp pressed the "play" button on the screen, and she held her breath as the message played.

Yeah, this is Guy Nelson. Can't take your call. Leave a message.

Her eyes met Sharp's over Yvonne's head as the message finished, and she raised an eyebrow.

Is that it?

He gave a small nod before his gaze fell to Yvonne.

'Can you play it again?' the woman asked.

'Of course.'

Sharp reached across and hit the "play" button once more as Kay moved next to him, her heart racing.

She tried to read Yvonne's expression.

The woman had paled, and was twiddling the strap of her handbag between her fingers as she listened once more.

The recording stopped.

Silence descended on the room.

After a few moments, Sharp coughed politely.

'Any thoughts, Yvonne?'

Yvonne sat back in her chair, and lifted her gaze to first Kay, then Sharp. She shook her head.

'That's not him.'

Chapter 25

Kay stepped to one side, and held the door open for Yvonne, thanking her for her time.

'I'll see Mrs Richards out and arrange for a car to take her home. Gather the team. I'll meet you in the incident room in ten,' said Sharp as he passed her, and then winked. 'You were right. Well done.'

She exhaled. The elation of being right quickly gave way to the reality that they still had no idea who Guy Nelson was working with, and who had, in all likelihood, orchestrated Melanie's murder.

She let the door slam back into place on its automatic closer, and hurried towards the incident room.

Four faces turned as she burst through the door.

Barnes had the desk phone to his ear, but quickly ended his call as Kay hurried over to the whiteboard.

'Yvonne Richards has confirmed that Nelson isn't the man who phoned them in relation to Melanie's kidnapping,' she said.

A shocked silence filled the room.

'So, he *was* working with someone else?' said Barnes.

Kay nodded. 'Yes, and we need to step up the effort going through those CCTV recordings, Gavin.'

'Ma'am. Sorry – Kay.' He gave a shy smile.

She acknowledged it with a wave of her hand. 'Think outside the box, Gavin. Think like our murderer.' She turned to the board, and drew a question mark next to the photograph of Nelson. 'Whoever he is.'

'Are we definitely looking for a bloke?' asked Carys.

'I think so,' said Kay. 'But keep your options open.'

'Right,' said Sharp, entering the room and pulling his tie away from his collar. 'Where are we up to?'

He rolled up the tie, and threw it onto his desk before approaching the whiteboard. He stood, hands on hips and glared at it.

'Back to the CCTV images,' said Kay. 'We're only halfway through them so far.'

Sharp nodded. 'How did you get on at the garage this morning?'

'That was interesting,' said Kay. 'Darren Phillips said Nelson was a complete computer game fan. That's all he spoke about during his breaks. Yet, we didn't find any trace of a console at his flat, right?'

Barnes shook his head. 'Nothing at all.'

'So who took it? Or, did he lend it to someone?' said Kay. 'Phillips said he was only a casual employee, and the last time he saw him was on the Friday before last – pay day. Apparently Nelson said he was going to take a week off. He never made it back.'

'Okay. Carys? Organise a couple of uniforms and go back to the Richards' neighbours. Take copies of Nelson's photo. See if anyone recognises him,' said Sharp. 'Even better, find out if any of them have had a chance to recall anyone acting suspiciously around the street.'

'Sir.'

Sharp directed his gaze at Barnes. 'Same for you. Go back to Nelson's flat. See if anyone was seen with a computer – laptop or otherwise – any time during the past two weeks.'

'Boss? If Guy Nelson had the money, it means our mystery suspect didn't bother going there to take it. He'd have found out about the guy's suicide, surely?' said Barnes, and held his hands up. 'So, what's his motive?'

'We have to consider revenge,' said Sharp. 'Maybe for something to do with Yvonne Richards' business. Kay – when we're done here, give Sheila Milborough a call. Find out if the business owes anyone any money, or has received any threats of late. Things that wouldn't show up in their accounts systems.'

She nodded. 'Will do.' She made a note on a pad next to her. 'What about power as a motive? He, or she,' she added, acknowledging Carys's earlier remark, 'went to a lot of trouble to set this up. Based on the post mortem report, his intent seems to have been to scare Melanie to death.' She shrugged. 'I'm simply wondering if it was revenge, why didn't he kill her some other way?'

'Too elaborate this way, you mean?'

'Yeah.' She leaned back, and pointed at the photographs of the biosciences facility pinned to the board. 'That took a lot of planning and preparation. He certainly didn't act on a whim.'

'Power's certainly a possibility. There could be a sexual element too,' said Sharp. 'Although, the post mortem confirms that Melanie hadn't been sexually abused.'

'But there was a camera there,' said Kay. 'He was watching her all the time.'

'Have the digital forensics team come back to us with anything?'

'Not yet,' she said, and scribbled on her notepad again. 'I'll chase them up.'

'Okay,' said Sharp. 'That's enough for now.' He checked his watch. 'We'll reconvene again at six o'clock.'

Chapter 26

Kay picked up her notebook, and settled into her chair, energised by the renewed sense of urgency that galvanised the team.

She dialled zero for an external line on her desk phone, and drummed the end of her pencil on the desk while she waited for an answer.

'Richards Furnishings, can I help you?'

Kay smiled, recognising Belinda's voice. Evidently the twenty-something was already begrudging the lack of an afternoon receptionist.

'Belinda?'

'Yes?'

'It's DS Hunter. May I speak to Sheila, please?'

'Oh. Yeah. Hang on.'

Kay pulled the phone away from her ear as a loud rustling filled the line, and guessed Belinda had held the receiver to her shoulder.

She strained her ears.

'It's her. The detective. Wants to speak to you.'

A pause, then—

'Hang on. I mean, one moment please.'

A melodious series of *pings* came on the line, and Kay looked up as Gavin hovered nearby.

'What's up?'

'Can't find Sharp. I think he's gone to a meeting. When you've got a minute,' he said, and jerked his chin towards his computer, 'I need to show you something. On the CCTV.'

'Okay.' She held up a finger as Sheila Milborough's voice broke in.

'Hello?'

'Sheila? It's DS Hunter. I'm sorry to trouble you, but I wondered – in Yvonne's absence from the office – whether you could help me?'

The woman was silent for a heartbeat, then spoke, her voice full of efficiency.

'Of course, Detective Hunter. What do you need?'

Kay bit her lip. The woman was so desperate for gossip, a flare could've gone up.

'I must insist this conversation is treated with the utmost confidentiality.'

'Of course.'

Kay doubted it, but ploughed on regardless. 'I wondered if you were aware of any threats made in recent months with regard to the business. Before Melanie's kidnapping.'

Sheila sucked in her breath, though again, Kay couldn't tell if that was through shock, or excitement.

'Well,' she said, eventually. 'I'm not aware of anything, that's for sure.'

'What about any debts to the business? Anyone causing issues there?'

'No. No – we're very lucky with our client base.' She paused. 'And we use a post office box for correspondence, so no one knows where we are.'

'That's good,' said Kay. Satisfied, she changed the subject. 'How are you coping? It must be hard at the moment.'

'Oh, we're fine,' breezed Sheila. 'Yes, it's busy, but the days go by fast, you know?'

Kay finished her call, and dropped her pen.

She glanced over her shoulder.

Gavin had disappeared – she suspected for a cigarette break – and so she looked up the number of the cybercrime team on the internal directory, and dialled the number.

''Lo?'

'Grey,' she grinned. 'It's Kay.'

'Bloody hell, bird – you back on the job?'

'Certainly am.'

'I knew they'd find nothing on you,' he said.

She smiled. 'Given the surveillance capabilities of your department, I do hope that comment is based on a personal observation instead.'

A shocked silence filled the air before the digital forensics expert choked out a laugh and swore. 'Very funny. What do you want?'

'That camera set-up we brought in from the Melanie Richards crime scene. Any progress?'

'Ah – the girl down the drain,' said Grey, absently. 'Hang on. I didn't work on that one, so the report might still be with admin. Two secs.'

Kay waited, hearing the sound of computer keys being hit.

'I've got a copy of the final draft on screen. It was a basic home security set-up – the sort you can put in your home, and then watch from your mobile or a laptop. Very common, so hard to trace beyond the shop selling it. You can check with them, but—'

'It was purchased online, we think.'

'You're stuffed, then.'

'Thanks.' She sighed. 'Any chance we can trace where it was being watched?'

'This is Kent Police,' said Grey. 'You've been watching too many James Bond movies.'

'No fingerprints or anything?'

'CSI said it was impossible to get anything off the surface. It had been thoroughly cleaned with—'

'Bleach. Yeah. Figures.'

She thanked the digital forensics expert, and put the phone down. She rubbed at her temples, then stood and stretched before she noticed Gavin had returned. 'Gavin. You wanted a word?'

'Could you come over and look at this?'

She wandered over to his computer. 'What's up?'

He held up a document. 'This is one of the calls that came through via the Crimestoppers appeal after the boss's television appearance. A woman reported seeing a County Deliveries courier van going into the industrial estate where the biosciences place is. She said she saw it a couple of mornings, but then once late at night as well, on Thursday last week.'

Kay frowned. 'What was she doing around there at that time of night?'

'She's a nurse. Uses the industrial estate as a short cut home.'

'A courier van?'

'Yeah, I know.'

'Have you checked the CCTV images?'

He pointed to the screen. 'Yeah. It took me a couple of attempts to find it, even after I'd phoned the nurse to get an idea of timings, but it's there.'

'Where's this camera?'

'On Westmead Road.' He tapped the screen. 'The entrance to the industrial park is just up there.'

'Play it.'

Gavin clicked the "play" button, and the recording began.

Sure enough, on the grainy image of the CCTV camera, a van emerged from the industrial estate, heading in the direction of the camera. On the opposite side of the road, a small white hatchback passed by.

'That's her,' said Gavin.

Kay remained silent.

She heard Barnes finish the call he was on before he joined them, his elbow brushing hers. 'Got something?'

She pointed at the screen in response.

The van drew closer to the camera, and then turned right. As it did, she got a clear look at the courier company's logo emblazoned down the side.

'Can we see the driver's face?'

'No. He's wearing a baseball cap pulled down low. No distinguishing marks or tattoos on his hands. Can't see a watch or a wedding ring.'

'Registration number?'

Gavin turned his notebook towards her. 'Yes.'

'What's going on?' said Sharp as he entered the room.

'We've got CCTV images of a courier van leaving the industrial estate on the evening of last Thursday,' said Kay. 'Gavin was going through the call logs from the Crimestoppers appeal. A nurse reported seeing a courier van entering and leaving the estate on three occasions, once at night. This is the night-time event.'

Gavin replayed the video as the team watched on in silence.

When it finished, Sharp nodded. 'Good work, Constable.'

'I take it there's been a development?'

They all turned as DCI Larch strode through the doorway and across to where they sat.

'Sharp?'

'Angus.' Sharp stepped away from the computer, and brought the DCI up to speed.

'Boss? When I was at the garage this morning, they had a lot of courier vans there. Darren Phillips said his dad won the contract before handing over the business to him,' said Kay. She pointed at the frozen screen. 'That can't be a coincidence.'

'We'll need to formally interview him – and his employees,' said Larch.

'I'll phone the County Deliveries depot, too,' said Kay. 'Find out who that van is assigned to.'

'Better still, Hunter, find out who it's assigned to, and bring him back here for questioning,' said Larch.

She glanced at Sharp. 'Sir?'

'Might be a bit hasty, Angus, with all due respect,' said Sharp.

'Do it,' said Larch, and jutted his chin out. 'We need results here, ladies and gentlemen – and fast.'

He checked his watch. 'I have a meeting with the chief superintendent,' he said. 'I'll join you at the next briefing for an update.'

Kay watched him stalk away, and cursed under her breath.

Sharp rubbed his chin, then sighed. 'Tread carefully, Kay.' He pointed at the frozen image on the screen. 'That's all we've got to go on at the moment.'

'I understand.'

'Then, go.'

Chapter 27

Eli traipsed away from the van parked in the lay-by, the tall grass swishing against the hem of his trousers.

The overgrown hedgerow to his rear provided ample cover from the road, and any passing motorists would simply think the van had been temporarily abandoned while its driver took a break.

He shifted the heavy canvas bag on his shoulder, a jangle of metal reaching his ears as the equipment slipped around, and picked up his pace.

Overhead, a lone crow soared on the air currents, its sorrowful caw receding as it flew across the edges of the urban sprawl.

Eli sniffed.

A tang of ozone filled the air, a promise of the heavy rainfall forecast for the coming days.

He clenched his fists, and tried to ignore the ache below his belt.

Soon, it would be time.

As he made his way to the padlocked entrance gate, he extracted a key from his pocket. The buildings had been deserted mid-construction, the developer running out of finance before the complex could be completed. Now, the abandoned apartment blocks awaited a resolution between the banks and the council, and stood derelict while awaiting their fate.

The plans had been easily accessible from the council's website, and Eli had spent his week off poring over the details while ignoring Melanie's pitiful pleas for mercy.

Once he'd committed the plans to memory, he'd burnt them, filling the old animal laboratory with smoke.

Melanie had screamed, convinced the building was on fire, and he'd crawled to the hole and lain down, listening to her sobs.

Now, he opened the padlock he'd procured, loosened the chain around the fence, and slipped through.

He ignored the construction signs warning him to keep out, and moved swiftly through the site, the layout committed to memory.

The developer's money had been sucked dry once the building company had begun to dig the foundations, and discovered an old maze of Victorian drainage systems criss-crossing the ground. Arguments ensued, blame apportioned, and construction stopped.

That was six months ago.

Eli pushed a sheet of plastic to one side, the material crackling under his touch before he let it drop back into place.

The ground floor of the first of the two apartment blocks housed little more than a screed floor. Above his head, the concrete and steel framework of what would have been the floors of accommodation units lay open, the grey sky darkening with impending rain.

Eli ducked around a pillar, stepped over a pile of abandoned plastic piping, and lowered his bag to the floor.

He tugged the zip open, rummaged inside, and pulled out a large torch. He switched it on, and re-shouldered the bag. He swept the beam left and right, and then found what he was looking for in a darkened corner of the space.

The concrete steps led down to what had been intended to be a fire exit to and from the basement car park. Access to that from outside was impossible – the construction company had barricaded it for fear of the local kids getting hurt, or more likely, vandalising the place.

Instead, the car park and the bowels of the building could only be accessed through these steps, and now Eli descended them, his free hand placed on the wall to steady himself.

After a few moments, he found himself in the car park itself. The torch beam couldn't reach the far end of the space, but Eli gained his bearings quickly, and hurried towards the left hand corner.

A metal gate had been set into the wall, which had been inaccessible until two days ago when Eli had taken a blowtorch to its hinges. Now, he placed the torch on the floor facing it, wrapped his fingers around the steel, and pulled it to one side.

Water glistened on the rough surface.

He retrieved his torch, and ducked under the low entrance into a short passageway that dropped steeply away from the basement level.

The beam bounced off red brickwork, chipped and worn, before coming to rest on a dead end.

A wide opening gaped in the floor of the passageway, an entrance to a centuries-old labyrinth.

Eli dropped the bag to his feet and crouched, then rested his forearms on his knees, and inspected the opening.

A steady *drip-drip* of water reached his ears.

'Perfect,' he murmured.

Chapter 28

Kay loosened her seatbelt as Barnes swung the plain-coloured sedan left and into the visitors' car park of the County Deliveries depot.

Despite the lateness of the day, a number of spaces were still available.

As she got out of the car, Kay ran her eyes over the low-set structure in front of her.

To her right, a high, wire mesh fence separated the visitors' car park from an area filled with the familiar red outlines of courier vans. On her left, a separate parking area had been sectioned off for staff members. As she watched, two vans drove into the sectioned off area, the drivers hurrying across the asphalt towards the back of the depot.

Barnes stopped mid-stride across the car park and waited for her. 'Ready?'

She nodded. 'Let's speak to the depot manager first,' she said, 'and let's not mention to him our suspicions about the van straight away, okay?'

'Sounds good.'

She locked the car and followed Barnes to the glass double doors at the front of the building.

A simple reception desk took up the back wall of the small area, and they signed in while the receptionist phoned through to the depot manager and announced their arrival.

She turned at the sound of a door closing to her right.

A man approached them, his hand outstretched.

'I'm Bob Rogers. I'm the depot manager here. What's this about?'

Kay introduced herself and Barnes. 'Is there somewhere we can speak in private?'

'Of course. Follow me. There's a small meeting room along here we can use.'

They followed the man along a short corridor that ran across the front of the building. He stopped and held open a door to his left for Kay, and she led the way into a sparse meeting room.

It was evident the room wasn't used much; a thin layer of dust covered the round table in the centre, and only three chairs remained, the others no doubt poached and removed to other offices. A desk phone had been placed on a small cabinet in the corner.

The depot manager gestured to the chairs. 'Sit down. How can I help you?'

Kay passed across her business card, and waited while Barnes did the same.

'I'd like to ask you some questions about the vans that you use here,' she said. 'First of all, are vehicles assigned to a particular courier? Or are they assigned on a first-come first-served basis?'

Rogers pulled out a chair and sat down. He scratched his chin. 'The vans are assigned to a particular route. So the courier doing that route uses the same van every day.'

'What happens at the end of the day?' said Kay. 'Where are the keys kept?'

'When people return from their shifts, they hand in their keys. All of the keys are kept in a secure place.' He frowned. 'What's this all about?'

Kay ignored his question. 'What security measures do you have here? Is the security gate manned at night?'

'No. The gate is locked in place by security at six o'clock.'

'Is there only one gate?'

'Yes,' said Rogers.

'And the fencing is secure?'

He frowned. 'I believe so, yes.'

'You don't seem sure.'

'The security guards check it every week. I haven't heard any reports that the fence isn't secure.'

'What about CCTV cameras?' asked Barnes.

'We have cameras on each side of the building.'

'Do any of the cameras cover the car park where the vans are?' asked Kay.

'There's normally one camera that covers the car park. But it was broken a couple of weeks ago.' Rogers scratched the side of his nose, and leaned back in his chair. 'Our procurement guy hasn't been able to get the parts yet. The supplier told him it's going to be another week. I haven't told everyone, as I don't want any of the staff to know. They're mostly trustworthy, but I wouldn't want to risk it, just in case, y'know?'

'How did the camera break?'

Rogers shrugged. 'Kids I expect. The lens has been smashed.'

'Did you report this to the police?' Kay asked.

His gaze fell to the floor. 'No. I didn't.'

'I'll need a copy of the purchase order.'

Rogers sighed, then picked up the phone. 'Colin? Could you print off a copy of the purchase order you did for the CCTV parts and bring it to me?'

He returned the phone to its cradle.

'Who else has access to the place where the keys are kept?' said Kay.

Rogers looked at her in bewilderment. 'No one. Before I got here, the keys used to be left in the sorting area. Now they're kept in a safe in my office, and I lock that when I leave the depot.'

Barnes leaned forward. 'Could anyone have accessed the safe before you left the office?'

'Even if they did go to my office, they don't know the combination—' He broke off at a knock on the door. 'Come in.'

Kay turned as the door opened, and a stocky man walked in, his face an ugly mess of sores, his entry announced by a strong nicotine and body odour mix that invaded the space the moment he closed the door behind him.

'That purchase order you wanted, Bob,' he said, and handed over a sheet of paper.

'Thanks, Colin. That'll be all.'

The man ran his eyes over Kay as he left the room, and she resisted the urge to shiver.

'Who's he?' she asked, as the door swung shut.

Rogers grimaced. 'Colin Broadheath. Does all the procurement and maintenance scheduling for the depot.'

Kay turned in her chair, and looked out at the vans in the car park beyond the window. 'What about the maintenance?' she asked. 'Do you do that on site?'

'No,' said Rogers. 'We use a local garage.'

'Which one?

'Phillips Repairs.'

'Can we have a look at the maintenance log please?'

'Of course. Wait here.'

Rogers left the room, and pulled the door closed. Barnes swivelled in his chair to turn to her.

'What you think?'

Kay exhaled. 'I don't know. At least we know the vehicles here all go to Darren Phillips, but if all the van keys are kept in a secure safe here, and Rogers locks his office at night, and he's telling the truth about that, then we need to find out if there was another way to get to the vans. Phillips also keeps the keys in a locked box while the vehicles are at his premises, so that rules out anyone getting hold of them there.'

She held up a finger at the sound of footsteps in the corridor outside, and then the door opened.

Rogers entered with a large hard-backed book in his hands. He closed the door, and set the book on the table.

'It's a bit old-fashioned,' he said, 'but we still keep the maintenance log in hardcopy as well as on the system.'

Kay reached into her bag, and pulled out a photograph of the van taken from the CCTV footage at the industrial estate. She slid it across the table to Rogers.

'This was taken just after one-thirty last Thursday night,' she said.

Rogers' eyebrows raised. 'That's impossible.'

'Has this van been to the garage recently?'

Rogers squinted at the registration number, and then began to paw through the pages of the logbook, a frown creasing his brow. He paused, and then ran his index finger down the left-hand page.

'Here,' he said. 'Six weeks ago. Needed a new water pump.'

'How long was it at the garage?'

'Three days. They had to order the parts from the supplier. They didn't have one at the garage as we'd had another vehicle in a couple of days before with the same problem.'

'Which route is this van assigned to? Who's the current driver?'

'Hang on. I'll go and check.'

Kay suppressed a sigh as the man disappeared from the room once more.

Barnes drummed his fingers on the table surface.

Kay glared at him.

'Sorry,' he said, and stopped.

They both turned in their seats as Rogers returned clutching a printout.

He held it out to them. 'Here you go.'

Kay took the page from him and scanned its contents before handing it to Barnes.

She waited, and then he lifted his head. Kay met his gaze, then turned back to Bob Rogers, and tapped her finger on the page.

'We'd like a word with Neil Abrahams, please.'

Chapter 29

Kay stepped to one side, and let Neil Abrahams into the interview suite ahead of her.

Sharp rose from one of the chairs at the table, and gestured to the seat opposite.

'If you'd like to sit, Mr Abrahams. I'm Detective Inspector Devon Sharp, and I'll be leading this interview.'

Abrahams pulled out the chair, sat, and clasped his hands together on the table, his eyes shifting between Sharp and Kay. He swallowed, an audible sound, and his Adam's apple bobbed in his throat.

Sharp leaned across and hit the "record" button on the machine below the frosted pane of the window, and eyed the man sitting opposite.

'Neil Abrahams, I'll begin this interview by reading you your rights,' he said. Once finished, he sat back. 'Please confirm your full name, address, and occupation for the record.'

'Neil Jonathan Abrahams. 14 Bolt Drive, Maidstone. I'm a courier.' He paused. 'What's this about?'

Kay flipped open the case file, and pushed three large photographs taken from the CCTV images across the table.

'Do you recognise this van?' asked Sharp.

Abrahams' brow creased. 'Um, yeah – it's a courier van.'

'Look at the registration number.'

He plucked one of the photos from the table and held it closer. His face paled. 'That's – that's impossible.'

'Please tell us what you were doing at the Westmead Industrial Estate last Thursday at one-thirty in the morning,' said Sharp.

'I wasn't there!'

Kay watched the man's eyes flicker over the remaining two photographs, then he jerked his head at Sharp.

'I can't explain this. That industrial park isn't even on my route.' He snorted, a nervous explosion from his lips. 'And why would I be driving around there at night?'

'We were hoping you could tell us,' said Sharp.

Abrahams leaned back in his seat and exhaled. 'I was out with friends that night,' he said, pointing at the darkest of the three photos.

'Are you able to supply details of an alibi?' asked Kay.

'Yes, I can.'

She slid a sheet of paper and a pen across to him, and waited while he wrote down two names and mobile phone numbers, his hand shaking.

She took it from him, and rushed from the room, handing over the details to Barnes who was waiting in the corridor. 'Text me as soon as you've got something,' she said. 'This is urgent.'

She returned to the interview room, and took her seat next to Sharp.

'How long have you been a courier?'

'Eight years.'

'And where have you been based?'

The man shrugged. 'All over. Most of the villages around here.'

'Have you ever worked outside of the Maidstone area?'

'No.'

Sharp leaned forward. 'Neil, would you have any idea as to how someone could be driving your van if the keys to it are kept secure?'

The courier driver shook his head. 'No. The depot is fenced, and has security cameras, so if someone did take it, they'd be seen.'

'I understand you enjoyed flirting with Melanie Richards when she helped out on reception at Richards Furnishings,' said Kay.

'What?' Abrahams recoiled in his seat. 'Wait – no way. I didn't kill her! That was just a bit of fun.'

'You're, what, fifteen years older than her?' she said. 'And you thought you'd charm her, is that right?'

'Did she lead you on?' asked Sharp. 'Was that it? Did she agree to meet up with you, and it went wrong? Did you lose your temper and decide to teach her a lesson?'

'No – no, I never met up with her!' Abrahams leaned forward, sweat patches appearing under his arms.

Kay's phone vibrated, and she checked the message before sliding it to one side.

'DC Barnes spoke to the two people you provided as alibis for Thursday night,' she said. 'Neither of them can vouch for you after eleven o'clock.'

She pointed at the time stamp frozen at the footer of the CCTV photograph. 'This is your van at one-thirty a.m.'

Abrahams worked his jaw, but remained silent.

'Unless you can give us the name of a solid alibi for your whereabouts between leaving the pub at eleven and appearing here,' Sharp tapped the photo, 'two and a half hours later, Neil, it's not looking too good, is it?'

'Why were you also at the Westmead Industrial Estate on the mornings of Friday and Saturday?' he added. 'What about these two daytime angles?'

'I wasn't there!'

'Neil, we've got two friends of yours who can't account for your movements after eleven o'clock that night, and evidence of your van being in the same area where Melanie's body was found,' said Kay.

'It wasn't me, I swear.'

'Then where were you between eleven and one-thirty on Thursday night?' asked Kay.

'I – I can't say.'

Kay tapped the van in the photograph. 'This is you, isn't it Neil?'

'It's not me.'

'Then who the hell is it?' Sharp slammed his hand on the desk, and Abrahams jumped in his seat.

'I have no idea.'

Sharp leaned over and snatched the folder from under Kay's elbow. He drew out another photograph, and shoved it in front of Abrahams.

'Are you proud of this?'

Abrahams' eyes widened as his gaze fell to the image.

'Oh, my god,' he whispered, and drew back, horror contorting his features.

'Now, I don't know what your sick little game is, Neil,' Sharp snarled, 'but I do want to know where you disappeared to after eleven o'clock on Thursday, and I want to know why your van was photographed leaving the Westmead estate at one-thirty.'

Abrahams ran a shaking hand over his mouth, his face pale. He finally tore his eyes away from the image of Melanie's lifeless body and spoke, his voice little more than a murmur.

'I wasn't at the Westmead estate that night because I was at a motel near Hollingbourne with someone else,' he said.

Kay's eyes dropped to the ring on Abrahams' left hand. 'We're going to need a name,' she said.

'I can't,' Abrahams pleaded. 'She's married, too.'

'Name,' said Kay, and leaned forward. 'At the moment, you're the only suspect in the kidnap and murder of a young girl.'

'Oh, god.' Abrahams wiped at his eyes, then told her the name, and gave her a mobile number.

Kay moved to the door, closing it behind her.

She dialled the number, and looked up as Barnes approached.

'Well?' he said.

'Got a new alibi.'

She held up a finger as the call was answered.

'Sandra Clark? Detective Sergeant Kay Hunter from Kent Police. I understand you know Neil Abrahams.' She paused and listened. 'Yes, he gave me your number. Frankly, I don't care about your relationship with Mr Abrahams, Mrs Clark. Can you tell me if he was with you on Thursday night? What time did he arrive?' She waited. 'He was? What time did he leave? What about Friday morning and Saturday morning?'

She nodded at Barnes. 'Thanks, Mrs Clark. That will be all.'

She hung up. 'I'll meet you back in the incident room,' she said, and pushed the door to the interview room open.

'Thank you, Mr Abrahams,' she said. 'Mrs Clark confirms that you were with her between eleven o'clock and one forty-five on the night in question.'

'Right,' said Sharp. 'Now we've got that cleared up, does anyone have access to the keys to your van?'

'No,' said Abrahams. 'When we finish our shifts, all the keys are handed over, and they're kept in a safe in the depot manager's office until we need them again.'

'And you drive the same van every day?'

Abrahams nodded. 'Yeah. For the past four months. My route changed, so I got a different van.'

'Why?'

'I don't know. I used to do the circuit around Larkfield, but there was an internal shuffle or whatever, and now I do the one for Harrietsham.'

Kay tapped the photographs from the CCTV camera. 'What about here?'

Abrahams shook his head. 'Never had a route there, no. In fact, none of us do these days – I think the last business that used to have a collection from there closed down months ago.'

Chapter 30

Kay leaned against the wall of the corridor and rubbed at her eye.

She blinked, and watched the retreating figures of Sharp and Abrahams as the courier driver was led out of the interview suites.

'Excuse me, Sarge?'

She turned at the sound of Gavin's voice. 'What's up?'

He moved to one side to let one of the office administrators walk past, and lowered his voice. 'I've been checking the CCTV footage from the courier depot. Bob Rogers was right. The camera above the secure parking area was damaged by kids.'

'How?'

'There's some rough ground with a couple industrial waste bins on the other side of the outer boundary fence. We've got footage of a group of four youths clambering up onto one of the bins to get up on the fence. They break the camera by throwing rocks at it, but then seem to lose interest.' He shrugged. 'They can be seen on one of the other cameras, leaving the same way they came in after about five minutes.'

'Identities?'

'Already passed on,' he grinned. He checked his watch. 'They should be getting picked up in the next fifteen minutes or so. We'll charge them with criminal damage.'

'Thanks, Gavin.'

He nodded, and then headed back in the direction of the incident room, leaving Kay to her thoughts.

If kids, and not the driver of Neil Abrahams' van broke the camera, then there had to be another explanation for the vehicle being seen at the industrial estate the night of Melanie's kidnapping.

Lost in thought, it was a moment before she heard the footsteps behind her.

'Causing trouble again, Hunter?'

She stopped, closed her eyes for a moment, and then turned.

DCI Larch stood in the corridor, his wide bulk taking up much of the space either side.

'Sir?'

His top lip curled in a sneer. 'I really don't know why Sharp puts up with you,' he said, drawing closer. 'You're not exactly a team player, are you?'

Confusion filled her mind. 'I'm sorry, sir – I don't understand.'

'Perhaps if you gathered evidence properly regarding this case, we wouldn't have wasted valuable time bringing in an innocent man for questioning, hmm?'

'But—,'

'DCI Larch, can I help you?'

Kay almost sighed with relief at the sound of Sharp's voice.

DCI Larch spun on his heel. 'No, Sharp. You can't.'

Kay sidestepped as he pushed past her and disappeared up the corridor, the door to his office slamming shut.

'Problem?'

'Seems bringing in the wrong guy for questioning is all my fault.'

Sharp chuckled. 'He's not going to let that failed Professional Standards investigation go easily, is he?'

'Doesn't seem that way. Seems to have affected his memory, too,' she said, attempting humour. 'It was his idea to bring in the driver of the van, after all.'

'Hang in there. He'll find someone else to taunt in time.'

She managed a thin smile, and then fell into step beside him. 'What do we do next?'

Sharp pushed open the door to the incident room, and the rest of the team stopped mid-conversation.

Sharp checked the door had closed behind Kay, and then tore his tie from his neck. 'Well, that was a monumental disappointment, wasn't it?'

Barnes led the murmur of agreement that bounced off the walls. 'What next, boss?'

'Team meeting,' said Sharp. 'Pub. Ten minutes. First round on me.'

Chapter 31

Emma Thomas teetered on her too-high heels and stepped back in shock as the taxi splashed past her, the light on its roof flickering off.

'Dammit.'

She slicked back her hair from her face and shivered, then hitched her bag back up onto her shoulder, hugged her arms around her chest, and stepped off the kerb.

She'd managed to slip from the house three hours before, unseen.

The moment her mother's voice had become muted, and the bass tones of her stepfather's response quietened, she counted the minutes until she heard the sound of his steady snoring filter through their closed bedroom door.

Tanya's parents were away in Ibiza for a cheap last-minute break, and the girls had planned a night out clubbing in Maidstone.

'It'll cheer you up,' insisted Tanya.

Emma had taken a few seconds to consider the idea, and then agreed. What better way to forget her grief for a while than a dance, a drink, and maybe some harmless flirting?

Now, she rued her recklessness.

Tanya had tumbled into a car with a twenty-year-old she'd been having an on-off relationship with for the past three months and some friends of his, thrown Emma a cheery wave over her shoulder as she landed, giggling, on top of him in the back seat, and then the car door had slammed shut and the vehicle took off.

She'd stood at the top of Gabriel's Hill trying to avoid the leers from the groups of men who wobbled their way past her before disappearing along the High Street, and then cursed as the first large drops of rain began to pelt the pavement at her feet.

She'd waited for a taxi for another half an hour, but it was no use – the town was simply too busy at that time of night with all the clubs emptying at the same time.

At that point, she'd had enough of waiting, the rain had started to fall harder, and so she'd begun to walk back towards Bearsted, the *clack-clack* of her heels soon slowing as her feet grew sore.

Emma had made it as far as the railway bridge that crossed over the Ashford Road before blisters had started to form on her heels and toes.

She'd wrenched the shoes from her feet, and now stood with the straps looped over one wrist while she padded barefoot along the pavement, miserable.

She sniffed, and wiped the back of her hand across her nose.

She raised her eyes from the pavement at the sound of a vehicle approaching. A dark-coloured car flashed by, its rear lights receding as it rounded the bend, a resounding *splash* in its wake at the same time as a puddle of water exploded over the footpath in front of her.

She cowered away from the fresh onslaught.

'Bastard,' she slurred.

In her drunken state, her thoughts returned to Melanie, and she shivered.

She'd never considered Yvonne Richards to be rich, but then what did she know? The woman lived in a suburb of the town a couple of miles from where Emma lived, and she and her husband had driven nondescript cars – nothing too flashy; simply vehicles that were no more than a couple of years old.

Kidnappings only happened to rich people, didn't they?

So, why Melanie?

Emma shivered again, and tried to walk faster. She pushed aside the thought of what she might be walking in, and instead rubbed her hands together to try to seek some warmth.

She cursed her own stupidity. Right now, she could have been curled up in her bed, listening to the rain as it pounded onto the thatched roof of the extended cottage.

She swallowed.

Vince, her stepfather, was so much better for her than her father had ever been.

She didn't mean to get into trouble by sneaking out tonight – she had simply found being around her mother so much these past few days too stifling.

All she wanted to do now though was get home, sneak back to bed, and wake up to the smell of Vince cooking one of his famous breakfasts.

Her stomach rumbled at the thought.

A streetlight wavered above her head, the wind rocking the metal structure from side to side. She held her wrist closer to her face, and tried to read the time on her watch dial. It was now well past one o'clock. There'd be no way she'd get a taxi now.

She dropped her arm, and tried to pick up her pace. Behind her, the sound of another vehicle approaching caught her attention.

She checked over her shoulder, and saw the headlights of a van as it splashed through the water covering the road under the railway bridge. She stumbled, and turned her attention back to the pavement in front of her.

She heard the vehicle slow as it approached. Part of her wanted it to stop, for the driver to offer her a lift. The other part of her began to worry. No one knew where she was.

Now, the vehicle drew nearer, the driver keeping pace with her. She stepped back from the edge of the kerb, away from the road, glanced to the side, and noticed the passenger window roll down.

'Do you want a lift?'

'I'm fine,' she said, and turned to walk away.

'Listen,' said the driver, his voice carrying over the rain, 'I live just up the road. You're going to get soaked. Let me give you a lift.'

It seemed tempting.

She heard the ratchet sound of the handbrake being applied, and then the driver's door slammed shut.

Suddenly, he was standing next to her, towering over her as she moved from foot to foot, undecided as to what to do.

She glanced from side to side. There was no one else around. No vehicles could be heard. Her eyes met his. She frowned.

'I know you, don't I?'

Before she could react, his hand shot out and grabbed her wrist.

'Hello, Emma. I've been looking for you.'

He held what looked like a syringe in his other hand, and then stabbed it into her stomach.

She cried out in surprise and pain.

'Let me go!'

A malevolent smile flashed across his face, a split second before his arms wrapped around her and pulled her towards the vehicle.

She struggled, trying to kick him, but it was no use. He was just too strong. As she fought, she heard the sound of a metal door creak on its hinges, and opened her mouth to scream. His palm across her face silenced her before she could cry out.

She continued to thrash, but her efforts began to wane as the drug started to course its way through her body.

The man shoved her, hard, and she fell into the back of the van, striking her head on the metal surface of the floor.

As darkness enveloped her, and she tried desperately to hang onto the last moments of consciousness, terror engulfed her.

This was what it would have been like for Melanie.

Chapter 32

Kay woke from an uneasy sleep to the sound of a persistent ringing next to her ear.

Groggy, she opened her eyes.

Running water reached her ears, and before she flicked back the curtains to see how hard it was raining, the water stopped, and she realised Adam was already up, using the en suite shower.

The ringing continued.

She lashed out with her hand, knocked a paperback off the bedside table, and wrapped her fingers around her mobile phone.

''Lo?'

'Hey, Sis. Thought you were never going to pick up!'

Kay bit back a groan as her head hit the pillow. 'Hi, Abby.'

'Did I wake you?'

'Yep.'

'Sorry.'

Kay rubbed at her eye. 'How sorry?'

Her sister laughed. 'It's six o'clock in the morning. I can't remember the last time I had a lie-in!'

A squeal of delight burst down the phone, and Kay wrenched it away from her ear, scowling.

'Charlotte says "morning", too.'

Kay bit back a retort. Charlotte was six months old. For all her sister's assertions about her daughter's wonderful language skills, she couldn't help thinking that the baby had probably just dirtied its nappy and was currently celebrating.

Adam emerged from the en suite in a cloud of steam.

Her heart leapt at the sight of him, and he grinned, before he proceeded to show off his muscles like a bodybuilder while Kay stuffed the sheet in her mouth and tried not to snort.

'Isn't she funny?' said her sister.

'What? Oh, yeah.'

'Anyway,' said her sister, her tone turning business-like. 'Silas and I were wondering when we're going to see you? It must be, like, four *months* since we last caught up?'

'Is it?'

Kay swallowed, fearful of what was coming.

'Yes, it is,' said her sister. 'Emily is three next weekend – can you believe it? I've got no idea where the time has gone. Mum's coming over, and there's going to be some friends of mine with their little ankle-biters.'

She laughed, a harsh trill that made the skin on Kay's arms prickle.

'So,' said Abby. 'You and Adam need to come. I won't take "no" for an answer,' she laughed.

'Um, yeah, Sis?'

'Oh, no you don't, Kay,' scolded her sister. 'Mum said you would do this.'

Kay sighed. She could visualise her sister's bottom lip sticking out, the same as it always did when she didn't get her own way when they were children. She could imagine her stamping her foot, the start of a tantrum only seconds away.

'Abby, I'm in the middle of a murder investigation,' she said, and concentrated on keeping her voice calm. 'I can't promise anything at the moment.'

'For goodness' sake,' said Abby, her voice rising. 'It's your niece's bloody birthday party.'

The baby started wailing.

'See, you've made Charlotte cry now as well.'

Kay caught Adam staring at her, all the fun gone from his eyes, and shook her head.

'I'm sorry, Sis. I've got to go. I have to be at work in an hour.'

She ended the call before she could hear her sister's response, slid the phone across the bedside table, and closed her eyes.

She bit her lip, angry at the tears that rolled down her cheeks.

'Hey, hey.' Adam crawled across the bed and curled up next to her, wrapped his arms around her and kissed her hair.

'I'm sorry,' she whispered. 'I know you're hurting, too.'

He didn't reply, and gave her a squeeze instead.

'I just don't know how to tell them now,' she said, and gulped another sob back. 'Christ, here I am – trying to prove to my bosses that I can be a detective inspector, and I can't even get my shit together around my own mother and sister.'

Adam released his grip, and then tilted her face towards him. His eyes glistened.

'When it feels like it's the right time, you tell them,' he said. He kissed her forehead. 'Until then, it's just you and me, kiddo.'

Kay bit her lip. 'I don't remember much after we got to the hospital. When I went to interview Yvonne Richards there, I could remember the smells and the sounds, but that's all.'

'You know as well as I do that's your body's way of dealing with it. You can only remember bits and pieces.'

'What about you? What do you remember?'

'Being utterly powerless as they took you away. It seemed like an age before anyone came to get me. There was nowhere to go. I ended up sitting on the floor in the corridor, just waiting.' He wiped his eyes. 'All that keeps going through my head is the thought that I came so close to losing you as well.'

Kay cupped his face in her hands. 'But you didn't.'

He pulled her to him, and held her tight. 'Thank god,' he said, closing his eyes.

'I love you.'

'I love you, too.'

She lay for a moment, the rise and fall of his chest against her face. She snuggled closer. 'You smell nice.'

'Really? I thought you were getting used to essence of horse poo.'

Chapter 33

Eli ignored the muffled noises that echoed off the damp brickwork, and rifled through the contents of the teenage girl's faux-leather handbag.

The lurid pink of its surface offended his senses. It was too bright, too cheap, too feminine.

Guilt threaded its ways through his veins as he worked. His mother had caught him going through her handbag once.

His mother's bag had been black, the leather cracked and worn, with a zip that had fought against his efforts to open it, snagging the lining until he'd managed to free it.

Cigarette odours clung to the inside, a chemical stench that mingled with the stink of stale beer from her nightly visits to the local pub. She'd still been able to leave the house on a regular basis then, unhindered by the ravages that alcohol would take over the next twenty years.

He still couldn't say what had made him open the handbag that day. He'd known, if he was caught, the consequences would be dire, but there was something thrilling about finding out more about his mother's private life.

For a seven-year-old, it was simply too tempting.

He'd found a half-used packet of strong breath mints, a crunched up paper tissue, a condom packet, and her purse. Her cigarettes were nowhere to be seen, and that had been when the hairs on the back of his neck had prickled.

He'd tasted bile on his tongue, but not before he'd placed everything carefully back in the bag, taking care with the zip when he re-sealed it, and turned.

She was standing, leaning against the frame of the open back door, the fingers of her right hand holding a cigarette between them as if she was leaning against a bar, waiting to be chatted up.

'Find anything, you little shit?'

Her voice settled somewhere between his heart and his stomach. He shook his head, and lowered his gaze to the floor.

Her heel crunched the cigarette to death on the back step, the sound reaching his ears as he debated whether to run and face the beating later, or get it over and done with.

She moved too fast for him to make a decision.

He lifted his eyes to face her at the same moment her open hand connected with his ear.

He crashed to the floor, the pain unbearable, but she took no notice. Instead, she hauled him to his feet, and aimed punches at his face and shoulders. He held up his hands in defence, and tried to block the hands that moved too fast for him to counter. The edges of his sight began to darken, and he sank to the floor, waves of nausea consuming him.

She'd given up then, and aimed a kick at his backside that caught his coccyx and made him yelp, and then she had snatched her bag from the worktop and stormed from the room.

He'd waited until he heard the front door slam shut before he started crawling towards the kitchen sink, soothing his bruises with cold water, and making sure no blood dropped to the cheap linoleum-covered floor.

He wiped at his cheeks, angry that tears blurred his vision. He could still remember every single punch and kick from that day, and all the other days.

No wonder his dad had walked out on her when Eli was only five years old.

He'd never been able to work out why he could never fight back. He knew it was the alcohol that made her the way she was, but he had nowhere else to go.

That much had been made clear to him.

Very clear.

Eli sniffed, and glanced at the beige colouring that now stained his fingers.

One of his secondary school teachers had suggested using make-up to cover his bruises when she'd heard the bullies one morning in the playground.

She'd taken him to one side, placed a small innocuous-looking tube into his palm, and wrapped his fingers around it. 'Try this,' she'd said. 'Maybe, if they can't see them, they'll leave you alone.'

He'd nodded, grateful and slightly confused. It had taken a further three days before his mother left the house long enough for him to try the foundation cream. He'd been amazed at the results, and though the bullying didn't stop completely – his mother's alcoholism was a running joke at the secondary school – at least he didn't stand out so much.

He clenched his fist. Until Melanie Richards and her stupid friend, encouraged by the girl's father, had started teasing him for wearing make-up.

It wasn't his fault. It had been raining that day, and when the older woman who worked in the warehouse had handed him a towel to dry off his hair after he'd run from the van, he'd accidentally wiped the make-up from his arms and face, too.

He'd lowered the towel to see Melanie staring at him, mouth open, before she'd laughed, and pointed out the make-up on the towel to her brute of a father and a friend of hers. The friend had turned around and raised her smartphone, committing his discomfort and embarrassment to social media history.

The older woman who ran the warehouse had blushed, snatched the girl's phone from her and deleted the image, much to the rancour of the teenagers. She had tried to make light of it, and told him not to worry as she helped him to the door with the parcels.

He had smiled, told her it was nothing.

He'd battened down the fury until he'd stalked across the forecourt to his vehicle. He'd thrown the parcels into the back of the van, not caring about the contents, and vowed his revenge.

He'd show them what happened to bullies. He might not be able to control his mother, but he could stand up for himself away from her clutches.

Another groan reached his ears.

Eli checked over his shoulder. The girl had knocked her head on something, and he didn't know what. There was blood on the side of her face, and while she was still unconscious, he'd checked and found a cut under her hair. Satisfied that it wasn't life-threatening, he relaxed. He wanted her on his terms.

He reached into the bag and pulled out the contents, lining them up along the plastic covering of a narrow brick shelf that ran along the wall next to him.

Lipstick, mobile phone, purse – no notes, just change – a small box of tampons, and—

His fingers wrapped around a flimsy article, and as he extracted it, he realised it was a polaroid photograph, the sort people took in photo booths for passport photos.

His thumb rubbed across the face of the man in the photograph, and a smile twitched at the corner of his mouth.

Things were going even better than he had imagined.

Chapter 34

Kay and Barnes turned at the sound of the door opening behind them.

'Thanks for seeing us at short notice,' said Kay.

Bob Rogers shook her hand. 'No problem. I'll use the meeting room here,' he said to the receptionist.

'Sorry, Bob,' she said. 'David's got that one booked for the next hour.'

Rogers grimaced. 'Okay. We'll have to use my office.' He beckoned to them. 'Come on through.'

He swiped his card, held the door open for them, and then led the way down a windowless corridor.

About halfway down, he pushed open the door to his office, and led the way in. 'Excuse the mess. I'm trying to get some statistics together for head office.'

He gestured towards the chairs opposite his desk. 'Take a seat.'

He moved around the desk, closed an open laptop computer, and pushed it out of the way before gathering up the paperwork strewn across the desk.

'If I don't do this now, I'll end up doing it tonight at home.'

'We're sorry to interrupt your work,' said Kay. 'But I was hoping you could help me.'

'Of course,' said Rogers, sitting down. 'What do you need?'

Kay reached into her bag, pulled out a photograph before handing it to Rogers. 'Do you know this man?'

Rogers frowned as he looked at the image, and scratched his chin. 'He looks familiar.'

'His name is Guy Nelson,' said Kay. 'He works at Darren Phillips' garage.'

Rogers grunted. 'That's why I recognise him. Yes, I remember now.'

'Did you ever see him away from the garage?'

Rogers handed the photograph back to her. 'Just the once, I think. We had a barbecue a few weeks back, for some of our suppliers.' He jerked his thumb in the direction of the car park. 'It was all very informal. A couple of the lads brought in barbecues from home, and I stumped up the bill for the food.' He smiled. 'We had to move the vans out the way because some of them decided they wanted to use the car park for a game of cricket.'

He leaned back in his chair. 'What's the problem?'

Kay put the photograph back in her bag. 'I can confirm Neil Abrahams has provided us with alibis, and isn't a suspect in our enquiries, but it bothers me that, despite your keeping the van keys in your safe here, and Darren

Phillips doing the same, someone has been driving around in a County Deliveries courier van. And, I'd very much like to speak to that person in relation to our enquiries concerning Melanie Richards.'

Rogers' eyebrows shot upwards. 'But none of our vans have been stolen. So, how is that possible?'

'Either someone had access to those keys without your knowledge,' said Kay. 'Or someone had access to the vans, and managed to duplicate the registration plates for the vehicle Neil Abrahams drives.'

She flicked through her notebook. 'How long do you keep the vehicles for?'

'What do you mean?'

'Most of the vehicles out there look quite new. How often do you change them?'

'Every ninety thousand miles. Or every five years. Whichever occurs first, unless a vehicle is involved in an accident.' He held up his hand. 'We haven't had one of those for quite a while, thank goodness.'

'How are they disposed of?'

'If they're still considered roadworthy, we auction them off. The rest are scrapped.'

'And the paperwork for these?'

'All with head office,' said Bob.

'When was the last auction held?' said Barnes.

'About twelve weeks ago.'

'Who runs the auction?'

'A company up near Sheerness. They do all the auctions for post vans, police vehicles, that sort of thing as well.'

'Have you got a contact name for them?' said Kay.

She wrote down the name and phone number that Rogers retrieved from a diary next to his phone.

'How long will it take to get the paperwork from head office for the last auction?'

'I'll phone them this afternoon for you. The bloke who runs the department isn't in the office in the mornings. Once I put the request in, it'll take a few days.'

Kay rose to her feet. 'We'll wait to hear from you.'

***

Kay slung her bag under the desk, and gratefully took the steaming mug of coffee from Gavin.

'Right,' she said, and blew across the surface of the hot liquid. 'Going on the basis that Neil Abrahams' van was in for a new water pump, and the possibility that while it was at the garage Guy Nelson replicated the licence plates, I went back to the courier depot with Barnes. Chatting to Bob Rogers, it sounds like our suspect might have managed to get hold of a courier van that was auctioned off. The last auction was about twelve weeks ago.'

'At least that goes some way to explain the vehicle on the CCTV images,' said Gavin. 'Plus, if the suspect bought an auctioned courier van, he wouldn't have to worry about spraying it or anything to make it look like a real one. And he could easily create decals to go on the side with the logo on.'

'Exactly.'

Kay leaned over, and wiggled her mouse to wake up the computer. She opened a new website page, typed in a general search screen, and sipped at her coffee while the internet connection began to load the results.

'Have you got the records from the previous auction?' Gavin moved around the desk so he could see the screen.

'No,' said Kay. 'Rogers is going to phone his colleague at head office this afternoon and request them for us. We might not get them for a couple of days.' She checked her watch. 'We've got a few minutes before the afternoon briefing. Let's take a quick look at something.'

She tapped the sixth name down in the search results. 'This is the company that auctions the vans for them.'

She clicked on the website address, and moved the mouse back and forth while it connected.

The page loaded eventually, and she scrolled through the home page, skimming over the sales jargon until she found what she was looking for.

'Here we go. Ex-County Deliveries vans. Let's see how many they have for sale before the next auction. At least it'll give us some idea of the numbers before those records turn up.'

She clicked on the link, and then groaned as the page finished loading.

Gavin choked on his coffee. 'Christ, there must be about fifty vehicles.'

Kay swore under her breath. 'Nothing's ever easy, is it?'

Chapter 35

He loosened his tie and tossed it onto the desk, then strode across to the door and twisted the key in the lock.

He switched off the lights, and pulled the blind down over the glass window set into the door.

His breathing was already heavy as he wandered back to the desk and ran his hand over the top of the laptop.

He reached out and tweaked the cord for the window blinds. He'd checked once, before locking the door, but he knew it paid to be paranoid.

Besides, it was part of the routine – a way to pace himself before savouring the main course.

He snatched the desk phone from its cradle and placed the handset to one side, before he reached into his pocket and checked his mobile phone was switched off.

Unprofessional, especially as he was on call, but he had a well-prepared excuse should he need it.

He was ready.

He powered up the computer, then selected a program linked to a shortcut displayed on the screen.

A delighted gasp escaped his lips.

There she was – and the picture quality was perfect.

He ran his tongue over his bottom lip and leaned closer, his hand shaking as he tapped a key to activate the zoom.

The lighting at the location cast an iridescent glow over the girl's skin, but even from here, he could see the effect of the insulin.

Sweat beaded from every pore, and he knew that right now, the girl's heart rate would be accelerating, pushing the muscle to its limits.

He raised his eyes from the screen, and listened.

Rain continued to pound the roof of the building, and the forecast predicted the deluge wouldn't relent for at least another two to three days.

The timing was incredible.

He rested his elbow on the desk, and cupped his chin as his gaze returned to the girl.

His finger tapped the keyboard again, and returned the camera lens to its original position.

He frowned at the sight of blood on her shoulder, and clenched his fist.

The rules were that no blood should be seen around the head, neck, or shoulders. It would detract from the viewer's enjoyment of seeing the terror in her eyes as her predicament become clear.

However, the injury seemed minor.

He'd make a note to mention it, though.

For next time.

The girl shifted her weight, and strained against the bindings at her wrists. The movement was weak, and after she attempted it one more time, she gave up.

He checked his watch. There was no need to worry, he thought. The date rape drug would be working its way out of her system for another hour or so yet.

She'd become feistier as the effects wore off.

He hoped.

He ran a hand lovingly over the keyboard.

The last one had been incredible. Such memories!

He'd seen fire in her eyes, right up to the moment her heart had given out and she'd slipped from the rung of the ladder, her will to survive almost outwitting her panic.

This one, well – he'd have to wait and see, wouldn't he?

He reached out, and ran a finger across the image of her shivering body, then sat back in his chair and groaned.

A shadow passed the door of the office, then stopped.

He covered his mouth with his hand, and held his breath.

Had he been heard?

He slapped the laptop closed with his other hand.

He'd never tested his theory that the glow from the screen wouldn't be seen through the combination of frosted glass and the cloth blind, and now he silently rued the oversight.

The door handle turned, before being released, and the shadow moved on.

He exhaled, and opened the laptop.

The tiny clock in the bottom right-hand corner caught his eye. Of course – the cleaners would be doing their rounds.

His shoulders relaxed once more, and his eyes locked onto the girl on the screen.

He shifted in his seat as the material of his trousers tightened across his groin, and settled in to watch.

Chapter 36

Eli checked his rear view mirror.

The road behind had been empty for the past mile, the soft orange glow of the town receding on the horizon as a steady rainfall began to pelt the windscreen.

He leaned forward, and retuned the radio. He hated the cheery pop music that the local paint-by-numbers station played during the day, and it seemed that their night-time programming featured the same repetitive drivel. Even the presenter had run out of steam over an hour ago and reduced his chatter to small talk, only offering a time check after the obligatory three adverts that played out every twenty minutes.

He found a station playing classical music instead, and sat back in his seat.

He turned his wrist until the luminous dials of his watch were visible. His shift started in four hours, before dawn broke, and he was keen to get a couple of hours' sleep at least. Bob Rogers had already commented earlier in the week about the state of his sunken eyes so soon after a supposed holiday, and it worried him that his appearance had been noticed in such a way. He did his best to stay out of the way while at the depot, not wanting to draw attention to himself, yet if he wasn't careful, it would be more than his use of make-up to hide the bruises on his face and arms that gave people an excuse to stare.

He just had to keep going.

Especially now.

He ran the back of his hand under his nose and sniffed.

The new site was perfect.

He'd scoured the internet, tracing the previous structure's history. Far enough away from the town that kids wouldn't trespass; the security fencing first put in place around the building by the contractors had remained intact.

Until Eli had taken care of it.

The van rumbled over a series of potholes, and the tools in the back of the van clattered across the metal flooring.

He inched his foot away from the accelerator.

He'd had to improvise, of course. The girl was bigger than the last one; large bones, his mother would say, and he had to be sure she'd be secure during the day.

The mother would have been home by six o'clock; the father stuck at work until at least eight or nine if his pattern reflected that of the previous few weeks. And the girl had a habit of staying out late with friends, often returning after her parents had retired to bed.

Not tonight, though.

A warmth flushed through his lap, and he swallowed as he tried to ignore the sensation.

It had been five days since the girl and her father had died, and the memory excited him.

At first, he had wanted to teach them both a lesson.

Then, when the Richards girl had roused from her drugged slumber to find herself in the hole, tied to the flimsy ladder, and tried to scream through the rag covering her mouth, the terror in her eyes had almost sent him into sexual oblivion, and it was all he could do to turn away and fight the urge to ejaculate.

She'd seen the look in his eyes though, and despite the balaclava that covered his features, he'd sensed that she'd recognised him. She had begun breathing heavily, panting behind the dirty rag as he'd circled the hole, his gaze never leaving hers.

'Do you know why you're here?' he'd asked.

She'd shaken her head.

'You will,' he'd said.

Her eyes had widened with hope as he'd bent down and removed the coarse rag from her lips, but then he had straightened and wrapped his fingers around the drain cover, and she'd begun to strain at the bindings that secured her ankles and wrists to the ladder.

She'd tried to plead with him as he'd dragged the heavy, steel grille across the hole, and babbled words that he couldn't make out, nor needed to.

Then, as the grille fell into place and his footsteps receded to the door, her muffled screams had reached his ears, and a smile twitched at his mouth before he'd flicked the lights off.

He'd camped at the site of the old animal testing laboratory, safe in the knowledge that the soundproofed walls that once camouflaged those poor souls' screeches of pain masked his captive's pitiful attempts to communicate with him.

Eli only had to wait another forty-eight hours before the girl's parents returned from holiday.

He was driving along the road towards the house as a taxi had pulled into their driveway, and he'd slowed to a stop halfway up the lane to watch them exit the vehicle, already arguing as they paid the driver and pulled their suitcases over the doorstep.

He'd waited until the taxi had disappeared from sight before putting the van into gear and gliding past the house, sweat on his palms, his heart racing.

He'd made his way back to the industrial park as fast as possible, his eyes flickering between the road and the dashboard, terrified he'd be pulled over for speeding.

On reaching the disused laboratory an hour later, he'd paced back and forth in the atrium, trying to fight down the adrenalin that was coursing through his system.

Eventually, he'd pulled the balaclava over his face, strode across to the steel door to the chamber, wrenched open the door, and crouched next to the steel grille.

She stank.

She'd been in the hole for nearly three days by then, and a fetid stink of faeces and fear emanated from below ground.

At first, he'd recoiled, before reaching out and lifting the grille from its housing.

She'd blinked in the light, her voice rasping.

'Please. Let me go.'

He'd ignored her, and pulled a small knife from the back pocket of his jeans.

She'd opened her mouth to scream, and then clamped her lips shut as he reached out and sawed through the bindings that held her right hand.

'Your parents are back. We're going to make a phone call.'

Tears had welled in her eyes, pooling before streaking over her dirty cheeks.

He'd held out a pay-as-you-go mobile phone. 'Dial your dad's mobile number.'

A shaking hand snaked out from the hole, and then she'd dabbed at the screen with her index finger.

He'd held a finger to his lips. 'Not a word. I'll be the only one who speaks. You understand?'

She'd nodded, her face eager. 'Yes.'

'If you try anything, you'll never see your parents again.'

She'd paled, but nodded once more.

He'd straightened, and connected the call, leaving it on speakerphone.

It rang four times before a breathless man answered.

'Mel? We're home. Where are you?'

'Mel's with me,' said Eli.

A silence followed for a moment, then—

'Who is this?'

'No more questions. Do exactly as I say and you'll get her back alive.'

'Please,' said the father. 'Don't hurt her.'

Eli had heard another voice in the background, female, and realised the mother was asking the man who he was talking to. 'Shut her up. I won't repeat myself.'

He'd given the father the instructions about the money, where to drop it off, and not to go to the police.

The man had agreed, fear in the grunted acknowledgement of the instructions.

During the second phone call, however, a struggle had ensued at the other end of the line before the woman's voice cut through the air.

'What have you done with my daughter, you bloody animal?'

His lips had thinned. 'You were told to be quiet. Maybe you need a stronger message.'

He'd bent over and placed the phone on the tiled floor, then straightened and moved closer to the hole. He'd flicked the knife up. 'Give me your hand.'

216

The girl whimpered, and shook her head, trying to twist away from him.

His hand had shot out, wrapped around her right wrist, and raised it until it was above her head.

Behind him, he could hear the parents' voices, shouting, pleading with him to pick up the phone.

He'd ignored them and raised the knife.

The girl's screams echoed off the tiled walls as he sliced through her little finger, before he tossed it down the hole.

Blood spurted from the open wound, splashing across the floor.

He'd turned his back on her and picked up the phone.

'You've got your instructions. Make sure you obey them.'

His fingers clenched the steering wheel as the memory washed over him.

The parents had been hysterical by the time he'd ended the call, and it had taken the next hour to first bandage the girl's finger and then swab the floor clean.

He'd acted on impulse, but the instructions were always clear.

No blood.

He'd apologised of course, an awkward phone conversation that had made him cringe. After that, he'd phoned Guy Nelson with confirmation about the ransom money, and where it would be found.

Since that day, he'd watched a replay of the video on the laptop he'd taken from Nelson, but it wasn't the same – he knew exactly how the final moments of her life ended.

He needed fresh footage.

Live footage.

Eli stretched his neck from side to side, checked the speedometer, and turned right into the narrow lane that swept upwards across open farmland towards home.

His next fix was ready.

A burst of static then spat from the radio, before the headlights died and the van was plunged into darkness.

Eli swung the van hard to the left, the suspension bouncing across the soft verge as he brought the vehicle to a sliding halt.

He sat for a moment, shocked, and then swore and punched the steering wheel.

Chapter 37

Bernard Coombs bunched the sleeve of his fleece jacket over his fist, leaned over the steering wheel, and wiped at the faint sheen of condensation that stuck to the windscreen.

His breath fogged in front of his nose, and he shivered as he drew his hand back, wrapping his fingers around the wheel before the thirty-year-old vehicle splashed through a puddle, the ancient suspension creaking as the wheels sank several inches into a deep pothole.

He swore under his breath, and cursed the local garage for not returning his two-year-old Range Rover that day as promised.

He flicked the wipers up a notch, then squinted through the rain assaulting the yellow beam of the headlights, and tapped the brakes.

Ahead, a van had left the road, its nose into the verge while the tailgate hung precariously into the path of approaching traffic, one of its back doors ajar, and the driver's door wide open.

He slowed further, the vehicle in darkness save for the reflectors at each end of its back bumper that shone red as he drew near.

Swinging the vehicle out further into the lane to avoid a collision, he held a straight course as he drifted past, and craned his neck to see through the passenger window.

He breathed a sigh of relief as the edge of the headlight beam afforded him a glimpse through the open driver's door to where a figure lay prone across the seats, working under the dashboard.

His gaze drifted to the illuminated dials of his wristwatch.

Twelve forty-five.

For a split second, he considered driving on. The figure wasn't injured, after all.

Then guilt set in, and he pulled the four-wheel drive to the left, braked hard, and killed the engine.

Rain hammered on the roof, a deafening assault that hadn't seemed so bad when he'd been barrelling along the lane.

He reached out and flipped open the glove compartment, his fingers wrapping around the torch he kept there for emergencies, then he flicked up the hood of his jacket, and launched himself out into the night.

The wind buffeted the door, and he fought to stay upright as his thumb hit the power switch for the torch. The beam shone across the divide between his vehicle and the van behind, and then fell upon the figure's feet as they protruded from the driver's door.

Coombs kept the beam low as he approached the drenched figure, and he pulled his jacket tighter around his chest.

'Are you okay?'

He realised it was a man, of slim build, and only an inch or two shorter than himself, and gave a silent prayer of thanks that it wasn't a woman stuck out here on her own. The man was wearing a hooded sweatshirt, which threw a shadow across his features in the torchlight.

His response was tugged away by a gust of wind, and Coombs cupped his hand behind his ear.

'Say again?'

'Fuse has blown.'

Coombs gestured to the glove compartment where the figure worked, then shone his torch at it.

The man gave him a half-hearted thumbs-up, and turned his attention back to the work at hand.

Coombs watched as the man deftly wrenched out one fuse at a time, held it up to the light, and then replaced it before moving onto the next.

He sniffed.

The next gust of wind carried a distinct aroma of sweat from the figure next to him, and he took a step to his left, keeping the torch beam focused on the glove compartment.

The man worked in silence, a stubbled chin jutting out from under the hood of his jacket, and made no effort to strike up a conversation.

Within a minute or two, the malfunctioning fuse had been located, and the figure withdrew a spare of the right colour from his pocket.

'Does it all the time. Intermittent short blows the fuses,' he said. 'I keep spares.'

'Good thinking.'

As soon as the man dropped the replacement fuse into place, the van's headlights burst into life.

'Hang on,' said Coombs. 'I'll go round and check your brake lights.'

Without waiting for an answer, he burrowed deeper into the folds of his jacket and hurried along the length of the van, the torch beam bobbing alternatively between the sodden asphalt and the panels of the vehicle.

He was glad the man had been able to fix the van – the thought of having to offer a lift to him and try to make polite conversation while he drove him to his destination filled him with an introvert's dread. He'd stopped to help as it was the right thing to do in the circumstances, but he had no desire to prolong the encounter.

He rounded the open door, the sound of the glove compartment being reassembled reaching his ears. A moment later, both brake lights flashed on.

He bent down and looked through the length of the van. 'All good,' he called to the driver. 'Try the indicators.'

Coombs stepped back, away from the open door and nodded to himself as first the left, then the right indicator blinked. 'Okay.'

He reached out to close the door, and then stopped.

The torch beam wavered, and he blinked.

A dark stain covered the back corner of the van, nearest the door hinges, and he frowned as his eyes travelled over a streaked pattern that spread across the floor of the vehicle.

The van rocked as the driver turned around in his seat, his face still in shadow. 'Everything alright?'

Coombs swallowed. 'Yes. All good.'

He slammed the door shut, and hurried the length of the van towards his own vehicle, holding a hand up in farewell to the driver before the man could get out of the driver's seat.

Reaching his four-wheel drive, he thumbed the off switch on the torch, threw it onto the passenger seat, and slipped behind the wheel, locking the door.

His eyes found the rear view mirror, and he almost cried out.

The figure was standing at the front of the van, his silhouette haloed by the headlights blazing behind him, his hands in the pockets of his sweatshirt.

Coombs reached out for the ignition key, and then cursed the starter motor as it choked.

'Come on,' he urged.

He checked the mirror.

The figure had begun to walk towards the four-wheel drive, his outline growing larger.

Coombs twisted the ignition key once more, and gasped when the engine caught.

Throwing it into gear, he released the handbrake and floored the accelerator, sliding off the verge and onto the asphalt before regaining control.

He honked the horn once, then exhaled, surprised that he'd been holding his breath.

His heart rate thumped painfully between his ribs, and he forced himself to take a couple of deep breaths. Despite the chill air, sweat poured from his brow, and he wiped at his face with the back of his hand.

A rabbit skittered away from his headlights. When he glanced down at the dashboard, he saw he was driving twenty miles over the speed limit.

He checked his mirrors.

The van remained stationary, receding into the distance.

Coombs eased off the accelerator, tightened his fingers around the steering wheel, and resolved to get home in one piece.

Chapter 38

Kay sat at her desk, and tried to fight down the frustration at the lack of progress.

The calls to Crimestoppers had begun to slow down, which meant the team could get on top of the leads that had come in to date, but also meant the public were beginning to lose interest.

They were losing valuable time. The golden time for collating information was long past, and people's memories had a tendency to fade quickly.

She flicked open the internet browser window on her computer, and brought up the link to the auction site she'd found yesterday.

Her eyes travelled down the list of vehicles for sale once more, and noted there were new advertisements since her last search. She tweaked the search string to omit the larger vans until she was left with vehicles that resembled the one they'd seen on the CCTV footage.

That still left eight pages of vehicles.

She noted some were for sale by private owners. She wondered whether to ask Carys to chase up Bob Rogers for the auction records from his head office, and then discounted the idea. Carys would tell her when the records came in. She would just have to wait.

She blinked, and read the listing at the bottom of the second page again.

'Interesting,' she murmured, and clicked on the advert.

It had been placed by Darren Phillips' garage. She hit the print button, and then walked over to Carys' desk with it.

'Can you get on to Darren Phillips, and ask him to provide us with the details of all the auction vehicles he's sold on behalf of County Deliveries in the past three months?'

'Will do.' Carys frowned. 'I thought all their vehicles were sold by that company at Sheerness?'

'Exactly. And he didn't volunteer the information when I spoke with him the other day, either. Let me know what you find out.'

'Sarge?'

Kay glanced over her shoulder to see Gavin Piper peering around the doorframe. 'What's up?'

'There's a bloke in reception. He wanted to speak to Inspector Sharp, but he's in a meeting at the moment. He'd seen him on TV on the media conference about Melanie Richards. He seems agitated, so I thought he could speak with you.'

'Who is he?

'Bernard Coombs. Says he's a farmer out Coxheath way. Alleges he has information that might be to do with Melanie Richards' kidnapping.'

'No problem,' said Kay. 'On my way.'

***

Kay showed Bernard Coombs into the interview suite and left the door ajar.

'We'll get started as soon as DC Barnes joins us,' she said, removing her jacket. She slung it over the back of one of the chairs, and gestured to the seat opposite, dropping a file onto the table between them. 'Please – make yourself comfortable.'

Coombs sat, shuffled his weight on the chair, and exhaled. 'I can't help thinking that I'm overreacting.'

Kay smiled. 'Let us decide that. It's much better to tell us about something you're concerned about than let it fester away. You'll only worry about it otherwise.'

He nodded. 'True.'

The door was nudged open, and Barnes appeared, three Styrofoam cups of coffee balanced in his hands.

Kay shut the door as he distributed the drinks onto the table, then took her seat next to him. She reached out for her coffee, and blew across its surface.

'Now,' she said, as Barnes flipped open his notebook. 'Why don't you take us through what you saw? Our desk clerk said you'd been travelling near Straw Mill Hill after midnight last night – why was that?'

'I've got a small flock of sheep up there. One or two of them are showing signs of an infection, so I went up to check on them.' Coombs leaned back in his chair, his coffee cup hugged to his chest. 'Found a broken fence post while I was there, so it was pitch black by the time I finished mending that. It started raining as I got there, and the track was pretty slippery. Took me an age to get across the field to the lane.'

Kay flipped open the manilla folder, and unfolded an A3-sized map of the local area. 'Can you show me where that field is, and where you stopped to help the man with the van?'

The farmer put his cup down and pulled the map closer, then reached into his jacket pocket and pulled out a pair of reading glasses.

'The entrance to the field is here,' he said, stabbing his finger on the page. He waited while Kay placed a small cross with her pen next to his finger, and then moved it across the map. 'And this is the lane I was driving along when I came across the broken-down van.' He tapped the page twice. 'Here.'

Kay added another cross.

'Is that lane often used by motorists?' she said. 'Looks a bit narrow.'

Coombs shrugged. 'I've always used it to get from home to the fields. It's a rat run during the day sometimes if there's a crash on the main road, but I don't often see anyone along there at that time of night.'

'Okay, so you're driving along. What time is it?'

The farmer shook his head. 'It was about twelve forty-five. I remember looking at my watch a moment after I saw the van pulled over to the side of the road. I wondered who'd be out at that time of night.'

Kay nodded, pleased that the farmer's recall was sharp. 'Go on. Walk me through what happened, as you remember it, and I'll ask any questions I might have at the end.'

The farmer nodded, cleared his throat, and then continued. 'I slowed down to pass the van – the lane is really narrow there. At first, I thought it might have crashed, but then I noticed the driver's door was open, and a figure was lying across the front seats. I couldn't see much because it was so dark, but I was glad it wasn't a woman out there on her own.' He paused to take a sip of his coffee. 'I parked in front, grabbed a torch, and went back to see if I could help. The man was trying to work in complete darkness. All the lights on his van had gone out, and he said it was something to do with one of the fuses. He had a spare, and was working his way through them.'

Coombs put his coffee cup down, and leaned his forearms on the table, his brow creased. 'I didn't think anything was wrong until the lights came back on. I told him I'd check the rear lights for him – he'd left the back door open, to get tools and stuff out I suppose – anyway, the lights came back on, and I was just about to shut the door for him when I looked down and saw blood on the floor of the van.'

'How can you be sure it was blood?' asked Barnes.

'I'm a farmer. I've seen plenty of blood in my time. I know what I saw.'

Kay held up her hand to pacify him. 'What happened next?'

'The man was in the driver's seat,' said Coombs. He shivered. 'I don't know. There was something that *changed* the moment I'd paused to shut the door, as if he knew I'd seen something.' He swallowed. 'He asked if everything was okay. I said it was, slammed the door shut, and hurried back to my car as fast as I could.' He shook his head. 'I didn't want to hang around. As I was starting the engine, he got out of his van. He stood there in the headlight beam as I drove away.'

'Can you describe him?'

Coombs frowned. 'He was slim. I couldn't see his eyes – it was too dark. About five foot eleven, I suppose. I couldn't see his hair. He was wearing a sweatshirt with a hood.'

Kay resisted the urge to sigh. 'Did you see what colour van it was, given it was dark?'

The farmer nodded, and reached into his trouser pocket. 'I did better than that,' he said, and passed her a folded piece of paper, then pointed at it. 'Registration number.'

'Thank you.' Kay checked her watch. 'What time did you get home?'

'About one-fifteen.'

'It's now ten forty-five in the morning. What made you change your mind about reporting this?'

The farmer sighed. 'At first I tried to convince myself it was nothing. But I saw the news reports about that girl who'd been killed.' He shrugged. 'I don't know. There was something about the way that man acted. It didn't feel right.'

'Did he mention at all where he'd been, or where he was going?'

'No. Nothing. The only times he spoke to me was to explain about the fuses, and then to ask if I was okay when I was by the back door of the van. Nothing else.'

'Mr Coombs, I think we've got enough to look at for now, especially as you've given us the registration number,' said Kay. 'Detective Barnes here will sort out a statement based on our conversation for you to read and sign. Are you okay to wait while we do that?'

'Certainly.'

'Thank you,' said Kay. She shook hands with the farmer, and retrieved her jacket and the folder. 'I'll leave you with Detective Barnes, and I'll be in touch if we need to speak with you again.'

She excused herself, and hurried back to the incident room, handing the registration number to Gavin as she passed.

Sharp spun in his chair to face her as she dumped the folder on his desk.

'Well?'

'We're definitely looking for someone who's a local and knows the area,' said Kay, tapping the end of her pen on the desk as she stared at the large map on the wall. The two locations the farmer had pointed out had been added, transcribed from the mark-ups she made during the interview. She leaned across until she could see Gavin sitting at his computer. 'Anything on that registration number yet?'

'Not yet. Computer's bloody slow this morning, and apparently there's a backlog of enquiries since the weekend.'

'As soon as you can, then.'

Sharp rubbed his chin. 'Do you think this is our man?'

Kay frowned. 'If he isn't, he's still got some explaining to do.'

Chapter 39

A new burst of energy engulfed the team, and as Kay pored over an enlarged map of the area where Bernard Coombs had reported seeing the stranger's van, she felt the familiar adrenalin rush of the expectation of a breakthrough in the case.

Carys wound her way around the desks towards Kay, and held up a stapled bunch of paperwork.

'I got the auction records emailed through from Darren Phillips,' she said. 'None of the vans he's sold locally in the past three months are our vehicle.'

'How many has he sold around here?'

'I've spoken to the owners of the three that were,' said Carys. 'One was purchased by a market trader at Whitstable who has a strong alibi, one was written off in a car accident five weeks ago, and the other was bought by an elderly couple near Wrotham Heath who rescue greyhounds. They've got alibis as well – they were staying at their daughter's house over at Croydon last week.'

'All right,' said Kay. 'It was worth a shot.'

As the detective constable walked away, Kay could sense the other woman's disappointment. It seemed that every time they felt they were getting close to a breakthrough, they ended up taking two steps back. However, that was often the case with investigations of this nature.

She rolled her shoulders, and began to flick through the notes she'd taken to date.

A hubbub of noise filled the incident room – raised voices on phones, shouts across the office between members of the team, and somehow, somewhere in amongst all that, a mobile phone cut through the air with an eighties pop-rock ring tone.

Kay glanced over her shoulder at a loud whoop.

Gavin threw his mobile phone onto her desk, and spun his chair to face the rest of the team.

'Eli Matthews,' he said. 'Twenty-six years old. Van's registered to a street off Queens Road.'

Kay frowned. 'That's mostly shops and offices along there, isn't it?'

'Yes, but there's also a block of garages owned by the council up at the far end,' said Gavin, and held up the notes he'd been taking. 'And that's where the van's registered.'

'Good work,' said Sharp. 'Right, you lot – I want everything you can find out about Eli Matthews. We have an address for where his vehicle is kept, but where's he living? Find out if he's on the national systems already. If he isn't, check with other divisions near here, just to be sure.'

He approached Kay. 'Can you deal with this? The chief superintendent's asked DCI Larch and myself to brief her on this case, and I'm already running late.'

'Sure, no problem.'

'Okay – phone me if you need me.'

***

Kay stretched her arms above her head, and winced as a muscle in her shoulder twitched.

The incident room had been quiet for the past twenty minutes, as she'd sent everyone out for a half-hour lunch break. They were all in need of some fresh air, and as she glanced out the window towards the entrance to the narrow cobbled street of Gabriel's Hill, she wondered if she should heed her own advice and go for a short walk, despite the inclement weather.

Instead, she wandered over to the whiteboard, her eyes running over the various words and lines that criss-crossed the surface.

Her gaze fell to the photographs of Melanie Richards. One, a normal teenager beaming at the camera, her freshly ironed school uniform immaculate. The second, a tortured soul whose life had been cut short by an evil being who didn't deserve to be roaming the area, free.

'Boss, you need to see this.'

Kay looked away from the whiteboard at the excited tone of Barnes' voice.

He pointed to his computer screen. 'Eli Matthews is a courier.'

'How do you know?'

'His name came up on the system for police checks,' he said. 'He applied in Suffolk, but as he's from here, he had to get clearances from Kent Police for his application with County Deliveries in Ipswich because of the confidential nature of some of the businesses they have contracts with.'

Kay's heart missed a beat. 'Print out a copy of his photograph.' She pulled her jacket off the back of her chair and swung it over her shoulders. 'Carys, you're with me.' She patted Barnes' shoulder as she dashed past.

'Nice one. We'll speak to Yvonne Richards, see if she recognises him. If she does, we'll bring him in for questioning. Go find Sharp and ask him to be ready in case we need him to request a search authorisation for that lock-up.'

Chapter 40

Eli placed the plastic cup under the hot water jet, and stared sightlessly at the brown liquid that shot from the machine, steam rising in front of his eyes.

His hand reached out to the small wicker basket on the counter to his left, and plucked out two sugar sachets. He blinked, picked up the cup, and wandered over to one of the white plastic tables against the café wall.

Exhaustion consumed him.

Between working early mornings and ensuring the site was ready, he'd had less than a few hours' sleep the past week, and it was beginning to show.

His manager had already had a quiet word with him yesterday, asking if everything was okay. Somehow, someone had figured out a while ago about the bruises on his arms and face, and reported it. He'd tried to cover them as best as possible, the embarrassment writhing in his veins, making him squirm every time one of his colleagues passed him and lowered their gaze.

He'd managed to avoid his mother the past few days – she'd been asleep, passed out, by the time he'd got back to the house, and he'd crept from the front door to his room, locking the door behind him before collapsing into a fitful sleep.

His back ached, and he pulled out a packet of painkillers from his pocket.

He was used to the weight of most of the boxes he lifted on a daily basis, but the girl had been heavier – and when she'd tried to squirm away from his grip as he'd been carrying her across the site, he'd felt a muscle spasm shudder down his spine. He'd cursed under his breath. In his hurry to continue his plans, he'd rushed and made a mistake with the dosage. He'd only managed to stagger through the tunnel and secure her before her eyelids had fluttered open and she'd stared wide-eyed at him.

He'd punched her a split second after she'd opened her mouth to scream, her cry cut off before it could echo off the brick tiles.

She'd struggled as he'd tied her wrists above her, wriggling and moving from side to side.

Silently, he'd wrapped a gag around her head, filling her mouth with the bunched material.

He'd retrieved the needles next, and the girl's muffled screams had echoed off the walls as he'd inserted one, then the other into a vein in her arm in quick succession before he'd leaned against the opposite wall, admiring his handiwork.

Her ragged breathing filled the space, alternating with his as he worked to get his breath back after the exertion.

He'd felt a grin stretch across his face as he'd watched her.

Terror filled her eyes, her face so pale it almost glowed in the pale light from the camping lantern he'd strung from the ceiling of the tunnel.

'You know what happened to the last girl,' he'd said, and straightened. 'What do you think your chances are?'

He'd turned then, climbing up the tunnel incline back to the exit to the underground car park, the girl's frantic muffled cries soon silenced by the twists and turns of the path. It was all he could do not to turn around and have her then, but he had to wait.

It had to be perfect.

He pushed the packet back into his pocket, swallowed the two white pills with the first mouthful of coffee, and ignored the next twinge that seized his back muscles as he hissed through his teeth.

The need to continue outweighed any regrets, though.

He wrapped his hands around the warm cup and closed his eyes.

'Are you okay?'

He jerked awake at the sound of a woman's voice.

She stood over him, concern etched across her features, a tea towel in her hand.

'I-I'm fine,' he managed, and rubbed his hand over his face. He'd only rested his head on his arms for five minutes.

'You look like you could do with a holiday,' the woman smiled, and went back to wiping down tables.

Eli checked his watch. He'd only been asleep for a few minutes, but he couldn't afford to draw attention to himself. Not now.

His shift ended in an hour, and he was ahead of schedule.

He stood, dumped the coffee cup in a waste bin, and ignored the waitress as he exited the café and hurried to his courier van.

As he pulled the door open and climbed in behind the wheel, his gaze drifted to the clouds scuttling across the sky.

'Soon,' he murmured.

Chapter 41

Kay jogged from the car across the gravel driveway, and headed for the shelter of the front porch as fast as possible.

She rang the doorbell and brushed water from her suit, hoping that she didn't look as wretched as she felt after the soaking. She peered up at the grey sky, and wondered if the past days' rain signalled the end of a summer that hadn't even started yet.

She turned as the door opened.

Yvonne Richards stepped to one side, and beckoned her in.

'Hello, Yvonne,' said Kay. 'Where's Dawn's car?'

Yvonne pursed her lips. 'She's gone,' she said, then shrugged. 'I sent her home.'

'Oh, I see.'

Hazel appeared from the kitchen, her brow furrowed. 'Morning, Detective.'

'Morning, Hazel.'

Kay shut the door behind her, and withdrew the photograph of Eli Mathews from her bag. 'Do you recognise this man?' she said to Yvonne.

'I'm not sure,' said Yvonne.

'He's a courier driver,' said Kay. 'Have you seen him before?'

Yvonne shook her head. 'Like I said, I can't be sure.'

'Maybe you've seen him here, near the house?'

'We don't get parcels delivered here,' said Yvonne. 'And all our personal mail goes to a post office box at Downswood.'

'What about at the business?'

Yvonne bit her lip. 'I'm sorry, I don't really get involved in the admin side of things. That's what I pay people for.'

Kay bit back an exasperated sigh. 'No problem. I'll head over there now.'

***

Carys had fought a losing battle with the windscreen wipers between the Richards' residence and the furnishings business.

She parked as close to the building as possible, and the two of them hurried into the warehouse as a roll of thunder filled the air.

Despite all the lights in the ceiling being on, the lack of daylight lent a gloomy atmosphere to the space, and it took a moment for Kay's eyes to adjust.

'Well,' said a familiar voice, 'it's nice weather for ducks.'

Sheila Milborough peered out from behind a pile of boxes, a role of packing tape in one hand.

They made their way towards her.

'I've got a few more questions for you, Sheila,' said Kay. 'Got a minute?'

'Of course,' said Sheila. She put down the packing tape, and wiped her hands down the front of her jeans. She indicated an old sofa at the back of the warehouse. 'Come on, we can sit down over here.'

She led the way past a row of metal shelves, and pulled out a battered, old wooden chair while indicating to the two detectives to take the sofa.

'Sheila, when we last spoke, you mentioned Melanie usually flirted with Neil Abrahams, the courier, didn't you?' said Kay, as she sat down.

The woman leaned forward on the chair and nodded. 'Yeah. They were really friendly.' She sat back and shrugged, her face crestfallen. 'I don't know. I thought, maybe, there could've been something between them, given time.'

Kay suppressed a snort. Given Abrahams' current marital problems, she wouldn't have been surprised. She pulled out the photograph of Eli Matthews. 'Do you recognise this man?'

Sheila's lip curled. 'Yes. He's been here a few times.' She handed the photograph back. 'He's a courier, too. Used to do the morning run, but there was some sort of shift change at the depot two months ago. Neil changed to our morning drop-off, and he,' she said, pointing at the photograph in Kay's fingers, 'became our afternoon collection.'

'Any problems with him?'

Sheila placed her hands behind her head, and re-tied her ponytail. She sighed as she dropped her hands to her lap. 'There was one instance,' she said, frowning. 'I didn't think anything of it afterwards, to be honest. Just told them not to be mean. Why?'

Kay sat up straighter. 'Can you tell me what happened?'

'It was a few months ago. We'd had one of those late afternoon showers.' Sheila jerked her head towards the open doors of the warehouse. 'Nothing like this, just an hour or so of rain. I was upstairs, sorting out the last of the orders to go out, so it must've been, what, about half past four? Melanie was sitting downstairs at reception, and I heard the front door go. I dashed downstairs because I didn't want to miss him – we had some urgent stuff to go.'

'The poor man was soaked through – he must've got drenched running in and out of businesses like this, so I grabbed the towel from the downstairs bathroom for him to use,' she said. 'When he wiped at his arms, there was a stain on the towel. Looked like make-up – you know, when you've been out late and you don't take it off so it stains the pillowcase?'

Kay nodded, but said nothing.

'Anyway,' said Sheila. 'I noticed then that he had all these horrible bruises on his arms, and one on his face. Before I could say anything, the girls started laughing at him, poor mite. Tony came downstairs at that point and joined in, and then Emma took a photo on her mobile phone.' The older woman shook her head. 'Awful thing to do.'

'What happened to the photo?'

'Melanie was telling her to put it on social media,' said Sheila. 'As soon as I heard that, I snatched the phone from Emma and deleted the photograph.'

'What about this man?'

Sheila sighed. 'He took the parcels and left. Couldn't get back to the van fast enough.'

'What happened the next time he came in?'

Sheila looked down at her hands. 'I felt sorry for him. So I made sure Melanie and Emma were kept away from the reception area at that time of day in future. Then he stopped coming here after a couple of days, and the other chap started collecting the parcels again.'

'You've been most helpful, Sheila – many thanks,' said Carys.

They both rose, and Kay straightened the creases in her trousers before glancing around the warehouse area. 'How are you doing?' she said. 'Are you managing okay without Yvonne?'

Sheila shrugged. 'We'll be fine,' she said, and waggled her finger at the photograph in Kay's hand. 'You just concentrate on finding who did this to her family.'

Kay nodded. 'We'll be in touch.'

'What next?' said Carys, as she unlocked the car.

Kay lowered herself into the passenger seat, and stared up at the office windows.

'I think we need to speak to Eli Matthews.'

Chapter 42

Kay held up a finger to silence Carys as the door behind them opened, and a man appeared, wearing a short-sleeved shirt and casual trousers.

'I'm Damien Ashe, the HR Manager here,' the man said by way of introduction. 'I'm afraid Bob isn't available right now, but I'll do my best to help you any way I can.'

Kay resisted the urge to snatch the papers out of his hands. Unless Eli was charged, she wouldn't have access to his personnel file. She could only hope his managers would let them have as much information as legally possible.

'That's fine, Mr Ashe,' she said. She checked her watch. 'When will Eli be back from his delivery route?'

'Another twenty minutes.'

'How long has he worked here?'

'About seventeen months.'

'Any issues with his employment?'

'Not really. He's a bit quiet,' Ashe said. 'Tends not to come along to social gatherings. We organise the occasional barbecue in the summer out the back of the depot, or a few drinks at the pub maybe every couple of months.' He shrugged. 'If he does turn up, he usually hangs around at the edges. Do you know what I mean?'

Kay nodded. 'Why do you think that is?'

'I don't know. Shy, maybe?'

'How does Eli get to work?'

'He has a moped. Parks it around the back of the depot. An old one, mind. I'm surprised it's still going.'

'When Eli transferred from Suffolk, were any issues noted?'

'None at all. Exemplary record. Same as here.'

'He's from Kent, though, isn't he?' she said. 'Any ideas why he was in Suffolk?'

Ashe shook his head.

'Was he based here before he left for Suffolk?'

'No. Suffolk was his first employment with County Deliveries.' He lifted a page from the bundle in his hand, his eyes flickering over the content. 'Before that, he was working at a printing firm here in Kent.' He replaced the page, and pushed a phone away from his side of the table before dropping the file onto it. 'They went into receivership two years ago.'

'Before or after Eli left?'

'After.'

'Well, thank you for letting us have some background about Eli, it's much appreciated,' said Kay. 'Obviously, I need to ask that you don't discuss this conversation with anyone else.'

'Of course. Is he in trouble?'

'We're simply seeking his assistance with some questions we have,' said Kay. 'The only address we have on file for him is non-residential, so we thought we'd come here.'

'He lives with his mother. I'm okay with giving you that address.' He shrugged. 'He'll tell you anyway.'

'Thanks,' said Kay, as she watched him write down the address on a sticky note before handing it to her.

She passed it to Carys, fighting down the excitement that was building.

If his employers knew Eli's home address, then it appeared the address of the lock-up garage was a secret that Eli kept from both his employers, and perhaps his mother.

The question was, why?

Kay resisted the urge to take out her phone and check for any missed calls or texts. She would have heard it vibrating in her bag if Barnes had called with the news that their search authorisation had been granted. She mentally crossed her fingers, and hoped Sharp's powers of persuasion had worked on the superintendent he'd sought the documentation from. They'd been hasty, yes, but given Kay's theory of two people being involved in the kidnapping and subsequent murder of Melanie Richards was beginning to take form, some of her colleagues were starting to wonder if she had a point.

The phone on the meeting room table rang. Ashe leaned across and picked it up.

'Hello? Right. Thanks. I'll let them know.' He replaced the receiver. 'Matthews has returned from his shift.'

'What's the normal routine when someone gets back?' said Kay.

'It depends. Eli keeps a change of clothes here, so once he's handed his keys in, he'll probably get changed before going home.'

'Okay,' she said. 'We'll give him a couple of minutes.'

She realised after the urgency she'd conveyed to the HR manager in the past half an hour he'd likely wonder at her instructions, but it was imperative that she didn't rush now.

Approaching Eli the moment he arrived back at the depot and taking him away for questioning would only cause a scene, and she knew until she could prove otherwise, he had to be treated as an innocent man.

Ashe glanced at his watch. 'Right, he should be in the locker room by now, so if you'd like to follow me.'

Kay and Carys followed him from the office, turning left instead of right along the corridor, and past the double doors through to the sorting office. The corridor truncated at the end, and they took the left-hand fork. By Kay's calculations, they were heading towards the staff car park.

The unpainted brickwork gave way to two separate doors, one labelled for men, the other for women.

'These are the locker rooms,' said Ashe. He pointed at the men's door, then crossed his arms and stood in the middle of the corridor, as if unsure what to do next.

'We can take it from here,' said Kay, and held out her hand. 'I presume we can exit through the staff car park?'

The man looked relieved. 'That would be good. We don't normally get any members of the public coming to the reception area this time of the day, but you never know. It'd certainly be a bit—'

'Awkward? Yes, I understand,' said Kay.

They watched as he walked away, then Carys settled against the wall opposite the locker room door, and Kay blocked the corridor in the direction of the car park.

Her heartbeat refused to settle.

She knew she was right. Knew Eli Matthews was the second kidnapper they were looking for. Knew he was responsible for Melanie's murder, and her father's death.

Her phone buzzed in her bag, and she swore under her breath. She pulled it out, and jerked her thumb at the locker room.

Carys nodded.

'Yes?' she murmured into the phone.

'We've got it.'

She exhaled, some of the tension fleeing her neck and shoulders. 'We'll be on our way shortly,' she said.

'We'll be waiting for you.'

She finished the call.

Carys raised an eyebrow.

'We're good to go,' said Kay.

They both turned at the sound of the door to the men's locker room opening, and the man from the photograph appeared.

A confused look spread across his features.

'Eli Matthews?'

'Yes?'

'I'm Detective Sergeant Kay Hunter, and this is my colleague, Detective Constable Carys Miles.' She advised him of his rights, citing the caution as she watched his face for a reaction.

His eyes narrowed. 'What's this about?'

'We'd like to ask you some questions at the station regarding the kidnapping and murder of Melanie Richards.' Kay pointed to the exit. 'We have a car waiting.'

Eli let the door close behind him, and followed Carys as she led the way through to the car park at the rear of the building.

As they hurried towards the vehicle, their shoes splashing in puddles, Kay placed her hand on his arm to guide him to the car, but he shook it off, a glare on his face.

She shrugged, opened the back door for him, and waited while he climbed in.

As she shut it, she frowned.

A beige-coloured stain covered the paintwork where her hand had been. She turned her palm over and stared, then raised it to her nose and sniffed.

'Interesting,' she murmured.

Chapter 43

By the time Kay returned to the incident room after booking in Eli Matthews with the custody sergeant, her colleagues were clustered at one end of the room, balanced on desks if a seat wasn't available.

Despite his faults, DCI Larch had finally convinced his peers to obtain more resources, and so the team had grown by three more people – all administrative staff who would help Sharp keep the increasing paperwork up to date.

Sharp nodded as Kay leaned against her desk.

'Hunter, good work. We'll talk about the interview strategy in a moment.' He turned his attention back to the rest of the team.

'Tasks for now – Barnes, get onto our colleagues in Suffolk. Find out if there have been any kidnappings, or unsolved murders that are similar to that of Melanie Richards. Debbie can help you follow up any leads. Carys – phone the County Deliveries depot in Ipswich where Eli was previously employed. See if there were any issues with his employment history there.'

Sharp's eyes flickered to a point behind Kay, and she spun round.

'Okay if I join you?'

A slender woman in her late fifties with short, grey hair cut into a fashionable razor-sharp bob peered through the door, a notebook clutched to her chest.

'Come on in, Fiona,' said Sharp. 'Everyone, for those who haven't met Fiona Wilkes before, she's our senior interviewing specialist.'

A murmur of greetings swept through the room before Sharp brought the meeting to a halt.

'All right, everyone. Heads down. We need as much of this information as soon as possible. DCI Larch is currently speaking to the chief superintendent to get us another twelve hours to hold Matthews, but until we hear otherwise, we have twenty-four hours within which to charge him. An application for a further search authorisation in relation to Matthews' residential address is currently under review, and Larch has indicated that should be approved within the next hour or so.'

As the team began to disperse and head back to their desks, Sharp beckoned to Kay.

'Come and join me and Fiona in my office. I want to get the first interview underway within the hour.'

Sharp stood to one side and let the two women pass before he shut the door, and gestured to them to take the two chairs opposite his desk.

He manoeuvred his way between the desk and a filing cabinet, and lowered himself until he could lean against a low, wooden cabinet against the wall.

'Okay, Fiona, you've had a chance to review what we've got to date on this guy, and our reasons for bringing him in for formal questioning. Any initial thoughts?'

The interview specialist cleared her throat, and flipped open her notebook.

'I've taken a look at the extracts from Eli's personnel file David Ashe provided,' she said, the soft Somerset lilt of her voice belying the canny strategist beneath. 'And you're dealing with a very intelligent person. Although he didn't finish any higher education, the interview process used by County Deliveries, and subsequent reviews with his manager from a career development perspective, indicate a shrewd personality.'

'Good at giving the impression of being harmless, while being otherwise, perhaps?' said Kay.

'I wouldn't put it past him,' said Fiona. 'As you say, Devon, you've got him for twenty-four hours, and hopefully you'll be granted the extra twelve on top of that, so my advice would be to use this first interview to establish facts and gauge his personality – let's see how he reacts to being questioned initially before we start to put the pressure on him.' She shivered. 'Bearing in mind the way the killer ended Melanie Richards' life, if Matthews is guilty, then he's meticulous, and may in turn think he's untouchable and that we don't have enough on him to formally charge him.'

'Do we tell him about the searches from the start?' said Sharp.

Fiona tapped her pen on the spine of her notebook for a moment. 'Yes. See what his response is to that, but don't push it. Let him have something to worry about if necessary, between the first and second interviews.'

'Okay,' said Sharp, and straightened before unbuttoning his jacket and setting it on the back of his chair. 'We'll do one interview tonight, and then a second one mid-morning. That'll give us time to see what information comes through from Suffolk, and the searches at the lock-up and the house. By then, hopefully Larch will have got us the extra twelve hours to continue our questioning as well.'

'What are you thinking?' he said to Kay, as Fiona wound her way past the desks and left the incident room.

She exhaled, and cricked her neck. 'When we picked him up from the depot, I put my hand on his arm to help him into the car. He jerked his arm away from me, but I was left with a substance on my hand afterwards. Make-up.'

'Make-up? You mean, like the stuff you put on your face?'

'Yes. Sheila Milborough at Yvonne Richards' place said that's what Melanie took the mickey out of him about.'

'Why?'

'I wondered that, but when we arrived back at the station, his sleeves were rolled down.'

Sharp frowned. 'The only reason he'd be wearing make-up is to hide something. Like a bruise.'

'That's what I'm thinking. But, I bump into things all the time. We all do. Why hide it by using make-up?'

'Depends how you got the bruise.'

'Exactly.'

'It's an angle.' He checked his watch. 'Okay. I'll go see if the approval for the search authorisation for the mother's house is through. Let's get started with the questioning.' He turned away, and then peered over his shoulder. 'You can lead this one. It'll do you good to get back into the swing of things.'

'Thank you, sir.'

He nodded. 'Get our man. I'll see you in interview room one.'

Chapter 44

Kay waited until Sharp pressed the "record" button, and then stated clearly who was present in the room.

A duty solicitor had been requested for Eli Matthews, and both men looked as uncomfortable as the other about the circumstances by which they'd been thrown together.

Eli wore a set of overalls, his own clothes removed for forensic analysis at the same time Harriet had taken swabs of his hands.

Kay briefly wondered how long the young duty solicitor would last before he changed his mind about practicing criminal defence law, and then turned her attention to their suspect.

'State your name, age, and occupation for the purposes of the recording, please.'

'Elijah Matthews. Twenty-eight. Courier driver.'

'I'll now read you your formal rights,' said Kay, and spoke the words from memory. '…do you understand?' she concluded.

Eli nodded.

'I need you to say that out loud for the purposes of the recording, please,' said Kay.

'Yes.'

'Thank you.'

Eli's whole body language remained relaxed, an almost languid expression on his face. His eyes travelled lazily down Kay's body, but she retained her composure, and ignored his attempts to unnerve her. He wasn't the first suspect to try to intimidate her, and no doubt, he wouldn't be the last. It was why she always wore a double-breasted jacket. She knew he couldn't see anything of interest.

Eli clasped his hands together on the desk and raised an eyebrow.

'Mr Matthews—'

'Eli, please.'

'Mr Matthews, where were you last Thursday night between eleven o'clock and one thirty?'

'At home.'

'Please confirm the address.'

Eli sighed, and recounted the address.

'That's your mother's house?'

He scowled. 'Yes.'

'And your mother will be able to provide you with an alibi for that time?'

'I doubt it,' he sneered. 'She was drunk at the time. As usual.'

Kay noted the solicitor jot something down out the corner of her eye. 'Do you own a van, Mr Matthews?'

259

He blinked. 'Yes.'

'And where is that van kept, Mr Matthews?'

He glared at her. 'At a lock-up. Off the Queens Road.'

'What do you use the van for?'

He shrugged. 'This and that.'

'Elaborate, please, Mr Matthews.'

He exhaled; an impatient huff that sent spittle flying onto the surface of the desk, and folded his arms. 'Why do you want to know?'

Kay leaned back, and pulled her notebook away from the blob of liquid. 'Answer the question, please. What do you use the van for?'

'Helping mates out. Moving stuff. That sort of thing.'

'What sort of stuff?'

He rolled his eyes. 'Furniture and that.'

'When was the last time you used it?'

'Don't know,' he said. 'A few weeks ago, maybe.'

'Who were you helping at the time?'

'Can't remember.'

Sharp slid the CCTV photograph of the van driving through the industrial estate across the table. 'Is this your van?'

Eli glanced down, and then smiled. 'Nah,' he drawled. 'That's not mine.'

'What happened to your arm, Mr Matthews?' said Kay, lowering her voice.

'Eh?'

'Your right arm. When we picked you up at the depot earlier, I placed my hand on your arm to guide you to the car. When I removed my hand, it had make-up on it.' She pointed at his long sleeves. 'You've since rolled down your shirt sleeves. What's wrong with your arm?'

Eli sneered, uncrossed his arms, and unbuttoned the cuff at his right wrist.

'Banged me arm,' he said. He rolled back the sleeve and held up his arm, turning it so she could see.

Sure enough, a bluish-purple bruise covered the lower part of his forearm.

'Looks painful.'

He shrugged, and then rolled the sleeve back down.

'How did you hurt yourself?'

'Knocked it loading the van last week.'

'Which van?'

He glared at her. 'The one at work.'

'You didn't report it?'

He snorted. ''Course not. It's nothing serious.'

'Why have you attempted to cover it up with make-up?'

His eyes blazed. 'I didn't want anyone making a fuss.'

'Where were you between the hours of four-thirty and eight o'clock on Tuesday morning last week?' said Sharp.

'At home.'

'Would your mother—'

'No. She wouldn't. She was drunk.'

'Why did you move to Suffolk?'

'Needed a change of scenery.'

'But you only stayed for two years. Why was that?'

'Didn't like the scenery.'

Sharp pushed two documents across the table towards Eli.

'Mr Matthews, these are copies of approved search authorisations signed by a magistrate,' he said.

Eli frowned, confusion clouding his features. 'Search authorisations? For what?'

'This one is for a property in Maidstone, specifically, number three Edward Street. Your mother's house. This one,' he said, pushing the page closer, 'is for your lock-up garage.'

Eli's jaw clenched.

The young duty solicitor paled.

'Now, Mr Matthews,' said Kay. 'Before we carry out these searches, is there anything you'd like to tell us? Anything we might expect to find at either of these two locations in relation to the kidnapping and murder of Melanie Richards?'

Eli rocked back in his seat.

'No,' he said, eventually. 'No, there isn't.'

Chapter 45

He took a long drag on his cigarette, and then squinted through the chemical-infused smoke as he exhaled.

He rolled his shoulders, conscious of his hunched position over the laptop computer these past few days, and a constant twinge that had formed at the base of his neck.

He refused to panic.

He'd received a phone call to explain that Eli had been taken into custody, and silently congratulated the female detective. His customers would appreciate her determination.

He removed the cigarette and wetted his lips. He wondered what price he could demand for footage of *that* one, if the opportunity arose.

He pinched the cigarette between his fingers, and knocked the excess ash away, then took another drag.

Eli's misfortune was of concern.

Luckily, the voyeur had the foresight to visit the lock-up garage before the police had learned of its whereabouts.

Eli's penchant for collecting things extended beyond young girls, and the voyeur had cursed under his breath as the beam from his torch had swept over a workbench at the back of the garage and onto the fake registration plates that lay there.

He'd found a laptop computer in a plastic storage crate under the workbench, turned it over, and swore as he read the name etched into the surface.

G Nelson.

In a box of assorted nails, he'd found other souvenirs, a worrying trend that he thought the youngster had overcome.

Especially after their last talk.

The man was like a magpie, as if he coveted shiny things.

The note was more worrying.

He'd had no idea Eli had followed Guy Nelson to Mote Park that night.

Their relationship had been purely professional – they'd simply engaged Nelson to provide the copy registration plates and collect the ransom money.

Eli had worried about that. 'What if he keeps it all?'

He had shrugged. 'Let him. It's a fraction of what I can get for this.'

Finding Nelson's original suicide note had sent a chill down his spine. It had implicated Eli by name, and alluded to the participation of others, but that didn't bother him –

the police had only found the replacement note Eli had left on the body.

What was more concerning was the fact Eli had kept the original note instead of destroying it.

The man's strange cravings, once an indulgent quirk he could use to his advantage, were fast becoming a liability.

Now, he reached into the pocket of his trousers and extracted a photograph, then rubbed his thumb over it as he inhaled the next nicotine fix.

'You've been a good boy, Eli,' he murmured, 'but you've been careless.'

He held the stub of the cigarette to the edge of the photograph until a flame caught the image and began to devour the glossy laminate with a crackle before the photograph disintegrated into ash.

He crouched, pushed the remnant into the small metal tray next to the door, and straightened at the sound of footsteps.

'Those things will kill you,' someone said as they passed, and then the door swung shut in their wake before he could turn to see who it was.

The voyeur smiled to himself as he peered out from under the eaves of the building, and tapped another cigarette out of the packet into his hand.

He breathed in the ozone-laced air before lighting up.

'Yes,' he murmured, 'but I'll die a rich man.'

Chapter 46

Emma blinked, tried to raise her head, and then groaned as the dull ache at the back of her skull that had woken her began to throb painfully.

Her eyelids were heavy, and a strong urge to vomit sent her stomach into convulsions. Something covered her mouth, a cloth that was sucked in through her lips with each panicked inhalation.

Her arms were raised, and when she tried to move her hands, she discovered they were held at shoulder height by something strong wrapped around her wrists.

She opened her eyes, the wall in front of her spinning as she regained consciousness. A light shone in her eyes, and she frowned while she tried to work out where she was.

She ducked her head to the left, and saw that the light came from a camping lamp that had been fixed to a bracket above. Its wavering beam illuminated her position and cast shadows over the walls opposite. She tilted her head back, and her eyes opened wide.

Her wrists were bound, tied to the bow-legged junction of a steel pipe that snaked across the roof.

When she looked down, she realised she was standing in water. She moved her feet, and the sound of sloshing echoed off the brick walls around her.

She squinted past the beam of light to the opposite wall, where a white stick protruded out of the water and ran up the length of the brickwork.

For a moment, she couldn't fathom what it was, and then she saw the black lines etched into its surface, and the numbers marking regular intervals.

The numbers began at "1" just below the level of her knees, and increased the further up the post they were painted.

She swallowed, her throat dry and painful, and tried to focus.

Despite the cold water, perspiration streaked across her forehead and between her shoulder blades.

She shivered, and strained at the bindings at her wrists once more.

A cry escaped her lips, its echo bouncing off the walls around her, amplified by the enclosed space and the acoustics of the arched brickwork.

She tried to recall what day it was, but the darkness of the tunnel prevented any light from reaching her, and she had no idea how long she'd been unconscious for.

She flexed her wrists, and then looked to her left hand. The material around it seemed more pliable, with more give in its woven seams.

Emma turned her head to one side, and wiped her face across her arm.

Christ, she was so damned hot.

She cried out as pain spread from her heart, jabbing her sternum, the sudden attack leaving her breathless.

She sank against her bindings, her breath escaping in pants.

She'd heard what had happened to Melanie, despite her mother and stepfather's attempts to shield her from the truth.

Only Monday night, she'd stood at the top of the stairs, listening as her parents shared a bottle of wine with their neighbours and spoke in hushed tones about the murdered schoolgirl.

That was why she'd left the note on her dressing table before leaving the house Wednesday night.

She didn't want her parents to panic; she simply needed time to let off steam before returning to school next week.

That was why she'd arranged to spend the rest of the week at Tanya's.

Would Tanya raise the alarm when she realised her friend hadn't returned to her home, and that the spare bed had never been slept in?

Or would she think her friend was sulking, back at her own home, after being dumped in favour of her twenty-year-old boyfriend?

The realisation hit her, hard.

No one knows I'm missing.

No one knows I'm here.

Then, she saw it – an unblinking red light to the right of the camping lamp, under which the cold dark lens of a camera peered back at her; a solitary eye that watched her every move, mocking her predicament.

Her knees gave way, and she felt her bowels move involuntarily as her arms took her weight.

She screamed.

Chapter 47

Ian Barnes checked his watch, and then gave a low whistle that turned heads.

'Okay, let's have a debrief,' he said. 'Sharp and Hunter are still in with Eli Matthews and his solicitor, so let's have a progress update on the other leads we're chasing.'

He turned to Carys as the rest of the small team gathered around. 'You start.'

'All right,' she said. 'I've managed to get hold of someone in the HR department at the Ipswich depot where Matthews was based until seventeen months ago. As with the depot here, there are no issues they can think of. I've requested a copy of his full personnel file, but apparently they need a senior manager's approval to release that to us, and he's not back in the office until Monday morning.'

A collective groan filled the room.

'I know,' said Carys. 'But they won't budge on that stance. I'll phone them first thing Monday to chase it up. They should be able to email it to us as soon as they get the authorisation.'

'Thanks, Carys,' said Barnes. 'Piper?'

'I spoke to Suffolk Constabulary to find out if there were any unsolved murders or kidnappings similar to Melanie Richards,' said Gavin. 'I had a phone call back from them half an hour ago. There's an unsolved kidnapping case from seventeen months ago.'

Barnes raised an eyebrow. 'Ties in with the time Eli Matthews left Suffolk to come here.'

'Exactly,' said Gavin. 'In that case, the girl managed to escape, but she wasn't able to give a full description of her attacker. All she can recall is a red van being used to take her from where she was grabbed. It was dark when she was taken – she was cycling home from a friend's house at the time – and she couldn't see her abductor's face.'

'How did she escape?' said Carys.

'The poor mite can't remember,' said Gavin. 'She was found wandering along a lane on the outskirts of Ipswich early on a Tuesday morning by a woman taking her dogs for a walk. She was only eleven at the time, and the doctors who treated her afterwards said it was likely the date rape drug used to pacify her when she was taken could've still been affecting her memory at the time she escaped.' He tossed his notebook onto the desk next to him. 'She has no recollection of where she'd been, or how she managed to get away.'

'Eli Matthews' former HR department confirmed he applied for a transfer only days after that girl turning up,' said Carys.

'What reason did he give them for wanting the transfer?' said Barnes.

'He said his mother was sick, and he wanted to return to Kent to be near her.'

'Any record of him applying for a transfer out of the Kent depot?' said Gavin. 'At least that might show Melanie's kidnapping was premeditated.'

Carys shook her head. 'No.' She frowned. 'Maybe he didn't mean to kill her.'

'Or he thinks he's got away with it,' said Barnes. He checked his watch. 'All right. Carys, get yourself over to Beryl Matthews' house and monitor the search there – see what CSI come up with. Gavin, call it a day.' He glanced around at the rest of the team. 'You, too. I'd imagine the first interview with Eli Matthews will go on for a bit yet. Get yourselves back here by seven-thirty tomorrow morning.'

'What are you going to do?' asked Gavin.

'I'm going to meet Harriet and her team over at the lock-up garage,' said Barnes. He held up a plastic bag containing a bunch of keys, and shook it with a grin on his face. 'Which isn't going to remain locked up for much longer.'

***

Ian Barnes stepped on the cigarette butt, ground the soft material into the pavement, then turned, and strode up the short concrete driveway towards the cinder block garages set behind a row of terraced houses.

He exhaled the smoke as he approached, savouring the last dregs of nicotine before he joined the crime scene investigators at a large, dark-coloured van being unloaded with equipment.

Two patrol cars blocked the entrance to the driveway, the uniformed officers doing an efficient job of maintaining a perimeter within which the forensic team could work in peace, as well as keeping any prying eyes from the operation.

They'd erected a plastic barrier around the entrance to the garage, while two floodlights on tripods shone above their heads. Another floodlight had been set up ready to be used in the garage itself.

The afternoon was drawing to a close, the early summer sky dark well before the cloud-covered sun would dip below the horizon.

Barnes' eyes roamed over the scuffed, aluminium roller door that concealed whatever lay beyond. Once blue, it had been chipped and scratched over the years so it now bore a speckled effect, much like its neighbours.

There were six garages in total, all leased by the council to a menagerie of tenants whose addresses originated from various parts of the county town.

'Makes you wonder what's tucked away in the other five,' he muttered.

Harriet smiled. 'But you only have a search authorisation for this one.'

'More's the pity.' He turned his attention back to the garage nearest them, and squared his shoulders.

'Ready for this?'

'Let's do it,' he said. He tugged on the gloves that Harriet handed to him, then pulled a bag from his pocket and emptied it of the keys Kay had taken from Eli Matthews.

He selected one, and inserted it into the lock.

It turned easily.

'Used regularly, then,' said Harriet.

Barnes didn't respond. Instead, he stood, then placed his fingers under the handle and pulled.

The door rolled back smoothly, exposing first a concrete floor riddled with cracks and oil spots, and then, as the door fell back into its housing in the ceiling, a red van.

Barnes frowned. 'Doesn't that look like—'

'A courier van? Yeah. It does.'

'Looks like we hit the jackpot, then.' Barnes stepped back to let Harriet and her colleague access the garage, and held his breath as they circled the van from either side.

A workbench and a row of shelves lined the back wall of the low-set building, and the crime scene investigators were already making a start on the contents.

'No room to open the back doors of the van in here,' called Harriet. 'We're going to have to move it.'

'Here,' said Barnes, and extracted another key from the bag.

Harriet walked back towards him, stepping sideways down the narrow path between the side of the vehicle and the cinderblock wall. She held out her hand. 'Thanks.'

Barnes stepped out of the way. 'Moment of truth,' he muttered.

Chapter 48

They'd phoned the duty solicitor two hours ago to confirm another interview with his client, the fourth in total.

Now both men wore a confused expression at the request relayed over the intercom that DI Sharp's urgent presence was required only thirty minutes after the recording had begun.

The major incident team had been working for a solid day and a half since Eli was brought to the station, re-checking the circumstantial evidence they had to hand while they tried not to look at the time as the hours passed. Nothing had been heard from the two crime scene teams that had been steadily working their way through Eli Matthews' lock-up garage and his mother's home.

Larch had obtained authorisation from a superintendent late the previous day for an additional twelve hours to hold Matthews for questioning on the basis of a convincing argument that Eli was withholding the truth from them, but despite their best efforts, they were getting nowhere, and they were running out of time.

Kay resisted the urge to look at her watch.

Unless they could obtain information from Matthews during the next few hours, they would have to release him without charge.

Sharp had sensed the team's frustration and exhaustion, and sent everyone home Saturday night, instructing Kay to report in early Sunday so they could resume interviewing their main suspect.

Now, Kay avoided Eli's intense stare as Sharp buttoned his jacket and left the room.

She'd arrived at the station early that morning, met the interview specialist and Sharp in his office for an hour, and now rued not taking up his offer of a coffee while they were preparing their notes.

The young duty solicitor twirled his pen between his fingers, and popped the nib in and out each time it passed his thumb, and then cleared his throat.

'What's going on?'

'I don't know,' said Kay.

'How long will he be?'

'Do you need to be somewhere else?'

The man fell silent.

Eli crossed his arms over his chest, slumped in his chair and closed his eyes, then rocked his head from side to side.

Again, Kay found herself fighting the urge to check her watch, and willed her heart rate to slow down. Something was wrong, she could sense it.

Footsteps in the passageway preceded the reappearance of Sharp.

Kay took one look at his face, and realised what was going to happen.

She spun in her chair to see Eli grinning at her, a manic look in his eyes.

'Mr Matthews, thank you for your cooperation,' said Sharp. He reached out to the recorder and pressed the "stop" button.

Eli pushed back his chair and stood, ignoring the hand his solicitor held out for him to shake.

'If you'd like to follow me,' said Sharp. 'We'll get you released and your belongings returned to you.'

He waited until Eli was in the corridor with his solicitor, and then turned to Kay. 'Stay here.'

She sank back into her seat.

Desperate to know what had happened during the searches, and why the decision had been made to let Eli go, she fumed silently as the minutes passed.

She checked her watch. Eli had been with them for slightly less than the thirty-six hours they'd been able to question him without having to seek an extension from a magistrate. During that time, he had volunteered no information. He hadn't been charged yet, but surely forensics would have found something to link him to Melanie Richards' kidnapping and murder? And from the way Matthews had ducked and weaved around every single question, surely Sharp could see now that Guy Nelson would've had to have had an accomplice, and that the accomplice was Eli Matthews? Why had he let him go before their allocated thirty-six hours had expired?

After a time, she heard someone approaching the interview room, and looked up as Sharp returned.

He pushed the door until it was almost closed, then turned to her, and thrust his hands in his pockets.

'They didn't find anything,' he said.

'What? Why not?' Kay stood, her heart racing. 'They found the van, right?'

Sharp nodded. 'Yes. They found the van.' He unbuttoned his jacket and pulled at his tie to loosen it. 'It had been wiped down with bleach.'

'Same as the post box.'

He shook his head, his eyes weary. 'But, unfortunately that doesn't necessarily prove a link between him and Melanie's kidnapping or murder.' He sighed, and leaned against the wall. 'Both the exterior and interior of the van had been wiped down. Nothing in the back of it. Nothing to link Eli Matthews to Melanie Richards or Guy Nelson in the lock-up garage or at the house he shares with his mother.'

'He can't be that good.'

'We were getting nowhere with him, Hunter, and there's no way we're going to get an extension from a magistrate based on our attempts so far. How long have we been questioning him for? Perhaps he's innocent. Thought of that?'

Her mouth fell open. 'You don't seriously believe that.'

He straightened, his eyes never leaving hers. 'We have a confession in the form of Guy Nelson's suicide note.'

Kay threw her hands up. 'From someone whose own death showed none of the violence or forethought that went into Melanie Richards' murder.' She paced the room. 'Eli Matthews could have socialised with Guy Nelson at the barbeque held at the courier depot.'

'But Nelson was the one who was found with the ransom money. Not Eli.'

'He must've guessed Bernard Coombs would get in touch with the police,' argued Kay. She swore. 'Damn it – why didn't he call us straight away? We lost hours. Plenty of time for Eli to clean the car.'

'It's too circumstantial, and like I said, DCI Larch wouldn't authorise us approaching a magistrate to hold Matthews for any longer based on the slim evidence we have.'

'They're still looking, aren't they?' she said. 'Please tell me forensics haven't given up that easily.'

Sharp exhaled. 'The van's at the pound. They brought it back here under the pretence of having it cleaned. The pound is closed to the public on Sundays.' He held up his hand to stop her interrupting. 'I've told Harriet she's got until tomorrow morning, or I'm going to let it go.'

'Thank you,' she murmured, and then spun on her heel as the door crashed open.

DCI Larch stalked into the room. 'You're both here. Good.' He glared at Kay, then at Sharp. 'Well, that was an unmitigated disaster, wasn't it?'

He didn't wait for an answer, and instead jabbed his finger at Kay. 'You do realise your *hunch* placed suspicion on an innocent man, and cost us two forensic teams to chase their tails in pursuit of zero evidence?'

He turned away from Kay, and directed his glare at Sharp. 'I told you she should've been dismissed. She's a bloody embarrassment.'

Sharp held up his hands to pacify the other man. 'It was my decision to bring in Eli Matthews for questioning, and to search his property,' he said. 'From a due diligence perspective, and procedurally, it makes sense to check all lines of enquiry.' His eyes hardened. 'And with all due respect, Angus, if one of my officers needs to be disciplined, I'll deal with it myself.'

DCI Larch snorted, wrenched open the door, then spun back to face them, his face flushed with anger.

'I'd be very careful if I were you, Sharp,' he said, barely keeping his voice under control. 'I'd hate to see you risk your career to save hers.'

Chapter 49

Kay rested her hands on the side of the sink, and peered out the window into the soaked garden beyond.

The path from the back door to the shed that housed a lawn mower and little else had become a quagmire, rivulets of water that had escaped the gutters now tearing across the patio and under the fence towards the neighbouring garden.

She pulled down the blinds.

A rumble of thunder sounded a couple of miles away, and the lights flickered.

Her eyes fell on Sid's glass case, and she shivered, then sprang into action and pulled candles and matches from the bottom drawer she and Adam reserved for emergency supplies – an assortment of batteries, and the candles and a box of matches.

Kay pulled out an old candleholder from another cupboard, took her supplies through to the living room, and set everything out on the coffee table before retrieving the glass of wine she'd left there.

With any luck, they'd miss the worst of the storm, but with the amount of rain they'd been having, there were plenty of places that would be starting to flood.

She didn't envy her uniformed colleagues who had to work tonight.

She glanced up at the sound of a key in the front door, and then Adam peered into the living room.

'You're home,' he smiled. 'I'll go and have a shower, and then I'll come and join you for one of those,' he said, pointing at the wineglass.

'See you in a bit.'

She sank back into the sofa, and jabbed the mute button on the remote control.

The screen fell silent, the presenter of the home renovation programme reduced to a silent mime as he showed a couple in their fifties around a dilapidated barn.

She took a sip of her wine, then leaned forward and placed the glass on the low table in front of the sofa before rubbing her eyes.

She dropped her hand, and tried to ignore the stinging sensation at the corner of her eyelids.

She knew it was just the myriad of emotions that were wracking her mind of late, but the knowledge didn't help.

Despite Sharp's best efforts, it seemed that every action of hers was being judged, weighed and considered, as if she couldn't be trusted any more.

Then, there was Eli Matthews.

She couldn't leave it alone.

She realised her jaw was clenched, and forced herself to try to relax.

The man was guilty, she was sure of that. He knew something about Melanie's disappearance and murder.

Yet he had outwitted her, and Sharp. His mannerisms seemed rehearsed, as if he fully expected to be arrested and had practised.

And he'd been too good for them.

She let out a groan. Her assertions about his guilt weren't helped by the fact that nothing had been found at the lock-up garage, or at his mother's house.

Frustration overwhelmed her, DCI Larch's final words going round and round in her head.

She'd had moments of doubt about her abilities before – it was natural in her line of work, especially with a case that wasn't straightforward, but this was different.

Now, she felt as if she was being singled out – set up. But, for what?

And why?

She'd known she'd have to fight her way back after the embarrassment of the Professional Standards investigation, but now she felt naïve – she'd completely underestimated the effect it would have on her integrity, despite being absolved of any wrongdoing.

She sniffed. If that wasn't bad enough, her application to become a detective inspector was now probably at the bottom of the pile.

Or in the shredder.

She sat back and wiped at her cheeks as Adam appeared.

He stopped in the doorway. 'Hey.'

'Hey.'

She pulled a paper tissue from the box on the coffee table, and blew her nose as he sat beside her.

He reached over and squeezed her leg. 'Shit day?'

'Yeah.'

'It happens.'

'I know.' She snuggled into his arms. 'It's still shit.'

'What did Sharp say?'

Adam had met Sharp at a few social functions, often trading stories over pints of real ale at the local pub frequented by the police.

'I'm more worried about what they'll do to him if he keeps trying to protect me,' said Kay.

Adam chuckled, and kissed the top of her head. 'He can look after himself.' He edged away until his eyes met hers. 'Which is why he believes in you. I get the impression he wouldn't do this otherwise.'

Kay bit her lip.

Adam was right, of course. He'd been as shocked as she was about the allegations, but he trusted her. Trusted her integrity.

She reached out, and squeezed his hand. 'Thank you.'

'What for?'

'Making me feel better.'

'Really? I was just here wondering where my dinner is. I'm starving.'

She swatted his arm. 'Come on. I'll fix something.'

She picked up her wineglass, and followed him out to the kitchen.

Soon, the aromas of fresh onion and garlic sizzling in a pan filled the space.

Kay pointed her wine glass at the snake's glass enclosure on the worktop. 'How much longer is he with us for?'

Adam turned from the hob. 'Another few days.' He smiled. 'It's good. He seems to be on the mend – certainly getting his appetite back.'

Kay shuddered, and held up her hand. 'Too much information.'

Chapter 50

Eli stood with his hands clasped over his head, his feet planted hip-width apart, and stared at the empty garage space.

The moment he'd been released by the custody sergeant, he'd been informed that his van had been taken by the crime scene investigators, and that he'd be able to collect it by noon tomorrow.

'Tomorrow?'

He'd tried to keep his voice calm, but the uniformed officer standing next to the water cooler had raised an eyebrow in his direction, and Eli had held up a hand to pacify him before lowering his voice.

'Why?'

'Well, sir, as you can appreciate, there's no one around at the moment to sign the release paperwork, and with forensic investigations there's often residual cleaning up to do, to ensure your vehicle is returned to you as we found it,' said the sergeant.

Eli's eyes narrowed at the glee that flitted across the man's face.

'"Residual cleaning up"?'

'Yes, sir. So, if you'd like to go to the vehicle recovery centre from about eleven o'clock tomorrow, your vehicle should be ready for collection.'

Eli had resisted the urge to snatch the paperwork from the custody sergeant, and instead had pushed his way past a thickset man with tattoos standing behind him in the queue and hurried out through the door.

Now, Eli reached out and pulled a string next to the doorframe, and a single light bulb hanging from a thin cord in the ceiling flickered to life.

He surveyed the space before him.

His space. *His* things.

That *they* had touched.

He knew they had to wear gloves, but it didn't help the feeling of being violated that made him shiver.

Eli ran his hand over the workbench. The thin layer of dust had been disturbed by the police search team, and his fingers followed in the wake of others.

He stopped, and stared into space for a moment, all his senses alert.

Then it hit him.

Where were the registration plates?

He'd removed them the afternoon he'd learned of Neil Abrahams being taken away for questioning, when he realised they were of no use to him any longer.

He frowned, and then his hand shot out and wrenched open the plastic drawers on the back of the bench.

His things were gone.

He tried to swallow, but his tongue rasped within a dry mouth.

His mobile phone blared out from his back pocket, startling him from his thoughts.

There was only one person who had the number.

He stumbled away from the bench, his hand fumbling for the phone before it stopped ringing.

'Hello?'

He cringed at the anger in the man's voice, but agreed with everything he said.

Finally, mercifully, the caller hung up, and Eli replaced the phone into his back pocket once more.

Hands shaking, he wracked his mind, and tried to think what to do next.

His throat constricted, and he fought down the urge to cry. He hadn't cried in several years, and he wasn't about to start now.

Instead, he clenched his fists until the tears turned to frustration, and then anger.

Even his mother hadn't known about the lock-up garage, though no doubt she would do now. The female detective who had interviewed him had informed him that his mother's house was also being searched at the same time as the garage.

He flapped his hand at an errant bluebottle fly that buzzed too close, and contemplated his options.

He'd have to find another vehicle, and quickly. The drugs would have worn off by now, and he wouldn't get the desired result.

His moped was no good, it would be locked behind the security gate at the courier depot by now, and he couldn't reach the building where he'd hidden the girl using public transport – a taxi was out of the question.

It was simply too risky.

Pain shot through the palm of his hand, and he glanced down to see that his fingernails had dug into the skin, leaving crescent-moon shaped dents.

He didn't have enough money to buy another van. In any event, the moment any paperwork was submitted to transfer the vehicle into his name, the police would probably be informed.

He groaned.

She was *there*, waiting for him.

It was only a few miles away, but it could have been another country – without a vehicle to get back there, without the insulin, it wouldn't happen. It wouldn't be perfect.

He *had* to get there, somehow.

He paced the floor, strode across to the worktop that he'd built along one side of the narrow wall. Dusty jars filled with old nails and screws jangled as he pulled out the drawers underneath one by one, his mood darkening as he pawed through the contents, trying to work out if anything was missing, whether the police had found anything.

He didn't think so. The man who had phoned him had been thorough. Otherwise, the female detective, DS Hunter, wouldn't have let him go.

Eli slammed the drawer shut, his eyes roaming over the power extension lead that hung on a nail he'd bashed into the wall. He ran his hand over it, and then turned away.

He swallowed as a thought occurred to him.

His mother had a vehicle. Given, it was a small car, but it would do.

And it was in her name, so he wouldn't be stopped by any police if he drove past them. They knew he didn't have a vehicle until tomorrow lunchtime at least.

There was no other choice. He'd have to walk to his mother's house in the morning – early, before she woke up, then fetch his meagre belongings from there, and take her car.

His stomach clenched painfully at the thought of having to return to the house and face her.

For now, he'd try to create a makeshift bed and get his head down for a few hours. He was too strung out, and the police might be watching.

He'd wait until the morning.

As it was, he'd have to find somewhere else to keep the van when he got it back. He'd get no privacy from the other owners in the garage block now the police had been here. For a start, they'd want to know why it had happened, and then they'd wonder if it would happen again.

He ran a hand over his weary eyes.

No, he'd have to sell the van, or dump it, and find a new place to base himself.

He sighed, and made his way across the bare concrete to the boxes that lined the back wall. He ran his hand over the lid of the nearest one, and then pulled it back, the scraping sound of the cardboard flaps pulling apart making him flinch.

He peered in.

Although the contents had been repacked with care, it wasn't the same.

They'd torn his life apart.

He picked up the box and threw it across the garage, the contents tumbling over the oil-specked floor.

Chapter 51

Emma's head rocked forwards once, jerking her awake.

She blinked, for a moment confused by the unfamiliar surroundings, and then she remembered.

She choked back a sob, and wondered how she could have fallen asleep.

Exhaustion swept through her body, and she realised the fear that had permeated every cell of her being had also sapped her energy.

She raised her head, and squinted at the bindings that still held her hands above her head. Her pink nail varnish glistened in the beam from the lamp, the skin of her hands and wrists a deathly white from the lack of circulation.

The cloth gag bit at the sides of her mouth where her captor had tied it too tight, and the coppery taste of blood filled the back of her throat.

She wondered what time it was, whether it was day or night, and how long it had been since she'd lost consciousness.

She had changed, though, she realised.

Whether it was because of her exhausted sleep, or the drugs the man had used to render her unconscious when he taken her had worn off, but she felt strangely refreshed.

Her vision had cleared, every detail around her was sharper, and her recollection had returned.

She knew her attacker.

She knew who had killed Melanie.

Emma bit back a scream. The camera's red light wavered above the lens, and she was determined not to let him have the pleasure of seeing her fear.

She shivered at the realisation that her heart rate no longer pounded painfully through her body, and her temperature had fallen. She frowned – was that the effect of being knocked out, or something else?

Her feet sloshed in the cold water that covered the floor of the tunnel, and she frowned, confused as the sensation of water lapping at her calves reached her brain.

She looked down.

The water that had once covered her feet had risen.

She cried out, the sound muffled by the gag, and raised her eyes to the white post set into the opposite wall, and the realisation hit her of its significance.

The lines were markings; old ones, in feet rather than metres, of the water levels recorded in the tunnel over the years.

And the water level had risen since she had first been brought here.

She realised then what she was standing in.

A drainage culvert.

Not simply a tunnel under a building, but a drain.

She tried to focus on calming her breathing, and strained her ears to hear the familiar rush of water further up the tunnel to her left.

It had been raining when he'd grabbed her, a hard, steady deluge that was already causing the storm drains along the sides of the road to overflow.

How long had it rained for?

Was it still raining?

She whimpered, and turned her attention to the steel pipe she'd been tied to. Bolted to the wall next to it was an old, iron ladder. She lifted her head once more, and tried to see how far up the ladder reached.

There were several rungs above her, but as her eyes adjusted away from the dull light of the lamp, she thought she could see where it ended. There seemed to be a metal cover at the top, but a glint of pale light encircled it, and she guessed it was a manhole cover.

She gritted her teeth, and tugged at the rope that wound through the rungs and around her wrists.

It failed to move.

She tried leaning her weight away from the ladder, then cried out as the tension on her shoulders became too much.

A faint *plop* sounded from the darkness and she held her breath.

Something squeaked.

The beam of the camping lamp wavered, the bulb dimming before returning to its sickly yellow colour. At the same time, a large rat paddled from her left, riding the water current.

Its nose twitched as it drew near, and then to Emma's horror, it altered course and crossed the stream to where she stood, helpless as its front paws scratched against her bare leg.

She screamed and kicked out.

The gag sucked into her mouth with every breath, and she started to cough, her chest muscles contracting as she tried to force air through her nostrils and into her lungs.

The stench of rotten vegetation – and worse – filled her senses, and she fought down the urge to vomit.

The rat powered away, scared by her movement, and she watched it, her breathing laboured, as its wake disappeared along the culvert.

Her eyes fell on the water level once more.

At first, she tried to convince herself that the water lapping at it was simply caused by the movement from her kicking out at the rat. Her unease increased as the minutes passed, and she realised the water was rising faster.

She was running out of time.

Chapter 52

By the time Eli reached his mother's house, he was soaked through to the skin.

His thin T-shirt clung to his back and chest, and he slicked back his hair to stop the water running into his eyes.

He had to get the keys to his mother's car.

He'd spent the past few hours camped out at the lock-up garage, mired in paranoid thoughts.

What if the police found something and had let him go to see where he went?

How was he going to explain himself to the one who mattered most in all of this?

Would he be allowed to keep his collection of things? Would he get them back?

He glanced over his shoulder, his eyes sweeping the neighbouring cars and houses.

No one followed.

In fact, the street was deserted, and despite being cold and wet, Eli figured the weather had at least made his job easier.

Now he had to return to the girl – and quickly, before the effects of the drugs wore off.

He slammed the garden gate shut, and stomped up the path towards the front door. Rivulets of muddy water ran from the overflowing plant pots next to the step, and streaked past him towards the street, the sound of water gushing from the broken gutter above the living room window reaching him as he inserted his key into the lock.

The door was opened before he could turn the handle, and his mother peered through the gap, her eyes flickering over the street behind him, before her glare found him.

'The police were here,' she said, and grabbed hold of his shirt.

She flung the door open, and yanked him inside.

He stumbled across the threshold before the door was slammed shut with such force that the window at the top shook in its frame.

Eli could smell the alcohol on her breath, and staggered back along the narrow hallway. He reached out and gripped the stair bannister beside him to regain his balance.

He'd forgotten how strong she could be when she was drunk.

Two years away from her had numbed the memories, though the ache in his left arm from where she'd fractured it when she'd pushed him down the stairs in a fit of rage when he was eight years old still ached in cold weather.

He'd only returned because he'd had to, after the incident in Suffolk. He'd been lucky to avoid police scrutiny then, and had nowhere else to go. Returning here was meant to be temporary, a chance to take stock, reinvent himself before moving on again. He frowned, wondering how he'd missed the signs and become complacent about her moods.

'You frowning at me?' she slurred.

Her hand shot out and slapped his right cheek.

Eli's eyes watered from the strike.

Her grip on his shirt relaxed, and he recoiled, turned his body away from her, and rubbed his face.

'No,' he mumbled.

'Why were the police here?'

'I don't know.'

'Bullshit,' she spat.

Although he stood a head taller than her, she was thickset against his skinny frame, and had used her weight advantage to beat him throughout his childhood.

She relied on verbal abuse as well as physical, belittling him on a regular basis, wearing him down until he believed every vicious word that escaped her lips. Often though, her fists would lash out at him.

He'd felt powerless until the first time he'd been tagging along with a group of kids after school when he was sixteen, the remnants of the boys no one else wanted to hang around with, and even then he was the bottom of the pecking order. They had psyched themselves up to mug an old lady in an alleyway off Wheeler Street, and Eli had felt the first flush of excitement as the leader of the group had dared the youngest to go first.

The look of terror that flashed across the woman's face had filled Eli with a rush of adrenalin and lust, and he'd suddenly understood why his mother was as she was.

Power.

His mother shoved him hard enough to send him sprawling onto the floor.

'You didn't hear a word I said, did you?'

He cried out as a well-aimed kick met his left shin.

'Get up!'

His mother turned to the small table against the hallway wall, her hand brushing against the telephone before she turned around and held up a business card. 'DC Carys Miles,' she said. 'Said she had authorisation to search the house. *My* house.'

'Sorry.'

'Sorry?' She advanced on him, her eyes blazing. 'Sorry? You have any idea what the neighbours are going to say?'

Eli shrugged. The neighbours never spoke to them, so he was at a loss for words.

His mother poked a pudgy finger into the soft tissue beside his collarbone, hard enough that it would leave another bruise. 'They left a mess. Because of *you*.'

Eli tuned out as she began to berate him for being useless, an embarrassment, all the things she usually dredged up, and let the words wash over him.

A fury began to well up within his chest, and his vision blurred for a moment.

And then he lashed out.

He couldn't recall afterwards whether she cried out before her head shot back from the blow, but he would always remember the crack as her skull hit the stair bannister a split second before her limp body sank to the threadbare carpet.

He stood for a moment as blood rushed to his head. His chest heaved with every breath.

'Shit.'

He crouched, rolled her body towards him with effort, and then recoiled as he saw the dent in her head behind her ear. A trickle of blood ran from her nose and dripped onto his shoe.

Eli pushed her away, stood, and ran up the stairs two at a time.

He held his breath as he entered her bedroom, the stench of urine and vomit too much to bear.

She'd clean up each time of course, but over the years, the stink clung to everything, and it turned his stomach.

He crouched and reached under the bed, and then pulled out her handbag and began to rifle through the small vials that she kept in an old make-up bag.

He removed two, and shoved them into his pockets, then grabbed more, just in case.

He straightened, ran back down the stairs, stepped over her body, and hurried into the kitchen. The car keys hung from a copper-coloured hook next to the internal door that led through to the single garage, and he swiped them off as he passed.

The small rusting hatchback sat in darkness, and he wondered when she'd last managed to be sober enough to drive – and whether there was any petrol in it.

He pushed past the protruding wing mirror to the garage door and wrested it open, ran to the bottom of the driveway, and pegged open the two metal gates.

Returning to the vehicle, he inserted the first key to unlock the driver's door, then inserted the second into the ignition, and twisted it away from him.

The engine stuttered, and then failed.

Eli swore, and then remembered the old car had a manual choke. He pulled the lever out halfway, and then tried again.

The vehicle puttered to life, and he threw it into reverse.

It charged from the garage, and Eli eased off the accelerator. The last thing he wanted was to draw more attention to the house than the police already had.

Eli swung the car out into the street, left it running while he ran back up the driveway, and closed the garage door.

As he returned to the car, a curtain twitched in the front window of the house opposite, and the man who lived there peered out.

Eli held his hand up, then got in the car, and powered away.

He needed to get to work.

Chapter 53

Kay drummed her pen on her desk, her eyes roaming the investigation reports.

She wouldn't admit to feeling desperate, not in front of her team, but Eli Matthews had been clouding her thoughts ever since she'd first listened to him in the interview room.

The man was a deviant, and she had no doubts about his intelligence or cunning.

During the interview, he'd been too self-assured, too comfortable. The only time she'd seen him falter was when Sharp had announced they'd obtained the search authorisations.

Eli had recovered quickly, but she'd seen the flicker of doubt cloud his eyes. Only for a second, but she'd seen it.

Frustration could cause mistakes, so she bottled it down, and forced herself to continue reading.

A coffee mug appeared in front of her, the contents steaming.

'Thought you might need that,' said Barnes.

'Thanks, Ian.'

She leaned back in her chair, and wrapped her fingers around the ceramic surface, her eyes drifting to the rain that pounded the windows of the incident room.

'Penny for your thoughts?'

She sighed. 'What have I missed, Ian?' She held up a hand and counted off using her fingers. 'He's got a van that was spotted late at night with no explanation of what he was doing there; it's a vehicle that's an old courier van, identical to the one in the CCTV footage; he hasn't got a solid alibi for his whereabouts on that night, and yet that's still not enough to hold him.'

'We need more, Sarge,' said Barnes. He perched on her desk and sipped his own brew. 'He must've made a mistake somewhere.'

'But the lock-up was clean – so was the house.'

'Maybe he's got somewhere else,' said Barnes.

Kay put her coffee mug down. 'I'm not giving up on him. I'm going to track down his old employers here in Maidstone. Find out why he left and moved to Suffolk.'

'You don't buy his story of a change of scenery, then?' said Barnes, a quirk at the side of his mouth.

'No, I don't,' said Kay. She wagged her finger at him. 'And nor do you.'

Barnes shrugged. 'We're clutching at straws though. He's going to get away with it, isn't he?'

'Not if I have anything to do with it,' she said. 'He's getting careless. That means he's getting desperate.'

'For another fix, you think?'

She nodded. 'I guess that's a good a name for it as any, yes.'

'How long do you think we've got before he grabs someone else?'

'I don't know. I—'

She broke off as a uniformed officer stuck his head around the corner of the door. 'Sorry to interrupt. Thought you should know – a triple nine call came in from a Mrs Evans. Next door neighbour of Beryl Matthews, Eli's mother, half an hour ago.'

Kay leapt from her chair and slung her jacket over her shoulders. 'What is it?'

'Uniform attended the scene immediately. Beryl Matthews has been found dead, and Eli is missing. Forensic team are on their way.'

'Thank you.' She turned to Barnes. 'Come on.'

Chapter 54

He relished the silence of his office, the door locked for now.

He could concentrate for a start.

Undisturbed, he could work for hours, without the hubbub of noise from other people. Without the constant interruptions.

He didn't mind the long hours that came with his role; after all, a successful business needed to be nurtured, coaxed along. His position brought with it a level of responsibility that he enjoyed.

He was more than worthy of the role.

He ran his eyes over the paperwork that covered the surface of the desk, and then his gaze fell upon the laptop computer pushed to one side.

He ran his tongue over his bottom lip.

He'd promised himself he'd finish the paperwork before he watched again.

A sigh escaped his lips, and he felt the familiar tightness in his trousers.

Dammit, the paperwork could wait.

He leaned forward, and pulled the computer towards him. He closed the file in front of him, slid the papers out of the way, and tapped a key twice to wake the computer.

Password?

He typed in a messy sequence of symbols, letters, and numbers that were nonsensical in nature, and the laptop whirred to life.

His fingers worked the keyboard until the internet explorer program opened, and he sat back in his chair with a groan.

She was awake!

He reached out and ran a finger down the screen, tracing her outline.

The date rape drug Eli had used had now worn off completely he realised, and tried to contain his excitement.

The girl – Emma, Eli had informed him – was staring at her feet, and as his eyes travelled down her body, he choked out a gleeful laugh.

The water was rising, just as Eli had predicted.

He watched as Emma struggled against her bindings, and for a moment wondered if she would escape.

But, no.

He relaxed as she stopped, frustration clouding her features.

She wouldn't be going anywhere.

He frowned, and leaned closer to the picture.

Despite her efforts, the girl wasn't out of breath.

He tapped a key, and zoomed the lens closer to her skin.

Goosebumps peppered her arms and legs.

He sat back in his chair, the furrow in his brow deepening.

She should be perspiring, her chest heaving from the effort, her heart rate accelerated.

Instead, she looked cold.

He watched as she took a deep breath, before she pulled at her bindings once more, using her weight to stretch the fabric to its limits.

Then he realised what was wrong.

'Shit,' he murmured.

He reached out for his phone, and dialled a number.

Chapter 55

Kay pulled on overalls and plastic booties before she locked her car and followed Barnes through the garden gate to Beryl Matthews' house.

Neighbours had gathered on the street; a small cluster who were all of an older generation and, Kay noted with a sense of relief, without smartphones to record the crime scene investigators at work.

A white tent had been erected at the front door, where two uniformed officers stood, one with a clipboard. Kay signed herself and Barnes in, and then crossed the threshold into the Matthews' hallway.

Lucas glanced up at her from his crouched position on the floor. 'Blunt trauma wound to the back of her head,' he said. 'Given the blood and tissue on the stair balustrade, I'd say she fell against that. Death was instantaneous.'

'Fell, or pushed?' said Kay.

His lips thinned. 'It would have been quite some force to cause that sort of injury.'

Kay turned to Barnes. 'Get a description of Eli out to all uniforms. He's our lead suspect in the murder of Beryl Matthews, and should be apprehended as soon as possible.'

He nodded, and pulled out his phone. He turned away to speak to the uniformed officers, and Kay turned her attention back to the pathologist.

Lucas straightened. 'Harriet's team found vials of insulin in Mrs Matthews' handbag. She was keeping them in an old make-up bag.'

'Was she a diabetic?'

'We'll find out from her GP in due course,' he said. 'But there appear to be some missing.'

'And they weren't spotted before?' said Kay. She tore her eyes away from the woman on the floor. 'Sounds as if he was raiding her supplies.'

'Maybe she suspected he was, and tried to hide them from him.'

'Perhaps.'

'I'll let you know if we find anything else.'

'Thanks.'

Kay shoved her gloved hands in her pockets and moved towards the front door, then stripped off the booties and overalls.

Barnes finished talking with the two uniformed officers under the shelter of the porch, and one of the officers rushed towards the patrol car parked at the kerb, his radio to his lips while the other maintained his presence on the doorstep.

Barnes saw her approaching, and pulled his phone from his ear.

'We've received a phoned-in report from a neighbour saying they heard shouting earlier this morning.'

Kay's gaze shifted to an elderly man who beckoned to her from the other side of the road, a large umbrella with a familiar golfing brand emblazoned over its surface held above his head, sheltering him from the steady downpour.

'I think someone wants a word with us.'

She led Barnes across the street at a jog, and the man held out his hand.

'I'm Felix Peters,' he said, and jerked a thumb over his shoulder. 'I live there.'

Kay introduced herself and Barnes. 'Was there something you wanted to tell us, Mr Peters?'

He nodded, his eyes moving to the white tent and the people moving to and from the Matthews' house. He held out the umbrella so it offered some shelter to them both. 'I saw him. A few hours ago. He took his mother's car.' His brow creased. 'She never lets him drive that.'

'Why not?'

'She doesn't let him do anything – except go to work,' he said. His shoulders sagged. 'It's the drink. It was worse when he was a kid. Couldn't protect himself, especially after his dad left when Eli was only five.'

Kay raised an eyebrow at Barnes. 'Did he see you?'

'Oh yes,' said Peters. 'He'd run down the driveway to open the gates. He waved, then went back, reversed the car out and drove away.' He rubbed his chin. 'Surprised it started. Must be years since Beryl was in any fit state to drive.'

'What's the make and model?'

Peters told them, and made sure he gave Barnes the registration number twice, to be sure.

'Thank you, Mr Peters, you've been very helpful,' said Kay. 'We'll be in touch over the next day or so, to get a formal statement from you.'

He called out as they began to walk away.

'She's dead then?'

Kay stopped and looked over her shoulder. 'I'm sorry, Mr Peters, but I can't discuss—'

'Good riddance to the bitch,' said the old man, and hawked into the gutter before turning on his heel.

'Sounds like Beryl Matthews was a right charmer,' said Barnes.

'She's still dead,' said Kay. 'And Eli Matthews is still our main suspect.'

As they reached the Matthews' garden and the taped-off cordon, she placed a hand on Barnes' arm.

'I'm going to have a quick word with the boss to bring him up to speed,' she said. 'Get that car registration number circulated. All patrols to immediately report any sightings and apprehend Eli Matthews.'

'I'll get Gavin to have CCTV onto it, too.'

'Good. Make those calls, and then we'll go.'

Kay headed to her car, her shoes splashing through the water in the gutter before she bundled herself behind the steering wheel and slammed the door shut.

She pulled out her phone, and hit speed dial, turning up the volume to compensate for the rain drumming on the roof.

Sharp answered within two rings.

'Kay?'

'We've got the details for his mother's car – according to a neighbour, Eli took off in it. We're checking CCTV, and all patrols have been instructed to keep a look out and apprehend on suspicion of Beryl Matthews' death.'

'So he kills his mother and takes her car? Sounds extreme.'

'One of the neighbours told us that Beryl Matthews was an alcoholic, and a nasty one at that. They've lived here since Eli was a kid,' she added, checking the notes she'd jotted down before leaving Felix Peters. 'Eli went away, but returned seventeen months ago unannounced. Ties in with his personnel record at the depot. Within a week, the neighbour noticed he had bruising to his face and arms, even though Eli tried to cover it up with make-up.'

'His mother hit him?'

'Apparently so. Used to beat him as a kid when she got drunk, and it doesn't sound like she ever stopped. His father walked out when he was five, and never came back.'

'So, is this self-defence?'

Kay bumped her fist against the car window as she mulled it over. 'I don't know,' she said. 'Maybe it was meant to be, but it took a lot of force – anger – to cause her head to snap back at the angle Lucas thinks it did. CSI found vials of insulin in Beryl's handbag. Looks like some of it's been removed.'

She glanced up as a shadow crossed the back window, and then Barnes began to open the passenger door before he looked at his phone and raised it to his ear.

'We're going to join the search,' she said to Sharp. 'We'll maintain radio contact, and I'll phone you direct with an update as soon as we have anything to report. At least, once we have him in custody, we can try to ascertain his involvement with the kidnapping and death of Melanie Richards again, too.'

She finished the call, and looked across as Barnes wrenched open the car door, his phone clutched to his chest.

His face was white.

'What is it?'

'That was Eli Matthews,' he said, his voice shaking. 'He's got my daughter. The bastard's taken Emma.'

Chapter 56

Kay threw the car around the bend, and ignored the grunt Barnes emitted when the side of his head smacked against the car window.

'I'll phone Sarah. Find out what the hell is going on.'

'Wait – what? Sarah Thomas is your ex-wife?'

'Yeah.'

'You never mentioned you had a daughter, Ian.'

He sniffed, and dialled a number. 'She hasn't wanted anything to do with me since I split up from her mother. She doesn't even use my surname.'

'But I interviewed her about Melanie Richards,' said Kay, dumbstruck. 'You'd have thought one of them would've mentioned you to me, surely?'

Barnes coughed out a bitter laugh. 'She hates me being a detective. They both do.'

'You didn't mention anything in the briefings about your being related, either.'

'I didn't want to get them involved. I was trying to protect them.'

Kay swore under her breath. There would be time for recriminations later, but for now, her priority was finding Emma.

'How does he know she's your daughter?'

'She had an old photo of me in uniform in her purse. He must've seen me at the courier depot and put two and two together.'

'Shit.'

'Hello?' Barnes turned his attention back to his phone as his ex-wife answered. 'Why the hell didn't you tell me Emma was missing?'

Kay bit her lip, and concentrated on manoeuvring the car through the traffic while she listened to Barnes' end of the conversation.

'When? For chrissakes, Sarah, you should have told me!' He sucked in a deep breath. 'He's taken her, Sarah. The same man who took Melanie. He's taken her!'

He ended the call, and threw the phone onto the dashboard where it slipped across towards Kay.

She grabbed it before it could fall, and handed it back to him. 'What's going on?'

'Sarah and Vince woke up Thursday morning to find Emma gone,' he said, his voice shaking. 'She left a note, said she was going clubbing with her friend Tanya the previous night, and was going to stay at her friend's parents' house for the rest of the week – said she couldn't stand being cooped up in the house any more. Said she'd be back this weekend, before she's due to go back to school.' He stopped, his chest heaving. 'Emma and Tanya often camp out at each other's houses, so Sarah didn't worry too much. Said she thought it'd probably do her good. When Emma still wasn't home by this morning, Sarah phoned Tanya. She hasn't spoken to Emma since Wednesday night. Oh god—'

'Wednesday night? Didn't her friend report her missing?'

Barnes shook his head. 'Apparently they had a falling out – Tanya went off with her boyfriend, leaving Emma on her own. When she got home Thursday morning and Emma wasn't there, she figured she was sulking and had gone home.'

'No ransom request?'

'None.'

Kay frowned, and then it hit her. 'He hasn't had time to phone them. He's been with us.'

She grabbed the radio from its cradle on the dashboard, and held it to her lips.

'This is DS Hunter. Do not – I repeat, do not – apprehend Eli Matthews. Maintain your distance if you find him, but he is not to be detained until I say so.'

She tossed the radio over to Barnes, who caught it and held it between his hands, his knuckles white.

'What did he say?'

'He's got her.'

'I know, Ian. Focus. What exactly did he say to you?'

She heard him exhale as she slowed to negotiate a red light, and put her foot to the floor as soon as she was clear of the junction.

'He said "if you want to see your daughter alive again, call off the search for me. She hasn't got long". That was it.'

'Background sounds?'

'He was driving.' Barnes frowned. 'There was a horn in the background – a train horn.'

'So he's somewhere near a railway line.'

'That doesn't help,' he snapped. 'There are two near here.'

'We can—'

Her phone interrupted. She pointed to her bag in the foot well next to the passenger seat. 'Get that.'

Barnes leaned forward, tore open the zipper, and put her phone to his ear. 'Ian Barnes.'

Kay pulled the vehicle up to the gate of the police station car park, and nodded to the security guard who waved her through. She glanced over at Barnes, and realised how sick he looked.

He finished the call and met her gaze.

'Uniform didn't get the call in time. They've arrested Eli Matthews.'

Chapter 57

Kay's mind raced as she and Barnes ran towards the entrance to the police station.

Sharp met them at the door. 'What the hell is going on?'

'Eli Matthews murdered his mother,' said Kay, as they hurried towards the incident room. 'He went on the run, and we put out a call for his arrest. Then, Matthews phoned Barnes to say he had his daughter, Emma Thomas, and implied he'd harm her if Barnes didn't call off the hunt. He said Emma was "running out of time".'

Sharp's eyes flicked to the older detective, who paced impatiently between the desks, his jaw clenched. 'How did he find out Emma was Barnes' daughter?'

Kay explained about the photograph. 'I think he got lucky,' she said, 'but we know he *did* get bullied by her and Melanie Richards.'

'And?'

'By the time we put the instruction through not to arrest him, it was too late. A uniform patrol picked him up.'

They turned at the sound of the side door to the station banging open, and a uniformed police officer appeared, leading Eli Matthews. A second officer brought up the rear.

'You bastard,' Barnes snarled, and rushed at Matthews.

The officer's eyes opened wide as Barnes barrelled into him, and aimed a punch at Matthews.

Eli ducked, his hands handcuffed behind his back, a sly smile on his face.

'Enough!' bellowed Sharp.

He strode over to where Barnes stood ready to take aim once more, and hauled him backwards. 'Enough, Detective. This isn't helping.'

He gestured to the two uniformed officers. 'Get Matthews to the custody suite. Now.'

They nodded, and led the man away.

'Come on, Ian,' said Kay. She put a hand on his arm. 'Come on.' She turned to Carys, who was watching, wide-eyed. 'Take him back to the incident room. Stay there.'

She stood back to let them pass, her gaze taking in the look on Barnes' face.

The man didn't look angry; he looked scared, and she suddenly realised that was exactly what Eli wanted.

Barnes was terrified.

She pushed the thought to the back of her mind, and faced Sharp.

'We'll get Matthews booked in and processed as soon as possible,' he said, in a low voice. 'I'll interview him with DCI Larch. Get Carys to coordinate the search. You act as liaison between observing the interview and helping Carys. We'll find her.'

She nodded. 'Sir.'

Christ, I hope so, she thought, as she tore back along the corridor to the incident room.

The whole team had assembled, gathered around Barnes as Carys tried to calm him down.

'All right, everyone,' she called. 'Enough. We've got work to do.'

She turned her attention to Debbie West. 'Go and speak to the uniformed officers who arrested Eli. Find out where they picked him up. Get back here as fast as you can.'

She pointed at the map on the wall as the young PC shot off. 'I'm hoping they were close to where he's keeping Emma.'

'We're never going to find her in time.' Barnes pulled at his hair, a vein on his forehead pulsing. 'She's going to die, isn't she?'

Kay pursed her lips. 'Look, Bernard Coombs said he found Eli's broken down van here,' she said, tapping the blue pin that had been stabbed into the map. She traced her finger across the surface. 'He favours abandoned places. Somewhere he won't be disturbed. Somewhere Emma won't be heard.'

'Wait,' said Carys. 'He said she's running out of time. He hasn't had the chance to do anything elaborate like he did with Melanie – we've been keeping him occupied.'

Kay's gaze wandered to the rain pelting against the window, then back to Carys.

'Get onto the council, and to local patrols. Make a list of any abandoned places within a three-mile radius of where Coombs saw Eli, and where he was arrested earlier. We'll start with that.

She turned to Barnes, who looked as if his knees were going to give way at any moment. 'Ian, you're formally stood down from this investigation.'

'Kay—'

'That's an order. We'll keep you updated with all developments, but your personal involvement is not going to help at this time.'

His gaze fell to the floor. 'Yes, Sarge.'

***

Kay watched the monitor, and nibbled at the corner of a fingernail as Sharp guided Eli into one of the plastic seats across from where DCI Larch sat, and waited while the duty solicitor fussed about with his coat and briefcase.

Once he'd settled, Sharp took a seat, reached over, started the recording, and made the introductions. He glanced at Larch, who gave an imperceptible nod, and began by cautioning their suspect.

'Do you understand?'

Eli smirked, and said nothing.

The duty solicitor cleared his throat. 'Mr Matthews, you do have to answer.'

Eli leaned forward. 'Yes. I understand.'

'Thank you.'

Kay watched as Sharp opened the manilla folder in front of him that they had put together. She knew he didn't need it; he knew the contents word for word, but it would help him control the pace of the interview, and given their previous encounter, they knew full well that Eli understood the game that was about to be played out. The last thing they could do was appear to be desperate. It's why Sharp had placed Eli and his solicitor in the seats facing the clock on the wall. He didn't want the temptation.

He folded his hands on the opening page, and lifted his gaze.

Eli's eyes snapped up to meet his, and for a moment, Kay thought she saw a glimmer of panic.

Good.

'Where is Emma Thomas?'

'Who's that?'

'Nice try, Eli.' Sharp shrugged. 'Very well. Let's talk about your mother.'

He flicked to the next page. 'Your mother's body was discovered earlier this afternoon, at the house you share with her,' he said. 'There was a struggle in the hallway. She was pushed backwards with such force, that her head smashed against the stair bannister. She was killed instantly.'

'The bitch deserved it,' said Eli.

Kay raised an eyebrow as the duty solicitor spluttered a retort to his client.

'Oh, shut up,' said Eli, rounding on him. 'Just sit there and shut up.'

Kay held her breath. She wouldn't admit it to anyone, but Eli unnerved her. He showed no remorse at all for his mother's death, had effectively dismissed it as a passing problem, and seemed utterly focused on taunting them instead about Emma's whereabouts. Sharp and DCI Larch would have to be ruthless if they were going to find the girl.

'Why did you leave Suffolk, Eli?'

Sharp kept his tone measured, refusing to react to Eli's outburst.

Eli's head snapped around, his rant at the duty solicitor cut off mid-sentence.

'What?'

Sharp smiled; a predatory expression on his features. 'What happened, Eli? Did you make a mistake? Did you have to run away?'

Eli's jaw clenched.

'Where is Emma Thomas?'

Eli smiled, and raised his gaze to a point above Sharp's head.

'We've been having a lot of rain lately, Detectives,' he said, his voice almost trancelike. 'I'd imagine Emma's feet are getting wet by now, don't you?'

'Where is she, Eli?'

'Will Detective Barnes find his daughter in time, do you think?' Eli continued, seemingly oblivious to the question. 'What's his health like, Detective?' He leaned back, and ran his tongue over his top lip. 'What do you think it will do to him when he finds her drowned, all bloated, and blue?'

He leaned back, and stared straight into the lens of the camera.

In the observation room, Kay jumped in her seat.

Eli winked. 'Tick tock, Detectives. Tick tock.'

Chapter 58

Kay glanced away from the screen at a knock on the door.

It opened without her having a chance to respond, and Gavin Piper stuck his head around.

'Sarge?'

'What have you got?'

'We've received a call from Harriet,' he said. 'She's found a partial fingerprint matched to Melanie's, from the van that was seized at the lock-up garage.'

'Where?' breathed Kay.

'Over the wheel arch on the inside of the van,' said Gavin. 'Harriet thinks Eli wiped away any traces where his hands would have been when he cleaned the van, but he seems to have overlooked the wheel arch. Harriet couldn't confirm it until she had the results back.'

'How the hell did she get the results so fast?'

Kay frowned – fingerprint matching normally took weeks with the backlog the lab usually had, and even an urgent request could take forty-eight hours to process. They couldn't afford to have to drop charges for Melanie's murder against Eli simply because an impatient CSI decided to cut corners.

'Apparently, she drove over to the golf course at Sutton Valence where the lab technician was playing nine holes,' said Gavin. 'She threatened all sorts of things, but got the guy to get in his car and drive over to the lab straight away.' He held up a printout of an email. 'Confirmation came through a couple of minutes before I interrupted you.'

Kay snatched the paper from his outstretched hand, her eyes scanning the page. 'Good work, Harriet,' she murmured. She leaned forward, and hit a switch.

'Sir? An urgent word, please.'

Sharp glanced up at the camera in the interview room, then leaned across and terminated the recording before hurrying from the room.

Within seconds, he appeared at the door to the observation suite.

'How do you want to run with this?' said Kay, after explaining what the forensic team had found.

'We charge him with Melanie's kidnapping and murder,' said Sharp, 'that'll shock him into giving up Emma's location. He might think he'll reduce his sentence if he helps us now.'

He spun on his heel and put his hand on the door handle.

'Wait.'

He glanced over his shoulder, and raised his eyebrow at Kay.

'I don't think mentioning this will help Emma,' she said.

She stepped closer, and lowered her voice. 'Eli Matthews thrives on scaring people to death. Melanie, Tony Richards, Guy Nelson. If we walk in there and try to get him to tell us where Emma is, he's going to know we're desperate.'

Sharp's hand dropped away from the handle. 'We *are* desperate. So you're going to have to do better than that.'

Kay ran her hand through her hair, and paced the corridor. 'Eli made a comment in there, just now,' she said, and pointed at the door. 'He said "it's been raining heavily for a while now", and then said Emma wouldn't have much time. Why?'

'Wherever she is, the water's rising,' said Gavin, stepping forward. 'If it's a drain, or a sewer, the water from all the roads in that area would pass through it.'

'That's it,' exclaimed Kay. She turned to Sharp. 'Can you hold Eli while we check this out?' She blinked. 'Sorry – boss?'

He nodded. 'Do it. Municipal plans for the drains and sewers in the area where Eli's van has been seen. Look for access covers, culverts. Relay the information to the teams out there. Hurry.'

'Thanks.' Kay took off at a jog.

'And Gavin?'

They both stopped and turned.

'Well done,' said Sharp. 'Now, both of you. Go.'

Kay took the stairs up to the next floor two at a time, cursed under her breath as her toe caught on the top step, and regained her balance before running down the corridor and into the incident room.

Gavin arrived seconds later, and hurried over to his desk.

Kay brought Carys up to speed. 'Those abandoned buildings – narrow it down to ones that could have large drains, or tunnels. Somewhere he can keep her near water.'

'The council has plans for the sewers and drains in that area on their website portal,' Gavin said, punching a series of letters and numbers on his computer keyboard to access the site. 'Hang on, I'll pull them up on the screen over there.'

Kay paced in front of the wall, the blank white square of the projector's beam taunting her. She glanced over her shoulder as Barnes joined her.

'What's happened?'

Kay took a split second to decide whether to tell him, and then jerked her thumb towards Gavin. 'Eli made a comment that makes us think he's keeping her somewhere close to water. Gavin hit on the fact that he's probably hiding her in a sewer or drain – it makes sense,' she added, 'given he held Melanie in a drain, but this time he's using nature to carry out his wishes.'

She shivered as her eyes fell on the damp rooftops beyond the window. 'If Emma's being held in a culvert or sewer, the water's going to rise quickly after all the rain we've had the past forty-eight hours. We need to find her, and fast.'

'Here you go,' called out Gavin.

The white square on the wall was replaced with a map of the south-west of the town, setting out the criss-cross pattern of sewers and drains that had been constructed over the years.

'Here,' said Carys. 'Where all the paper mills used to be, out past Tovil. Some were demolished, others are being redeveloped.'

Kay checked her notes. 'It tallies with where Coombs saw Eli's van, and it's close enough to where he was arrested.' She pointed at Gavin. 'Get the search teams over there. Now.'

'On to it.'

'I'm going,' said Barnes.

Kay spun around. 'What do you think you're doing?'

'I'm going out there,' said Barnes, swiping his car keys from his desk. 'I can't sit here while they're looking for her. I need to be there.' He jabbed a finger at her. 'The minute you find out anything else, you phone me, you hear?'

Chapter 59

Emma coughed and rubbed the side of her face against her shoulder once more.

The water level had reached her chest, distinct waves lapping at her body as the bindings to her wrists remained intact, despite her efforts to loosen them.

She'd changed tactics a while ago, and had started to work on the gag that had been tied around her head to cover her mouth. If she could get the gag off, she reasoned she could use her teeth to tear at the bindings on her wrists and escape.

She had no idea how long it had been, but the time taken for the water to rise from her thighs to her stomach couldn't have been longer than an hour.

The flow was faster, too – as it passed, the water had a distinct current to it, flowing from her left to her right.

She growled under her breath, and tried once more.

If there was a current, maybe it led somewhere.

Or maybe she should turn left.

But that was the way the man had gone when he'd left her. What if he was waiting for her?

Was that part of his sick game?

She shuddered.

She screwed up her face as a fresh wave hit her, and tried not to think of what might be floating in it.

The camping light still maintained its yellow beam, and gave her a clear view of her surroundings.

She blinked.

The red light above the camera lens flickered.

Emma held her breath.

The man hadn't been back for ages – was it a day since she'd last seen him, or longer?

She craned her neck, and tried to see behind the camera. It had been fixed to a pipe on the opposite wall with black electrical tape, but no leads protruded from it.

Her heart leapt.

The battery was running out.

If she could escape, he wouldn't know.

She froze, and the light flickered once more.

She breathed out, scared that he would come back now, would somehow wade through all that water, and change the battery.

She strained her ears, but only the sound of rushing water reached her from the left hand side of the tunnel.

She turned back to the camera.

Had the red light dimmed?

She cocked her head to one side, rubbed at the gag with her arm, and felt the material give. Her eyes fell on the white marker stick opposite.

There wasn't much space left between the present water level and the top of it, with only a foot in height remaining.

She rubbed harder at the gag.

It gave way suddenly, the material loosening under her right ear, and she frantically pushed it aside with her shoulder, her breath escaping in gasps.

At that moment, the red light went out.

A cry escaped her lips, and she turned her head towards the way out, the water coursing past her at a steady speed.

The bindings on her left wrist appeared weaker, so she used her teeth and began to nibble away at the material. She tugged and pulled until she'd managed to loosen the knot, and eventually managed to create a big enough space for her to pull her hand through and free it.

She turned her attention to the bindings on her right wrist, but the lack of circulation in her left hand made her movements clumsy. She couldn't feel what she was doing. She cried out in frustration, and then realised she would work quicker using her teeth once more.

It only took minutes to finally free the last of the bindings, and she stood for a moment rubbing her wrists and hands. Pins and needles shot through her veins and arteries, and she gritted her teeth in agony before shaking her hands to try to speed up the process.

As the numbness in her limbs subsided, she sloshed her way across the narrow tunnel to where the camping lantern had been placed alongside the camera, unhitched it, and swung it in front of her as she tried to get her bearings.

The ceiling curved at the end of the tunnel, and beyond her position, to the outer limits of the lamp's beam, she could see that it narrowed, the design forcing the water into a smaller space, obliterating the air pocket between the water surface and the ceiling.

She realised with despair that there would be no air left in the tunnel if she tried to swim away.

She was out of time.

Chapter 60

Kay leaned forward, her nose only inches from the monitor, her jaw set while she tried to block out the sound of the rain drumming on the roof above her head.

She'd have done everything in her power to bring Melanie's killer to justice, but now Eli Matthews had made it personal.

She thought back to the teenager she'd met only a few days before, the girl's distress at losing a friend to such a sadistic murderer.

Yes, the girl was a bully, but she didn't deserve to die. And not like this.

Everyone made mistakes in their lives, and Kay thought back to her own days at school. Her own bullies had damaged her confidence, affected her choices – right down to the exam subjects she chose at school, simply so she could avoid the constant tirade from the group of girls and their ringleader.

But, she'd healed. In time.

And if one of those girls had ever been in trouble, she knew in her heart she would have done everything in her power to help them.

The plans on the screen blurred, and she shook her head.

They had to find Emma.

She couldn't imagine what Barnes was going through right now. Or Emma's mother.

Her phone vibrated at her elbow, the movement jiggling it across the polished surface of the laminated desktop before she reached out and grabbed it.

'Hello,' she said, her eyes on the monitor.

'It's Grey,' said an excited voice. 'Got something for you, I think.'

'Okay, go on.'

'The purchase order for the CCTV equipment – the one you got from the courier depot.'

'What about it?'

'There's some stuff on here that doesn't make sense.'

Kay stood, and began to pace the carpet by her desk. 'In what way?'

'There's the replacement lens and some parts to house the lens at the top of the order, but there are three items on here that have nothing to do with the CCTV system. Well, not any CCTV system I've seen.'

'What could they be used for?'

'Home video recording.'

Kay stopped in the middle of the room, causing Debbie to almost collide with her. Kay held up her hand in silent apology.

'What are the parts?'

Grey read them out.

'Are you sure they can't be used in CCTV system?'

'Pretty sure. Certainly not for the system at the depot.'

'That's great, Grey.'

She ended the call, and slung her jacket over her shoulders.

'Carys – you're with me.'

'Sarge.'

Kay grabbed the purchase order they'd been given, took a photocopy of it, and shoved it into her bag as Carys joined her, a set of car keys in her hand.

'Where to, Sarge?'

'County Deliveries' depot. I want a word with Colin Broadheath.'

Chapter 61

Ian Barnes wiped a tear from his cheek, and turned in the hope none of the uniform officers who were traipsing across the construction site beside him would see.

They'd been told, of course, and he'd done his best to ignore the glances of pity that were stolen as the team assembled at the assigned meeting point to begin the search.

He gripped his mobile phone in his left hand, willing it to ring, for someone to tell him where his daughter was.

The rain had stopped fifteen minutes ago, but the water would take several hours to run off, drain away, and the sound of the last drops rushing through gutters and downpipes reached his ears as he rounded the corner of the next building.

The team had managed to triangulate a call made from Eli's mobile phone to this place, a deserted apartment block that lay unfinished, fenced off from trespassers and backing on to a field that gently sloped towards the main road a mile away.

He shuddered as he recalled the history of the site.

One of the uniformed officers had searched for it on his smartphone while they were organising teams to walk out across the site, and had told them it had once been the site of an old mill.

He'd gone on to recite the history of the new construction, including the work that had stopped once the labyrinth of Victorian-era drains and sewers rendered the place useless.

Barnes fought down the urge to panic, even though he knew it was a fruitless exercise. He knew Eli's game. He knew the man would get a kick out of him dropping from a heart attack out of fright, just like Tony Richards, or drive him to suicide like Guy Nelson, but he'd be damned if he'd give the freak the satisfaction.

He gritted his teeth.

As he stomped across the cracked concrete of the deserted site, he caught up with one of the uniformed officers.

Her eyes spoke volumes, and simply reiterated what he knew every one of them must be thinking.

Poor bastard.

He nodded, and moved past. He couldn't talk right now, couldn't pretend that he was okay, that he was holding up, that he still had hope they'd find Emma.

His mind returned to happier times. When Emma had been born, he and Sarah had been over the moon, and so had his uniformed colleagues at the time.

During a very drunk session after a shift to celebrate the new-born girl, his sergeant had weaved his way over, thrust another drink into his hand, and patted him on the back.

'Only real men have girls,' he'd grinned, a proud father of three.

Sarah had been devastated when the doctors told here there'd be no more children. Barnes had been too, but more so at his wife's sadness than the thought that he'd never have a son.

It had all been fine while Emma was a toddler. Of course, his shifts played havoc with her bedtime routine, and sometimes he'd arrive home so late, he'd only been able to peer around the corner of the bedroom door at the sleeping form of his little girl. But there had been weekends away on the coast, longer holidays in Wales and Devon, where he'd taught her to build sandcastles, play hide and seek, and build dams across streams. It was inevitable that he'd show her things he'd hoped to show a son one day, but she thrived on the adventure and never cried when she stumbled.

Then, when she started secondary school, he had chosen to pursue his ambition of becoming a detective, and somehow it had all gone wrong.

It had started with Sarah making snide remarks about his staying late at work. He'd never dream of having an affair, but that was what he found himself being accused of, despite his protestations.

And in time, Emma learned to mimic her mother. He'd return home to find his wife in front of the television, her hand on the remote control as she studiously ignored him, while Emma glared at him across her homework spread out on the kitchen table while he reheated his dinner.

Over the ensuing years, things had become worse, until one day, he found he didn't want to go home any more.

The divorce had been quick, and bitter.

And, he realised, it had affected his judgement during the course of the investigation. Why the hell hadn't he told Hunter that Emma was his daughter?

He clenched his fists. He'd do anything to find his girl.

His head snapped to the left as one of the uniformed officers held her radio to her ear, the static crackling in the air between them. He pushed his earpiece into place, and then his shoulders sagged.

Another building cleared, another search area confirmed to have no sighting of Emma.

He pulled out the earpiece, and raised his gaze to the grey clouds that scuttled across the bleak sky.

He'd never been a religious man, but as he watched the storm pass over the hills and towards the main road, he made a pact.

I'll quit. Just give me my daughter back, and I'll quit.

Chapter 62

Kay opened the door of the car before Carys had time to use the handbrake, and hurried towards the front of the depot, the footsteps of her colleague in her wake.

She burst through the glass reception doors, approached the desk, and held up her badge.

'I'd like to speak to Colin Broadheath,' she said. 'Now, please.'

The wide-eyed receptionist nodded, and adjusted her headset before passing on the message in hushed tones.

Carys joined her as the receptionist finished the call.

'He'll be with you in a moment,' said the receptionist, and gestured to her left. 'Would you like to wait in the meeting room?'

Kay nodded, and led the way into a small waiting area through an open door to the right of the reception desk.

The walls had been painted white, once, with an array of large photographs framed and hung on three of the four walls.

Carys hovered near the door as Kay circled the room a second time.

Footsteps approached, and she stopped as Colin Broadheath appeared.

The man looked even more rundown than the last time Kay had seen him, and she glared at him as he leered at Carys before turning his attention to her.

'Detective Hunter. How lovely to see you again.'

Kay unfolded the copy purchase order, and held it out to him.

'Mr Broadheath, please explain the purpose of ordering the last three items on this list,' she said.

He glanced over his shoulder as a mobile phone began to ring, then back to Kay.

Carys pulled her phone out of the bag, held up her hand to Kay, and stepped back into the reception area to take the call.

'I'm sorry, what?' said Broadheath.

Kay tapped her finger on the document in the man's hand.

'I'd like to know why the last three items on this list were ordered by you.'

The man frowned, pulled a pair of glasses from his shirt pocket, and perched them on his nose.

'I have no idea,' he said, and held out the paper to Kay.

She didn't take it.

'You're going to have to do better than that, Mr Broadheath. The top two items are the parts you ordered for the broken CCTV camera that overlooks the van parking bay. The other three parts you ordered here have no relationship at all to the CCTV system. Therefore, I'd like to know why you ordered them.'

'I didn't,' he said.

Kay raised an eyebrow.

'Look,' he said, his tone one of exasperation. He pointed to the top right-hand corner of the purchase order.

Kay moved closer, and tried not inhale the man's odour. 'What am I looking at?'

'This number here, that's my code. Identifies me as the person who placed the order, okay?'

'Yes.'

'We use an Enterprise Resource Planning system for procurement here.' His finger moved up the page. 'This number belongs to the person who requisitioned the items. The person requested via the ERP system that I order these items for them.'

'Whose number is that?'

He removed his glasses, and handed back the purchase order.

'Bob Rogers.'

Chapter 63

'Sarge? An urgent word?'

Carys hovered at the threshold, her gaze shifting between Kay and Colin Broadheath.

'Thank you, Mr Broadheath,' said Kay. 'Please don't leave the building. We may need to talk to you again.'

He nodded, confusion on his face.

'And, Mr Broadheath? I'd appreciate it if you didn't mention this conversation to anyone else at this time.'

'I understand,' he said, and hurried away.

Kay turned her attention to Carys. 'What's up?'

'I got a call from Gavin. He's just taken delivery of Eli Matthews' full personnel file.'

Kay felt a chill raced down her spine. 'And?'

'Bob Rogers was Eli's manager at Ipswich until eighteen months ago.'

'Eighteen months ago?'

'He left Suffolk one month before Eli,' said Carys.

Kay brushed past Carys, and into the reception area. 'Where's Bob Rogers?'

'Um, if he's not in his office, he'll be out the back having a cigarette break,' said the girl.

Kay pointed at the security door. 'Buzz me through. Now.'

She led the way down the corridor to Rogers' office, her mind racing as all the pieces of the jigsaw fell into place.

Why Eli's transfer from Suffolk to Kent had taken only weeks, whereas it would normally be months before a suitable position could be found.

Why it had been so easy for him to obtain fake licence plates.

Why Eli had been able to obtain a second-hand courier van with very little paperwork.

And why a camera had been found next to Melanie Richards' body.

'What sort of sick bastard—' muttered Carys.

Kay held up a hand as they approached Rogers' office. It was empty.

Kay's eyes fell to the desk. 'His laptop computer is missing,' she said.

'Laptop?'

'When I was here with Barnes, Rogers had a laptop computer in front of him,' said Kay.

'What for? He's got a computer there anyway.'

'Exactly.'

Kay's gaze shifted to the safe.

'Carys, seal this room as a crime scene. And phone for backup.'

She spun on her heel.

'Where are you going, Sarge?'

'To make sure this is the last private cigarette break Bob Rogers has for a long time.'

She ran along the corridor towards the back of the depot, pushed her way through the double doors, and into the sorting office. She ignored the stares of the small group of men and women standing by the racks of shelving, and made her way through the large space to a door set into the back wall.

It opened as she neared, and she slid to a halt.

A woman walked in, her face lined, and her permed white hair stained yellow at the front.

'Hello, love,' she said, cheerily. 'Desperate for a smoke, eh?'

She chuckled, and held open the door for Kay.

'Thanks,' she said, and hurried out.

She blinked as the sun slipped out from behind a cloud, and the door slammed shut behind her.

'Didn't take you for a smoker.'

She spun around.

Bob Rogers leaned against the wall of the building, and blew a smoke ring into the air.

A lazy smile stole across his face.

'Where's Emma, Bob? Where have you put her?'

He shrugged, and then took a long drag on the cigarette before answering.

'Buggered if I know. Eli was the talent spotter and location scout. I'm just the executive producer.'

Kay stepped closer. 'Where is she?'

Bob's hand shot out, and Kay gasped as he took hold of her jacket lapels and swung her round until her back was against the wall, his body against hers. He snatched the cigarette from his lips, and tossed it to the ground.

'I had a lot of money invested in this,' he snarled.

Kay clenched her fists, and tried not to gag at his fetid breath.

He shifted his weight, and then ran his hand down her face. 'You were next, Hunter.' His eyes hardened, and his hand moved to her jaw, his fingers squeezing hard. 'You were always next.'

Kay turned her head from side to side, and tried to put some distance between them.

If she could raise her knee—

Rogers sidestepped. 'No you don't, you bitch.'

She cried out as his palm met her cheek, and tasted blood.

She blinked away tears, and glared at him. 'Why d'you do it, Rogers? Those girls did nothing to you.'

His hand moved to her throat, his voice almost a purr. 'Eli has strange preferences. But, it works to my advantage, so no matter.'

'What happened in Suffolk?'

349

His grip tightened, and Kay tried to swallow. Her windpipe contracted, and she coughed.

'It went wrong, didn't it?' she said. 'Who messed up? You?'

'I don't make mistakes.'

'Oh, so it was Eli, was it?' She choked out a laugh. 'How on earth did you end up with that one, eh?'

Rogers' fingers squeezed tighter, and Kay's vision blackened at the edges.

Just a bit longer.

Her hands flew to his fingers, and she tried to prise them away from her neck, her breathing ragged.

He bared his teeth, and ground his hips into hers. 'Go on, bitch. Struggle.'

Kay fought down the urge to vomit, and instead reached out with her thumbs, aiming for his eye sockets.

His grip loosened, and he swept her arms away.

A second slap caused her vision to blur, and then his hands were back, squeezing harder.

Kay gasped out a breath.

'I don't think attacking a police officer is going to do your case any good, Rogers.'

He chuckled, kept one hand on her throat, and took a step back. He pointed upwards.

'Who's going to believe you?' he said. 'Camera's broken.'

Kay's gaze flickered to her right.

'Well,' she croaked. 'That's true. But *they* might have something to say about it.'

He frowned, his grip loosened, and he looked over his shoulder.

Two uniformed officers stood only a few metres away from him, Tasers drawn.

Kay didn't hesitate. She lashed out with her foot, her shoe connecting with Rogers' shin, and he yelped.

The larger of the two officers leapt on him, pinned him against the door, and slipped cuffs over his wrists.

'Bitch,' hissed Rogers.

Kay glared at him, then turned to the two uniformed officers and straightened her jacket. 'Good timing, lads. Thanks.'

Chapter 64

Ian Barnes peered through the mist that rose from the soaked undergrowth before he lowered his gaze to the phone in his hand and cursed.

The team at the incident room had emailed him the plans, but they were agonisingly small on the smartphone, and he'd taken a wrong turn.

He cast his eyes back across the field to the abandoned construction site, the fear rising once more as he watched the team move methodically along the boundary, their eyes to the ground as they conducted their search.

Barnes stumbled, and swore again.

He regained his balance, and then realised he'd tripped over one of the manhole covers that peppered the land here.

Fifteen minutes ago, they'd located an entrance to the old Victorian sewer system through the basement car park of the skeletal apartment block nearest to the boundary fence, but had been forced back by flooding.

Barnes had stood as water lapped at his shoes, and strained his eyes to see along the darkness of the narrow tunnel.

He'd called out, his voice echoing off the nineteenth-century walls before disappearing into the shadows.

Silence had fallen, and he and the two uniformed officers had waited.

There had been no response.

'Sir, we can use the plans to find out if there's another way in,' one of the officers had said, a light touch on Barnes' arms. 'We'll keep looking.'

Barnes had appreciated the gesture, and the words, but he heard the unspoken thoughts that passed between the two other men.

The faces of their colleagues spoke volumes as they'd exited the basement and reached the derelict lobby.

Until the water receded, there was no hope of reaching Emma via the construction site.

They had to find another way.

A re-examination of the plans showed the old sewer system had branched out underground like a spider web. In places, the cartographers had simply given up, and dotted lines were marked up with typographic entries to support this theory, stating "unknown".

So, the team had split up to cover as many of the known routes as possible.

Before the municipal council had approved the construction site, and years before the stubbly undergrowth that now covered the space, an old mill had stood on the site, until the decision had been made to tear it down for fear of trespassers becoming trapped within its maze-like drainage system.

The natural watercourse would have been a godsend for the mill owners, but also a curse, and so the drainage and sewer network had been created to draw excess water from rainfall away from what was now a field, towards the sewer that was under the construction site.

A uniformed sergeant wandered over to him, his jaw set.

Barnes steadied himself. 'What's up?'

'We've got another team of experts on their way,' said the man. 'They're bringing some equipment with them. Some sort of GPS stuff that will show exactly where these culverts are buried.'

'How long will they be?'

'About half an hour.'

Barnes closed his eyes.

'I'm sorry, Detective, that's the best they can do.'

'I know.' Barnes opened his eyes, and wiped away tears. 'I know.'

They both turned at a shout from the other side of the field.

A young PC was waving his arms at them, then turned and beckoned to one of his colleagues who was nearer.

Barnes took off at a sprint, the sergeant's footsteps close behind.

Oh Christ, what's he found?

Two other policemen got there before him, and as he stumbled to a halt, they crouched and began to rummage in the undergrowth, their heads almost touching.

'What is it?'

'Shh.' The young officer who had waved them over held up his hand, then blushed. 'Sorry, sir – I thought I heard a tapping noise.'

Barnes looked to where he pointed.

A steel manhole cover, similar to the one he had tripped over, lay encrusted with weeds and moss within the undergrowth.

He dropped to the floor, where the three uniformed policemen tried to prise it from its housing.

'Give me your baton,' he said.

The man next to him held out the telescopic weapon, and Barnes inserted the end into one of the indentations in the steel cover.

The other two policemen realised what he was about to do, and readied themselves to create the additional leverage.

'On three,' said Barnes.

He leaned against the weapon, and the edge of the cover shifted on its opposite side.

'Again,' said the sergeant, and dropped to his knees on the opposite side. He withdrew his own baton, and slipped it under the edge as it lifted.

A hiss of air escaped, the stench of centuries-old air wafting around them, before they managed to get a grip on the steel cover and slide it to one side.

Barnes peered into the abyss.

A ladder had been fixed to the side of the drain for ease of access all those years ago, its edges frayed with rust and wear.

'Daddy?'

His heart lurched.

'Emma?'

He saw her then, peering up at him, her eyes wide as she hung onto the rungs as water lapped at her feet.

'Emma!' He reached out his hand, stretching as far as he could. 'Come on – you can do it. You're nearly there.'

A sob escaped her lips, and she began to climb, every movement slow and methodical.

Barnes held his breath.

His daughter shivered uncontrollably as she lifted one hand, then the other, then a foot, then the other, and climbed slowly towards him.

Please don't let her slip!

Her hand brushed against his.

'Hold my ankles so I don't fall down there!' he said to the police officer nearest to him.

He launched himself down the hole, reached out with both hands, and wrapped them around Emma's wrists.

'I've got you,' he said. 'I've got you. Walk up the rungs. I won't let you go.'

He was dragged up, his stomach and chest scraping against the brick and mortar sides of the drain, and then hands were reaching down, grabbing hold of Emma.

The sergeant pushed him gently away, then took Emma by the arms and lifted her away from the drain.

Her hair clung to her face, a nasty cut behind her ear had started to congeal, and her dress clung to her, ripped and torn, but as Barnes regained his balance and rushed over to her, all he could think was how beautiful his daughter had become in the years since he'd last seen her.

'You're safe, my darling,' he murmured.

'Daddy,' she blurted, and fell into his arms.

Chapter 65

Kay ran a finger over the soft padded dressing that the doctor had taped to her neck, and tried not to think about the bruises that covered her cheekbones.

Earlier, she'd stood in front of the mirror, about to attempt to try to cover them when she'd clenched her jaw and shoved her powder compact back into her bag before returning to the incident room.

A shadow fell over her desk and she glanced up.

'Detective Sergeant Hunter.'

'Sir.'

She began to stand, but DCI Larch waved her back down.

'I wanted to congratulate you on the team's results,' he said. 'Sharp will address the team in full shortly, but he said you'd been injured during the arrest of Bob Rogers.'

'I'm fine, sir, really,' she croaked. 'The doctor says my voice will be back to normal in a couple of days.'

'You need to be careful, Hunter,' said DCI Larch. 'One day your impetuousness will get you into real trouble.'

He turned on his heel.

Barnes wandered over as DCI Larch left the incident room.

'Had to have the last word, did he?'

'Something like that.'

He grinned. 'Well done, Sarge. You got him.'

'We all did, Ian.' She smiled. 'Thanks for sticking by me.'

'Someone had to.'

'Yeah, I guess.' She chuckled, and then grew serious once more. 'How's Emma?'

'Dehydrated. They're keeping her in hospital for a few days – they were worried about the effect that cold water might have on her, but I spoke to Sarah a moment ago, and apparently Emma's already given her initial account to Debbie West. She was adamant she'd do her bit to see Matthews and Rogers put away for a long time.'

'That's good to hear, Ian.'

'Yeah. I'll have a quiet word with her about the bullying, too.' His voice wavered. 'I can't believe how close I came to losing her forever.'

Kay reached out, and placed a hand on his arm. 'You didn't lose her though. Don't play "what if", okay?'

He blinked away tears, and then glanced over his shoulder. The rest of the team were hanging around Sharp's office. He turned back to her.

'Listen, Kay. I made a promise out there today,' he lowered his eyes. 'I don't believe in a god or anything like

that. You know what it's like with this job.' He shrugged.
'I promised that if I got her back alive, I'd quit.'

'What?'

'I nearly lost her forever today. She never wanted me to
be a detective, neither did her mother.'

'Ian, you said yourself that was years ago.'

'I know, but I want to spend some time with her now. I
can't bear the thought of losing her again.'

Kay let her hand drop. 'Listen to me. You're one of the
best detectives in this room.'

'But—'

She held up her hands. 'Listen,' she repeated. 'Have a
word with Sharp. Take some time off to be with Emma, but
please – think carefully before quitting, okay?' She forced
a smile. 'Despite what everyone says about you, I kind of
like having you around.'

He snorted, and then grew serious once more. 'Thanks,
Sarge.'

They turned as DI Sharp strode into the room.

'All right, gather round,' he said, and stood in front of
the whiteboard. He checked his watch.

Kay grabbed a seat between Carys and Gavin, and
waited while the rest of the team settled.

'Twenty minutes ago, DCI Larch and I met with Jude
Martin from the Crown Prosecution Service and set out our
case against Eli Matthews,' said Sharp. 'He's been
formally charged with the kidnapping of Emma Thomas,
the kidnapping and murder of Melanie Richards, the

murder of Beryl Matthews, and charges associated with the death of Guy Nelson. And, thanks to ongoing evidence and witness corroboration by Emma Thomas, we expect Matthews to receive a significant sentence.

'Bob Rogers has been charged with assault of a police officer, as well as financing the kidnapping of Melanie Richards and Emma Thomas, and perverting the course of justice,' he said. 'I'm sure we'll be adding to that list as our enquiries continue leading up to the court case.'

His eyes met Kay's, and then fell to her neck. 'Should you be here?'

'Doctor said I'm fine, guv.'

'You sound like you could sing lead vocals in a blues band.'

It raised a chuckle, and Kay was grateful. They all knew how close they had come to having another murder victim, but it wouldn't do to dwell too closely.

Barnes winked at her from across the room.

'Did Matthews tell you why he moved to Suffolk?' asked Carys.

'I was getting to that,' said Sharp.

He turned to the whiteboard, and fixed a photograph of Bob Rogers at the top next to Eli Matthews.

'Felix Peters, the neighbour, told Hunter and Barnes that Eli's father walked out on Beryl Matthews when Eli was five years old,' he said. 'It appears Eli managed to track him down to Ipswich, where he was working at the County Deliveries depot.'

He drew an arrow from Eli's photo to Bob's.

Kay ignored the stunned murmurs that filled the room and leaned forward. 'If Bob Rogers was Eli's father, why didn't he let him stay with him? Why make him stay with his mother if he knew she still abused him?'

'Careful planning,' said Sharp. 'Rogers knew his son had a tendency to keep souvenirs, and didn't want to get caught. By keeping Eli away from his house, he protected himself while still having someone to snatch their victims.'

Gavin emitted a low whistle that cut through the shocked silence. 'The eleven-year-old, who was found wandering,' he said. 'She was their first one?'

Sharp shrugged, his face grim. 'Suffolk Police have undertaken to open all their old cases that show any resemblance to this. She might not have been their first, but that little girl was the only one we know who survived.'

Kay shuddered.

If Bernard Coombs hadn't reported the blood he'd glimpsed in the back of Eli's van that night; if Grey hadn't looked at that purchase order more closely, if—

It could all have turned out so differently.

Sharp tossed the pen onto the desk nearest to him.

'Good work,' he said. He glanced out the window as the sun began to part the clouds. 'Right, I think you've all deserved an early finish,' he smiled. 'I want you all back here at eight o'clock tomorrow morning.'

Kay said her goodbyes as the team left the room one by one, then wandered over to her desk, picked up her bag, and grabbed her car keys.

As she straightened, she saw Barnes approach Sharp, and then both men disappeared into the inspector's office, the door closing behind them.

'Damn,' she muttered.

Chapter 66

Kay turned at the sound of footsteps on the staircase, tied a towel around herself, and stepped out of the en suite as Adam walked into the bedroom.

'Hi,' she rasped.

Adam took one look at her face and neck and cleared the space between them in two strides, pulling her to him.

'You said it wasn't too bad on the phone,' he said, then cupped her face in his hands while he inspected the lacerations with a practised eye. 'What did they put on these?'

'I don't know, but it stung like hell.'

'Christ.'

He hugged her tight, burying his face in her hair. 'Did you get the bastard who did this to you?'

'Yes,' she mumbled into his chest. 'He's going away for a very long time. So is the other guy.'

While he stripped off his work clothes, she told him what she could about the case, and the fact that Ian Barnes' daughter had also been taken.

'She's a feisty one, though,' she added. 'I think she's going to be okay eventually.'

Adam bunched up his boxer shorts, and threw them into the laundry basket. He turned at the door to the en suite, and smiled.

'Fancy another shower?'

She grinned. 'Maybe.'

'I'll take you out to dinner,' he said, as she drew closer. 'It's been too long since we celebrated something.' He frowned. 'That is, if you're okay going out?'

She smiled. 'It sounds like a great idea.'

She stepped closer, and loosened the towel. 'Care for an appetiser?' she said, then laughed as he pulled her under the hot jet of water.

Later, she marvelled at how good Adam looked dressed in a suit and tie.

'I'd forgotten that you tarted up quite well,' she said.

He cocked an eyebrow. 'Don't look at me like that. We'll be late.'

She giggled, and then caught herself.

'That's a nice sound,' he said. 'I didn't think I'd hear that again.'

She stood on tiptoe and kissed him, then turned to pick up her earrings.

'But there's something still bothering you,' he said. 'I can tell. What is it?'

She sighed, and put the earrings in. 'You're not going to like it. It's about the Professional Standards investigation.'

'Come on, then,' he said, his face turning serious. 'Tell me. What's going through your mind?'

Kay sighed, and ran her hand through her hair. 'This'll sound crazy.'

'This is me you're talking to,' he said, and winked. 'Remember?'

She took a deep breath. 'I need to find out what happened to the gun that disappeared,' she said.

Adam's eyes opened wide a fraction of a second before she heard his sharp intake of breath.

'It obviously wasn't me. But someone took it. Made it disappear. *Knew* it was all we had to pin that death on that suspect.'

Adam leaned against the dressing table. 'Why?'

'I don't know.'

'Well,' said Adam, handing her a cufflink and turning over his wrist so she could fasten it. 'You're the detective. I guess you'll just have to figure it out.'

'I can't. If DCI Larch finds out I'm sticking my nose in, he'll lynch me.' She raised her eyes to his, and was faced with an intense stare. 'What?'

'You could always use the spare room. Run your investigation from here.'

She bit her lip.

'We have to get on with our lives at some point,' said Adam, and laced his fingers through hers.

'What about you?'

'I worry about *you*,' he said. He brought her hand up to his lips and kissed her fingers. 'If you're happy, I'm happy. And I think you need to find out the truth. For yourself, if no one else.'

'You don't mind?'

He shook his head. 'Do it.' He smiled. 'Just don't get any ideas about wallpapering photographs of your suspects all over the room, okay?'

Kay rolled her eyes. 'That only happens on television.'

He grinned, and kissed her fingers once more.

A car horn sounded in the street below.

'Taxi's here,' she said.

Adam squeezed her hand. 'Head downstairs. I'll be there in five minutes.'

Kay smiled, grabbed her shoes and padded down the stairs before slipping them on, not trusting herself to navigate the incline with heels on.

She opened her clutch bag as she made her way through to the kitchen to check the back door was locked.

Keys, cash, credit card, mobile phone—

She stopped, level with the microwave, her heart in her mouth.

The top to Sid's glass case was off-kilter, a large gap showing in one corner, and the salt shaker was on its side on the kitchen worktop, white granules strewn across it like a hailstorm.

'Oh, no,' said Kay, her voice shaking.

She backed up against the refrigerator, and then yelled.

'Adam? Where's the bloody snake?'

THE END

FROM THE AUTHOR

Dear Reader,

First of all, I wanted to say a huge thank you for choosing to read *Scared to Death*. I hope you enjoyed the story.

If you did enjoy it, I'd be grateful if you could write a review. It doesn't have to be long, just a few words, but it is the best way for me to help new readers discover one of my books for the first time.

If you'd like to stay up to date with my new releases, as well as exclusive competitions and giveaways, you can sign up to my mailing list at my website, www.rachelamphlett.com. I will never share your email address, and you can unsubscribe at any time.

You can also contact me via Facebook, Twitter, or by email. I love hearing from readers – I read every message and will always reply.

Thanks again for your support.

Best wishes,
Rachel Amphlett

CPSIA information can be obtained
at www.ICGtesting.com
Printed in the USA
LVOW11s1526130617
537962LV00003B/509/P